# HALF PAST HATE

## A Censored Time Novel

# Corinne Arrowood

First Paperback Edition, 2021

Published by Corinne Arrowood
United States of America
www.corinnearrowood.com

ISBN: 978-1-7368189-5-4 (paperback)
ISBN: 978-1-7368189-4-7 (ebook)
ISBN: 978-1-7368189-6-1 (Hardcover)
ISBN: 978-1-7368189-7-8 (Audio)

Cover and Interior Design by Gene Mollica Studio, LLC

# Contents

# MORE THAN WORDS

The pause was deafening as pictures flashed through her mind like those on a runaway film reel. Michael looked over at Rainie and could tell she was welled up with emotion and struggling to speak. He squeezed her hand gently and smiled. *This is really happening*!

"I do," she managed finally. She had never known such happiness. This man standing before her was everything she could have imagined, but more. He was handsome in a real kind of way—his sandy hair with natural gold and warm brown streaks set off his deep green eyes, which emanated love. And it was all hers—always had been. Somehow, she knew this idyllic feeling in her heart was forever, not just for the minute, the hour, or the day, but forever.

The pastor announced, "I now proclaim you husband and wife. You may now kiss your bride." Michael could barely contain his enthusiasm. What had only been a dream at one time was now his reality. Tom's flagrant adulterous ways were his gain. Rainie, the woman he had always loved, was now his wife.

He took her in his arms and ever-so-sweetly kissed her.

"And now, friends and family—" The pastor paused briefly. "I present Rainie and Michael Landry."

They turned to the sound of applause. Michael's mother, Missy, had a stream of tears running down her cheeks with a smile that could go on for days. Her precious boy had gotten his dream. What more could a mother ask for?

Though intimate, the wedding number had grown substantially from their initial family plus Mer, her bestie pregnant with twins, and her hubs, Paul, pushed the numbers to seventy-five. Missy had invited everyone from up and down River Road. Jack, Michael's dad, and his older brother, John, had invited some of their pilot friends, and the New Orleans contingency had arrived by party bus, adding another twenty-four.

Michael and Rainie were beaming as they walked arm and arm up the aisle.

"What gives? I thought you said you'd be the girl in the gold dress?" Michael arched an eyebrow in intrigue.

"Story for later," Rainie said. "Let's call it issues with the fit of the dress."

"No matter, you look gorgeous, and now you're my wife!" He could barely contain himself. He stopped and truly kissed her. "I have missed you all day, and last night was almost unbearable knowing you were a couple of rooms away. I felt like a kid wanting to sneak into the girl's dorm." His enthusiasm was contagious, and they both had a spring in their step.

Rainie wore her devilish grin well. "What were you thinking, Michael? Hmm? Save the thought for later, and maybe we can talk about it or give it a go," she laughed using his coined phrase from the first night that ignited their friends to lovers spark.

"Mrs. Landry, are you mocking me?"

"No, Dr. Landry, but I hope you'll be having me." She raised her eyebrows at him and winked.

"Rainie, are you kiddin' me? You're too bad, but no matter what I say, you're going to turn it blue." They continued walking hand in hand.

"Blue? Me?" She feigned aghast.

"Yes, you, my naughty wife." He smacked her on the bottom. "And, if you don't behave, there'll be more later tonight."

They went around the back of the house and then to the front of the tent. As they entered, there was a round of applause. The florist had done a beautiful job; everything was twinkling and most enchanting. The topiary arrangements towered on the tables and were designed with a simple statement of exquisite roses, their long stems entwined and tied in bondage. It was a favorite of many floral designers. *How appropriate,* she thought and giggled to herself.

The band began playing "All of Me." He took her hand and led her to the dance floor. "I'm lost in you. I'm the most blessed man to be dancing with the woman I love. I feel like we're alone, just the two of us, like in a wildly beautiful paradise. You've made me the happiest man alive."

"I love you, too, but it's not just the two of us...you're holding someone else in your arms, as well."

He looked curiously at her. "Huh?"

She took his hands and placed them on her stomach, then his eyes widened. He gazed into her eyes, asking without words.

"Yes, Michael. And baby makes three. Well, in our case with the boys, baby makes five." She grinned.

He hugged her tight but quickly loosened his hold. "How do you know? Are you sure? Oh, God, this is amazing."

"Yeah, I'm sure. When I went to put on my dress, Mer couldn't zip it up. This," she pulled at the fabric, "is your sister's dress. She and Mer did this look to each other, and I was like, 'what?' It was then decided Wendy would get the test, and Mer would calm my near hysteria. So, yep, no doubt." She was far more excited about the situation than she expected to be, and watching Michael's eyes gloss with happiness sealed her emotion as waves of bubbly flip flops pulsed throughout her body. Perhaps the immense thrill had something to do with sharing the information with someone that felt the same, if not more, excitement than she felt; it had never been that way with Tom.

"Who knows?" Now it was Michael who was animated. They danced in place, swaying with eyes focused on each other.

Rainie, with hands clasped behind his neck, said, "We made a pact we wouldn't tell anyone until I told you. Neither of our moms knows. I figured we could tell them all together tonight after the reception ends. That way, nobody feels slighted." She placed her hands on his face and kissed him. "I kinda figured it would be good news."

"You kinda figured right. It's the best news. Shit, you married me, and I find out you're having our baby on the same day. God is good,

Rai. You'll need to get to your doctor as soon as we get back, or do you want to postpone the honeymoon?"

"Michael, do you hear yourself? You, I should think, being a doc, know I don't need to see my OB yet. I haven't been drinking since before we slept together the first time. All is good." She patted his cheek sarcastically. The music ended, but they kept dancing, chatting away as though the music was still playing.

Rainie's father approached and cleared his throat. "Can I dance with my daughter? I think your mom is waiting for her dance, Mike."

Michael gave her hand to Henry but kept looking at her, smiling.

His mom was full of tears as he walked up to her and took her hand. "Mom, I know you've been waiting for this as long as I have. Let's dance."

"Michael, y'all look completely in love. Not saying you haven't all along, but even more now."

"All I can say, Mom, is I'm complete now. Isn't she amazing?" He was all smiles.

He twirled her beneath his arm. She looked up with happy tears. "My sweet boy, I think y'all are amazing together. God had His hand in this union. It was all part of the plan, I suppose."

The song ended. He kissed her cheek. "I love you, Mom. By the way, you did a terrific job on the wedding." He brought her to her seat and then went to Rainie's mom and put out his hand.

Jack had already made it to Rainie. For being such a burly guy, he was good on his feet. "Rainie girl, you've made one hell of a bride, and my boy looks like he's bustin' his buttons. I guess he'll finally move into the house."

"Yes, sir, you bet," she laughed. "It's about damn time."

After the dance with the in-laws, they gathered Rainie's two boys, and the four of them danced together. Yeah, she thought, he was the dad they needed. He was the man she needed, for sure.

Surprising as it was, John had not tried to chat up any of the girls from Michael's office or made any move on the River Road girls. He wanted to make sure all went well for Michael and Rainie.

After three hours, guests started to trickle out. It had been a complete success.

Rainie and Michael waved goodbye as the party bus took off. It was great having his staff at the wedding without worries of driving hazards. His team was good to him, and it made it perfect that they could be there. The wedding would be the talk of the office for some time to come.

The kids moved into the house to play while the adults talked. The band packed up their gear, and the bartenders left, but they savored the time. Michael put his hand on Rainie's thigh then tapped his water glass to gather attention.

He stood and raised his glass. "A toast to my beautiful bride. May our love continue to grow, and this night the beginning of a magical journey together. I look forward to many years of happiness." He took a moment—his emotions were on overdrive. He cleared his throat. "And as the icing on the cake, cheers to a new baby entering our life soon." His eyes had glossed over. "Thank you, my love. I love you now and for eternity."

It was dead silence at the table when Wendy blew a sigh of relief. "I've been dying all day. Thank goodness. I'm going to be an aunt, and I haven't been able to tell a soul." She looked at Rainie, "And I haven't, hard as it's been."

The parents exchanged glances. Jack finally spoke. "Am I right in understanding we're going to have another grandbaby?"

Michael beamed, "Yes, sir." Rainie's skin tingled with racing prickles hearing the words come from Michael.

Everyone raised their glass and toasted the pregnancy.

"Just think, Rai, if my two girls are friends with your little girl, it'll be like our threesome-you, me, and Rand." Mer winked at her. "Or if the baby's a boy, the girls will have a built-in protector." Their eyes met, and both she and Rainie had to swallow the hurt of missing Rand.

"Dang, Mike, whaddya gonna do if it's a girl?" Jack had a way of putting things.

John piped in quickly, "Pray she doesn't find the likes of either of us." He leaned back in his chair with a sarcastic grin on his face.

"No shit!" Michael was beaming.

The speculation went on until it was time for everyone to retire for the night.

As they went into the house, Michael sighed. "It'll be good to sleep in my own bed. No offense John, but I much prefer to be in my bed. Thanks for giving me your bed instead of the rollaway last night."

"Mikey, ya gonna be a dad, wow. Congrats. I definitely need to settle down. There was never any pressure but now you with a wife and a baby on the way."

Rainie held her dress off the ground in one hand, going up the stairs. "John, I know Miss Right is out there looking for you. She'll find you, and then playing the field will be history. You've already sown wild oats; your time is due." The three of them made their way up the stairs.

"Coming from you, it sounds good. I want to have what y'all have; only I'm twice as good as Mikey in the sack." He guffawed.

"You had to be a jackass John, couldn't let this be a Hallmark moment, could you?"

"Hell no, bro. Y'all getting all sentimental on me. Shiiit! Good night, and please don't keep me up all night with your heavy breathing." He laughed and went to his room.

Standing in front of their bedroom door, Michael looked into Rainie's eyes and smiled. "Carry you over this threshold or wait until we get home to Stella Street?"

"Both," she laughed.

He swept her off her feet, brought her into the bedroom, and placed her gently down. She turned her back to him, encouraging him to unzip the dress. "This is my sister's dress? You married me in my sister's dress? It looks great on you."

Standing before him, scantily clad in bra, lace garter belt, and stockings, she put her hands on her abdomen. "I can't believe I didn't know. Does my stomach look poochy to you?"

"No, your body looks perfect to me. You don't look any different, honestly. Did you keep the test?" His eyes were dancing in curiosity.

"Of course. I was going to show you and not tell you since you're into showing things." She danced her eyebrows at him with a laughing smile.

"I want to see it." During the wedding, someone had moved her bags into their bedroom. She opened her make-up bag and pulled out the indicator. Plain as day, it said, "Pregnant." He looked at it, looked at her, and looked back at it. "We're pregnant. I'm going to be a dad. It's a lot to fathom."

Michael put the test wand on the dresser, turned to her while pulling his tie loose. She stepped toward him and began unbuttoning his shirt, then undid his pants. His body was firm, with well-defined muscles, but not over the top, simply perfect. He dropped to his knees and kissed her belly. He held her hips and brought her closer to him. "Hello, in there," he whispered. "I love you."

It was a sweet moment, but she had to add some levity. "While you're down there on your knees..." Her laugh had a sinister sound.

He looked up at her but didn't say a word. He returned her devilish smile, then tenderly kissed the top of her thigh, tailoring his movements to the moment. Slow, gentle, methodical, it was all whispered touches. As he stood, his kisses moved up her body. He took her face in both hands and kissed her as he had with their very first kiss. He started gently, gradually increasing with passion then letting up. He picked her up and gently put her on the bed. "Precious cargo. Gotta handle with care."

She relaxed back in the bed and pulled him to her side. "You're too funny, Michael. Being a doctor, I would've thought you would know your sleeping baby is fine with our playtime. Remember, it's how he or she got there." She stroked his hand tenderly.

"I know," he thoughtfully said, "but it's different because it's ours. Give me time. I'll get used to it." He crawled in next to her.

"By then, I might have to be hoisted into a sling to find the sweet spot. My belly gets big. I guess because my hips are narrow, and it all goes straight out in front." She pantomimed how big her belly would get.

"Hoist you up in a sling? What the hell? I've never hoisted, hung, or swung anyone, even back in the dark days. No, I'm more hands-on." He slid his finger inside her bra, feeling her aroused nipple.

She pushed him onto his back. She playfully kissed his chest. Her throaty laugh made him laugh, "Oh, you think this is funny, mister, just you wait. Since you don't have a baby sleeping, as you put it, inside you, you better hang on. I've got one hell of a ride for you." She slid her body down his, kissing his happy trail.

He was hard and hot, but she wasn't going to jump right in. No, he needed a little teasing. She kissed his inner thighs, giving light wisps of her tongue on the always ignored jewels. She cupped them in her hands as she took them into her mouth, still only teasing with her tongue. His body was asking for more. She could feel it as his quads tightened. She took him with her other hand, gripping with force, and began stroking. She knew he wanted more, so she encircled his hardness with her tongue. He liked it rough, and she willingly obliged. It didn't take long for his release. She knew his body's needs and desires and how to fulfill them to perfection.

Rainie climbed up his body, putting a knee to either side of his shoulders. She smiled down at him. The movements were almost melodic. Holding her hips, he rocked her, bringing her closer to his mouth. He held back nothing as he slid his hands from her hips to her ass and gripped tight. While not what she had thought the lovemaking would look like the night of their wedding, this more than fit any bill. The tension mounted, she waited for the crescendo, but he wouldn't stop. He kept going. He had brought her to the pinnacle a couple of times with every nerve ending electrified. She held her breath, knowing the last release was going to be intense. The chills raged through her body. She slid next to him on the bed, completely sated.

He rolled toward her, gently sweeping her long red tendrils from her face. "You're insanely beautiful." He continued to look at her with dreamy eyes. "I can't believe we're having a baby. Did you have any idea?"

"Michael," she said, gazing upon his ruggedly handsome face, "when I tell you I was shocked, it doesn't even begin to describe how I felt. All I knew was something was wrong with my dress. I had tried it on before, and it fit, maybe a little snugger than I had remembered. When Mer and Wendy suggested I may be pregnant, I was like, 'no way.' Then Mer, in her dignified way," she laughed, "commented on our excessive sexual interaction. I've been beyond diapers and the like. I never gave it a thought when we were fooling around. I just thought we were having a good time; it never once crossed my mind we could be making a baby. I'm still in disbelief." Closing her eyes, then slowly opening them as though waking from a dream.

Michael twirled her hair around his finger. "I never even thought about it. Mind you, in my past; I didn't take it out unless I wrapped it up. Things with you were different—always have been. It's felt solid, if that makes sense?" With a sweet smile, she nodded. Thoughts whirled through her mind. *We acted with no regard, but what's done is done. It's time to enjoy the ride.*

She snuggled into his arms. He made her feel like she'd never felt before. She felt loved, protected, and happy. She looked forward to things getting to a norm and being back at Stella Street. The honeymoon was going to be great, but life with him forever was the ultimate.

They were whispering back and forth, gazing into each other's eyes. "Michael, you're going to have to love the boys as much as you do this baby. I know you know, but I'm worried about what the boys will think." Her breath hitched as she thought about all the uncertainties.

"Don't underestimate them. Thomas and Henry are going to be awesome. Boys don't dig babies as much as girls do, it's not a boy thing, but they'll be curious, and they'll be great big brothers, whether it's a boy or a girl. It'll be six years difference between the baby and Henry. The guys will be great."

"They won't have the same last name."

"And does it matter, Rainie? No, it doesn't. I give you my word. I will not love this baby more than the boys. I can't imagine loving another child as much as I do Thomas and Henry. I know they aren't my flesh and blood, but those boys are mine." He had conviction in his words that made her heart fill with happiness.

"Oh God, I wonder what Tom's going to say." She giggled nervously. "Even though he is the boys' dad, he wasn't happy with the news of either pregnancy at the time."

"Fuck Tom. Rainie, he's yesterday's news. I got this one, okay?"

Her eyes lit up. "We're gonna have to decorate a nursery. We'll have to find out the gender." She nodded in confirmation, punctuated by her determined ice-blue eyes.

"Go to sleep, Rai. You have to be beat. We have plenty of time for all the planning, but we need to get to sleep. Tomorrow's gonna be a long day for all three of us."

She smiled at him and whispered. "We got married today, ya know?"

"Yeah, I know. Pretty amazing." He looked content, like a cat with a saucer of cream.

&#x304F;&#x3294;&#x304F;

It had been a restful night's sleep, but out of the blue, there seemed to be some sort of commotion coming from downstairs. They threw on clothes and went down to see what the ruckus was all about.

Sitting at the table in the Hearth, which she would've called the family room, was a scruffy-looking boy, maybe all of twelve. Michael looked at his dad. "I see we have a new face around here." He looked to the boy. "And when did you arrive?" The boy looked down without answering.

"Good morning, Mike," his dad said. "Good morning Rainie. I trust you newlyweds had a good night's sleep. You have a big day today. What time y'all leaving here, so I can make sure Missy has enough hankies?" He chuckled. "I think she was happier yesterday than she was when she and I tied the knot. You've got her wrapped, you know, Mike. Yep, wrapped right around your little finger. Always have." He beamed, looking at his son.

The boy was fidgeting as they spoke. Jack had an eye on him the whole time. The boy would have been rather cute if cleaned up, but the cute was well hidden beneath layers of grime and matted, nasty hair.

Jack looked straight at the boy as he spoke. "Mike, this young man decided to take up residence in the old river house."

The look on Michael's face indicated the error of the decision. "Don't know what to say, but kid, you made a big mistake. Did you call the sheriff's office?" he asked his dad.

"Nope. I thought maybe we could handle it right here. He and I have some talking to do, and I know you two need to get some breakfast and then get going." He looked back at the kid. "My son, Mike, got married last night, but then I guess you already knew. You had to have heard the band. Did it ever occur to you that you were trespassing?" Jack's hands tapped on the table.

"Yes, sir, but I'd been watching the house for days. It didn't look like no one was there. It was empty. Mister, let me leave. I won't come back; I'll keep on my way. I don't want no trouble."

John came in through the kitchen door and into the Hearth. "Hey kid, you got a lot of cleaning to do down at the house. You have wrappers, dirty dishes, empty cans, and a lot of other stuff." John came across as menacing. She felt sorry for the boy having these three big men all watching him. "Mikey, this kid decided to move into grandad's old house."

Michael sat next to Rainie, who was watching him intently, looking at the boy. "I'm Mike, and you are?"

Silence.

"One more time, and you are? Answer the question, or I call the police." Michael seemed harsh.

"Sam."

"Well, that wasn't too hard, was it? So, Sam, where you from?" Silence.

"Mikey, Dad and I have been trying to get information from this young man. You at least got a name, but the real interrogator will be back soon. She's shopping." One side of his mouth twitched upward.

Michael looked at the kid. "Let me make this simple for you. Firstly, Sam, you trespassed; secondly, you trashed private property, and I'm willing to bet you're guilty of truancy, as well. You know you can be charged for all those things. The way I see it, you can answer our questions or take the consequences. Up to you, kid." He held Rainie's hand and squeezed it beneath the table.

The boy started talking. Not to anyone, in particular, or no one at all. "My name is Sam. I ain't got no mom or dad or family. It's me and me alone. I'm fourteen an' been on my own since before it turned cold. I been walking, sleeping under bridges, and movin' on. I walked down the side of the river when I came to your place. I watched it for a few days and didn't see no one, and I broke in. Sorry about the trash. I'll go clean it and be gone." The boy's shoulders slumped pathetically.

Jack asked, "Where you been walking from?" He was all business but with a slight warmth about him.

"Lafayette." Sam continued to look down.

Jack nodded. "You say you don't have a mother or a father.

Everybody has a mother and a father, maybe not a good one, and maybe they're dead, but everybody has one," Jack said matter-of-factly.

Sam nervously shifted his eyes. "I had a mother, but she left one night, and my father, she said, is in Angola. Ya know, the prison. Don't know why—she didn't say. She never said much of anything. When I was little, my grandma took care of me, but she died. So, like I said, it's just me." He looked around at the grown-up faces looking at him.

They heard the kitchen door open and the rustle of bags. Both John and Michael jumped up with a "Need help, Mom?"

"No, thank you," she said as she walked into the room. "I see you haven't washed up yet." She said to the boy. "I figured when I left you would've cleaned up some, talked to my husband and sons, and maybe gotten a bite to eat. You're nothing but skin and bones." While speaking to the boy, her face glowed. Missy took Michael's seat and sat next to the boy. She took the boy's hand in hers. "Son, you're a mess, but I can see some clean between the dirt." She looked him dead in the eye. It was apparent this was her forte, young boys in trouble. "When's the last time you had a proper meal? The only things down on the river were cans of soup and stale crackers. You look hungry."

Jack, Mike, and John glanced around at each other. Yes, Missy was the interrogator, but she went in through the stomach and the heart. By the end of their meal and conversation, she would have found out all there was to know and set the rules.

She got up, went into the kitchen, and came back with a damp and dry towel. "Now, wash your face and wipe up your hands. Cleanliness is next to Godliness." She went back into the kitchen.

Jack ran his hand through his hair and let out a sigh. Missy came back with two sandwiches, some chips, and a glass of milk. The boy's eyes showed emotion for the first time.

Michael stood behind Rainie and put his hands on her shoulders. He massaged them and mentioned they needed to get a bite. She was still baffled by the strange boy, the conversation Michael had with him, and the peculiar way Jack and John were acting. She got up from the table and nodded to everyone at the table, "See you in a bit, y'all." They left the house.

Rainie was quiet and to herself. "Remember how I told you about my parents and the Lost Boys? Dollars to donuts, Sam is the next Lost Boy. By this evening, he'll have several sets of clothes, new shoes, toiletries, and have moved into Neverland." They walked toward the grand tent.

"Seriously?" She raised her eyebrows and crinkled her forehead in curiosity.

"Seriously. I told you, and voila, you get to see it in person." He held her hand as they walked to the tent. The air was fresh, and the sun was shining—their slice of heaven.

"I wonder where my boys are and everyone else, to boot. It's like everyone's disappeared." Her thoughts rambled in her head. *This is the weirdest fucking morning. Twilight zone at its best.*

"I bet everyone's in the tent having breakfast. It's a Missy thing."

Sure enough, he was right, and everyone was seated with breakfast in front of them. Thomas ran up to them. "Mom, Doctor Mike, we've been waiting for y'all to wake up." Rainie found it odd Missy had gone shopping with guests, and John and Jack seemed oblivious to the group as well. It was all strange.

"You look most curious. Do you have a question?" He looked at her while bending down, hugging the boys.

"Later." She made her way around the table with plenty of hugs and kisses. Chatter was constant around the table. No one seemed to mention Missy, Jack, or John.

They moseyed to the buffet, filled their plates, and returned to join in the conversation. There were several empty chairs. Michael sat by her dad, and Rainie sat by Wendy. "Thanks for the use of your dress. You were a lifesaver, Wendy. Really."

"No problem. I'm excited for you and Mike. Have you told your boys yet?" She quivered in her seat, bursting with excitement.

"Not yet. We probably won't until I know how far along and we've passed the critical time. Michael was hilarious. He asked if I wanted to cancel the honeymoon. Being a doctor, you wouldn't think he'd be all nervous about the pregnancy thing." She stabbed a piece of fruit and popped it into her mouth.

"Oh, but no. Anyone else, Mike's cool as a cucumber, but you with his child, he's going to act like any first-time parent with no medical knowledge. Mark my words. When it comes to you, nothing is normal with Mike," she laughed, "never has been." She nodded.

"Your parents and John are—"

Wendy cut her off. "John was his usual self and up at the crack of dawn. He likes to go down to the river. He goes there to think." She rolled her eyes. "Anyway, he found a boy staying in grandad's old river house, and that's a big no-no. No one is ever allowed in there. John got Mom and Dad, Mom ran to the market for kid things, and now they're in the house with the boy. I know Mike has told you about the Lost Boys, right?"

Rainie nodded as she took a few bites of the eggs and grits.

"Looks like Mom and Dad have another Lost Boy unless he's a runner, but he'd be a damn fool. There were two from the past here at the wedding last night. I'm surprised Mike didn't introduce you. We get close, not like brotherly, maybe cousin-like, but they stay in touch with my parents." Wendy twirled a celery stalk in her bloody Mary, trying to coax an olive from the bottom of the glass.

"Michael told me, but to see it. Wow. Your parents are something."

"They are, and most people find it strange, but it's who they are. What can I say?" Wendy stuck her finger in and plucked out the olive.

"Does everyone here know about the boy?" She looked around at her parents, Mer and Paul, and nobody seemed any different. They were all eating, chatting, and generally enjoying each other's company.

"Yes. Dad apologized for not being part of the breakfast gathering and explained Mom had to get some new kid things and ready the room. I'm not sure why John feels the need to stay with them, but I imagine he's right in the thick of it. The way it works is my parents stop everything until they settle the new boy. It's always been the way. Mom references scripture. 'When I was a stranger, you took me in. When I was hungry, you fed me' and so on. It's the way she lives her life. There's not an ounce of bullshit in it. It's who they are, like it or not." She took a bite of the celery as she smiled at Rainie.

"How did my parents act? Were they freaked, or Mer and Paul?" Rainie whispered to Wendy.

"No. Dad's frank and tells it like it is, and everyone pretty much goes, 'oh, okay.' There's no big discussion, no need. Like they say, it is what it is. What time are y'all heading out?" Wendy's eyes gleamed with excitement.

"I guess within the hour. We aren't going to be gone for very long. You know Michael and his practice. He's thinking of taking on a partner. He needs one, but I can't imagine any of his patients seeing another doc. They all love Michael." Rainie's eyes lit up like a flame to a wick. She was proud of him, and it resonated in her voice.

Michael leaned in. "I'm not trying to break in on this conversation, but we need to start giving our hugs and good-byes. You know how long it can take with both our families."

"Good point." She looked at Wendy. "I can't thank you enough. You were a lifesaver for the dress, the test, and keeping the secret." She hugged her. "We'll see y'all in a couple of weeks for Christmas."

"Christmas it is. I can't wait. Love you." Rainie wasn't sure how to respond.

"You're too sweet." *There, an appropriate answer.* The word love was a big word for her. The feeling came more effortless than the word. She thought the shrink would probably have some witty comment about intimacy and trust. Or one of his favorites, "Why do you think you cocoon yourself?" Yeah, she had to admit, she was a hot mess. Maybe not as bad as she used to be, but still pretty dang fucked up.

They said goodbye to everyone in the tent with pleas to Mer— no babies until they returned.

It was time for goodbyes with her parents while Allie, the dutiful nanny, focused on the boys and their behavior.

She started her goodbye with Jack and Missy while Michael jogged up the stairs to retrieve their bags. John came out of the kitchen. "Where's Mikey?" Rainie pointed up. Right about the time Michael came down the stairs. John took one of the suitcases from Michael as they walked to the car. "It's been awesome being together so much recently. I'm gonna miss you. As soon as this contract ends, I'm gonna work the river, so I'll be back to a normal pilot schedule and maybe get a life." It was a touching moment between the brothers, ending with a full-on hug. "Love ya, Mikey."

"Love ya, big guy."

Jack had already gone back to the runaway boy. Michael and

Rainie went into the Hearth one more time. He patted the boy on the shoulder and told him not to screw up this chance. "Dad," Michael said. Jack got up and gave him one of his bear hugs.

"You take care of your lady, now." He side-hugged Rainie. "And you take care of my boy."

"Yes, sir, Jack. That's a promise. We'll call when we get back in town, and y'all can come for a weekend." Her smile lit up her face.

He winked at her. "Be careful, my Rainie-girl."

Michael spent a few moments with his parents. Rainie's parents had come out to the car, and it was another long goodbye. Michael had been right. They had not only one but now two long-farewell families.

"We'll bring back a souvenir for you two," she said to the boys, "if you behave. I'm going to be checking on you. Thomas and Henry, you hear me? Remember, moms have their ways of knowing." She kissed them both.

☜☞

The drive to the airport was filled with conversation regarding the boy, Sam. For the umpteenth time, Michael went over it with her.

"I get it, Michael. I've never seen anything like it before. The kid's a perfect stranger and probably screwed in the head."

"Wait until you see the difference next time we see him. Night and day." They sat in silence, wrapped in their thoughts for a few minutes.

"Penny for your thoughts, Michael." She clutched his hand tightly.

"Oh, that's easy. You naked. In the bed. Against the wall. In the bathtub. I love looking at you, especially naked." He grinned. She felt a rush of heat and a tickle that caressed every inch of her body. *Yowza!*

"Where are we going? Mer hasn't given me any hints, and I know y'all packed my bag together, and, no, I didn't look inside. Everything I needed for last night and today was either in my toiletries bag or on hangers. I love how you're always full of surprises, but I want to surprise you sometimes." She sat sideways, looking at him with anticipation.

"Every time you open your mouth, you surprise me. Meredith was quite right when she said I'd never know what might come out of your mouth. You come out with some outstanding ones," he laughed, then followed with a grin.

"Like?" she asked cocking her head to the side in a flirtatious pose.

"Where to start? You swept me away when you said 'Like in the movies,' or donning me 'Fifties' just because I'm a bit old-fashioned. It's just you, Rainie. Like the way you throw your hand up with that look—" He put his hand up. "Uh, I don't think so!" he imitated and laughed. "You don't even know how great and one of a kind you are." He was glowing as he regaled her idiosyncrasies.

"Wow, I sound dramatically exciting," she said, her comment thick with sarcasm. "To think you married me. You had your choice of women. Most of the single women in New Orleans would've given anything to have hooked you." She leaned in and brushed his thigh with her fingertips.

"Hooked me? I thought I was the lucky one. I hooked you. You, my love, were single but a day. I didn't give anyone else a chance. I was not going to let you go again. You know, I was nervous on our first date? I knew you only wanted to be friends, and it killed me, not to mention having to hide the boner the whole evening. It was hard for me not to hold you, kiss you, and tell you how much I loved you. Oh, and to absolutely fuck your brains out." There was quiet in the car. "Did I say something wrong?"

"No." She giggled. "Fuck my brains out? You thought that on our first date? Really? You know you could've said, 'Wanna fuck?' Back then, I'd have probably taken you up on your offer." She snickered.

"Now you tell me. All the courting and the getting married, and all I had to do was ask you to fuck?" Michael sighed. "You see, that's exactly what I'm talking about, with what comes out of your mouth. You're hilarious. I would no more have treated you like that than fly to the moon. No, ma'am, I wanted you, but I wanted you the right way. I wanted you to feel loved, comfortable, happy, and know how much I respected you, and if I could only have you as a friend, it was how it was going to be. I want to be your friend, boyfriend, lover, confidante, and partner for life. There's nothing you can't tell me or come to me about. I'll even listen to the girl-talk. I may not be the best conversationalist on the subjects, but I'll try." He smiled at her. They turned into airport parking. "Do you really want to know where we're going?"

"Yes and no," she deliberated, tipping her head from side to side.

"Gotta pick one," he said with a shit-eating grin.

"Okay, yes, tell me." She tightly closed her eyes in anticipation.

"Um, no," he said and laughed.

# ANOTHER DAY IN PARADISE

"Do you trust me?" he asked.

"Of course," she droned, feigning disbelief and frustration with his constant go-to question.

"Then humor me." He tied a scarf over her eyes. "Take my hand. I'll tell you what to do. Sound familiar?" She could hear the smile in his voice. He navigated her to the tarmac and a private jet. "I'm going to be directly in front of you. Take both my hands. Step up. Step up." She felt clumsy. "There are seven small steps. Keep going, five more." He led her into the jet and sat her in one of the roomy chairs. He took the blindfold off her.

"A private jet? Are you crazy?" She was giddy with glee.

The flight attendant handed her a champagne flute. She thanked her but declined.

"It's sparkling water," Michael added.

"In that case, thank you." She was puzzled, "Michael, I haven't bugged you, but where are we going?"

"Relax, Rainie, and breathe."

She grabbed his hand and pulled him to her. She whispered, "You realize with our little attendant, there will be no mile-high club."

"If that's what you want, I'll arrange it, but you won't get the usual in-flight service. Maybe you might prefer my in-flight service." He gave her a wickedly sinister grin.

*Oh, my gosh, I'm twitching between my legs, and he's mine!*

She laughed. "I don't know. It's like we're announcing what we're doing. Now I'm self-conscious." She covered her face with her hands.

He couldn't help it. He had to laugh. Teasingly he said, "I'll tell them we're on a mission and have top-secret information. We need the utmost privacy. You know, James Bond-like."

"You're an ass, Michael!" She pushed his bicep.

"Let's see what comes up, naturally. Sound good?" He tilted his head.

The flight attendant brought them a deli plate with different salami, cheese, crackers, and fruit. She pointed to a button and told them if they needed her to press it, otherwise she would see them upon their descent.

Rainie wondered if she had heard their conversation or if it was standard. She had never flown in a private jet.

Michael was seated next to her, looking out of the window. She could see him looking at her in the reflection of the window. She saw him smile when she changed position, getting ready to pounce on him.

"Excuse me, sir, is this lap taken?" He had a way of barely running his tongue over his teeth before coming up with some witty comeback. He blushed. He had nothing to add.

"Should I wager a guess?"

Determined, she fired back, "Yes. You. Should."

No matter what she said, it always came out with flair and an almost childlike air of mischief. She wriggled her skirt up and straddled his lap.

As quickly as she got the skirt up, he had himself ready for the adventure.

He gave her a grin. "At the ready, ma'am." He finessed his way inside of her, reclined the chair, watching her eyes as they opened wide. His penetration was complete.

In a fluid, slow movement, she rode him. He grabbed her hips, controlling her pace and rhythm. She felt the intensity and watched as he clenched his jaw, his pupils dilate, and then a slight quiver in his bottom lip. There was no doubt. He was getting off on the in-flight service. She could see him succumbing to the wiles of her body. With total concentration, she waited for his moment.

She leaned forward for a kiss. "Michael, do you consider these friendly skies?" Her gutsy laugh was a turn-on.

"The friendliest I've ever known." He exploded inside of her.

She climbed off him to hit the lavatory and freshen up. She sashayed back out to him. "Have you seen the bathroom? Not at all like the usual pissy-floor of commercial flights."

"Can't say as I have, but I'll get my chance now, I suppose." His shirttail was untucked, and his pants barely zipped. He looked disheveled.

"Michael, I'm usually the one with the 'just-fucked' hair, but—" She twirled her finger in her hair— "You have the 'do' going on. Looks good on you. For once, I feel coiffed and tidy instead of sporting tribal big crazy hair."

As Michael passed her, he commented he would have to take note; he had never given it much thought. "You're gorgeous no matter what that mane of yours has goin' on," he chuckled. "Just-fucked hair, that's a new one."

He went in and came out perfect. Rainie got up, tousled his hair, and pulled his shirttails out. "I like the look."

"You're too much, but whatever, I'm yours." She couldn't help but think, *yes, you are!*

The captain announced they were beginning the descent and should be landing in twenty minutes. The perfectly poised attendant appeared. She did a double-take on Michael. "Need anything else?" They said no. "It's a beautiful day out there, and the weather should be spectacular." As she took the empty flute from Rainie, she quickly gave her a wink. "By the way, congratulations, Dr. and Mrs. Landry." She disappeared to refill their flutes.

"Michael, she knows."

"Knows what?"

"That we, you know." She batted her eyes.

"I seriously doubt she cares, no worries." He took her hand and kissed it. "You gonna relax, or do I have to resort to relaxation techniques?"

"I thought your relaxation technique was only for back home, Michael."

"Maybe Pandora and her toys, but, believe me, I don't need toys to relax you."

"But I'm pregnant."

"Hah, I see, you're going to pull the 'I'm pregnant' card, now. A few minutes ago, I'd swear it was the last thing on your mind. Your condition is ever-present on my mind, however. I can't wait to go to our first appointment." They sat back in their seats.

"Really? You're going to go?" She seemed bewildered.

With disbelief, he answered, "Of course. Why wouldn't I? This is an us thing, Rainie. I'm not going to miss even one appointment. It's not up for debate." He straightened his shirt a little.

Her eyes teared up. "You're too sweet."

Gently touching the side of her face, he turned her face toward his. "What don't you get about this? I'm here for you, and our child, and our family, for it all. The vows I made to you, before God, were not just words, ya know? I meant every word I said."

"Yes, I do know, Michael. I love you." A single tear rolled down her cheek.

He wiped the tear. "I hope that's a happy tear." She nodded.

They could feel the descent of the aircraft as they approached. Landings had always been exhilarating to her.

❧

The sounds and vibrations transported her back to the flight to summer camp with Rand. It was the first time they had flown without their parents. They felt grown-up ordering Coca-Colas with cherries. They had opened all the bags of peanuts and made a pile on the tray. Ten years old and worldly, ha. They giggled and talked incessantly about plans for camp, debating about who would be back and who wouldn't. Those were great times.

She wondered who Rand would have grown up to be. Would both of them be in business with Mer? Rand always said she wanted to go work with her dad, so probably not.

After Rand died, she stopped thinking about what she wanted to be or anything about growing up. Indeed, a part of her had died with her twin. No matter how amazing Michael had been and the difference he had made in her life, that would never change. It was there forever.

〜

"A penny for your thought, lady." His smile with his sexy dimples made her heart sing.

"I'm fine. I think you worry too much. Now, what're we going to do about that, Michael? You need to relax and breathe." She flipped her hair to the side and squinted at him. "Hm?"

He took her hand and kissed it. "You're such a smart ass. I care about you. You seemed sad for a few moments. Just trying to be there for you, but never mind. God forbid I care about you." He smirked.

They touched down. Rainie looked out of the window, and all she could see was lush greenery, giant palms, little palms, and bright flowers. It was definitely tropical. There were a couple of hangars with other baby jets in them.

When the aircraft came to a stop, the attendant opened the door lowering the stairs. There was a car waiting with the trunk open ready for their bags. He gave her his hand. "Come on, Mrs. Landry. Our car awaits."

She stood up, straightened out her skirt and top. "I look okay? My hair okay?" she asked.

"You've got a just-fucked look." He laughed at her expense.

She grabbed him. "God, I love you. You're so bad but damn good at it."

They emerged from the aircraft and hurried into the car. Doors closed, trunk closed, and off they went. Evidently, she thought, they must be running late. The driver was hauling ass.

Michael could see her concerned expression. "Let off the gas. You're scaring my wife."

The man driving the car responded, amused, "No problem, sir, and sorry, missus." He had an island-y British lilt and was most pleasant. He asked the typical questions regarding the flight and their satisfaction thus far. Now that he wasn't driving at a break-neck speed, she could enjoy the scenery. There were no houses, no hotels, nothing but beauty and nature, from what she could tell.

"Michael, where are we?"

"We're on a private island in the Caribbean. There are several homes and quite a few schooners and yachts." He was watching just as eagerly.

"Oh, okay." She was still in the dark as far as where they were going.

"You trust me?" he asked, his eyes sparkling.

"You know I trust you." She squeezed his hand then ran her fingers along his, lightly skimming the surface. His hands were smooth and strong. She traced the outline of each finger. It was hard to fathom that his hands were skilled beyond measure, and he literally held lives in them. Her heart filled with immense love and respect.

"Then sit back and relax. We're going on an adventure. It's something I've always wanted to do, so rather than the Keys or Sandals, I thought we'd come here. I bet we won't want to leave, from what I understand. My parents have been here, and John, as well. They highly recommend it." He continued to watch out the window.

There was a single road from the airport. As far as the eye could see was nature, nothing man-made. Finally, the driver made a sharp left on a sandy road. When the car stopped, there was nothing around. Michael took off his shoes, rolled up his pants, and asked for her shoes. A small motorboat pulled up onshore. The guy driving the boat waved enthusiastically.

"You Mister Jack's son?" Michael nodded. "Welcome." The man shook Michael's hand and smiled. He had maybe half a mouth of teeth, but his whole face lit up. He put his hand out for Rainie to take and helped her into the boat. Michael helped him push it from the sand, and they both hopped on. The little speedboat took off at full throttle.

She could see a boat in the distance, and the closer they got to it, the bigger it looked. It had multiple sails, all down or coiled around parts of the boat.

Skip, the toothless boat driver, pulled alongside the schooner and jumped on board with great agility. He offered his hand to Rainie, and she gladly took it. Then he offered it to Michael, and up he popped. She could hear another boat flying up.

A few people were buzzing around on the boat. All with big toothy smiles, skinny, wiry bodies, very dark skin, and flowy white shirts, or no top at all. The vibe was very "Don't worry, be happy." She loved it.

A small man presented them with champagne flutes. He smiled and said, "Pineapple juice, m'lady." It was delicious. Michael could see her eyes sparkling with excitement.

"This is amazing, Michael."

"Yeah, it is, isn't it? John and Dad told me nothing in my imagination could compare to the real thing, and they were right. I've even seen pictures, but those pale in comparison." He looked off in the distance. "I remember you talking about you and Rand prancing around in your bathing suits when your parents went deep sea fishing. You gonna prance around here for me?" He grabbed her waist.

"You remember everything. That's crazy. To answer you, you bet I'm gonna prance. I'm not only gonna prance but dance and be decadently lazy." She swayed her hips to a mood-setting background steel guitar.

"I wish I had planned more time, but I—"

"Can't be away too long, I know. Besides, Michael, I can't because Mer's close, and you know they usually take twins early. Let's love it while we have it. Right?" She wrapped her arms around him and held him close. It was a slice of heaven.

The crew showed them to their quarters. The decor was luxurious and classy. Rainie opened her suitcase to see what they had packed – Bathing suits, sarongs, flowy tops, two hats, and a lightweight cotton dress, but no shoes or nightgowns. She also had hair ties up the wazoo. "Meets with approval, yes?" he asked.

"Yes, I'll have to figure something for sleepwear." She raised an eyebrow.

"Sleepwear? Against the rules. I want you always available." His bangs had fallen in his face, which she found sexy, and as he watched her, he ran his tongue across his smile. *Oh, do you now?* She thought.

"What's in your suitcase?" She sauntered to the other side of the bed. She pulled out each item. "Swim trunks, tee shirts, a white shirt, and a bow tie. A bow tie? I don't think I've ever seen you in a bow tie." It dangled off her finger.

"In case you wanted a more formal feel, I'd put on a bow tie."

"Oh," she answered quizzically, "to wear with what?"

All he could do was grin. She laughed.

They put on their bathing suits and headed out on the deck.

The schooner was magnificent and huge. Much bigger than it had looked when she'd first seen it, and they were moving at a pretty good clip. It was the same carefree feeling she had while riding horses on the levee. It invoked a sense of utter freedom.

The water was crystal clear, with the most beautiful cast of turquoise and blue hues. Dolphins playfully raced alongside the boat. The sails were stretched taut by the wind, and to her, it looked like something out of a movie. The staff, while attentive, stayed in the background, giving them their privacy.

She watched him as they lounged on the bow. Michael was a big man, not massive, but tall at six-foot-two, with a solid build. He kept in great shape. She had always thought he was cute in the all-American boy-next-door kind of way, but over the past year, she saw much more. Yeah, he was easy on the eyes. Many guys who worked out had muscular upper bodies but no legs. Michael had strong legs to go with his broad shoulders and defined arms. Everything was in perfect proportion. His skin tone was darker than hers, but then everyone's was darker than hers. He was the total package. He kept in shape because he wanted to, not for vanity. The superficial trappings of the perfect image emphasized by fashion magazines and Hollywood evaded him. It wasn't as though he passed judgment on others or came across with a "holier than thou" attitude. It plainly wasn't his deal. It was like he'd been there and done that and was beyond it.

He cocked his head in curiosity. "You seem pensive. What are you thinking?" She could see him trying to read her.

"Hardly." She smiled. "Looking at you with happy thoughts." She leaned toward him. "Do you have any idea how handsome you are, Michael? Everything about you is just right."

"I'll do in a pinch, I suppose, but I don't think about those kinds of things very often. Being in the business of plastic surgery every day, one would think I'd care a lot more about my appearance than I do. I want to look nice. Everyone does, I think, but it's not what makes up the big picture. Get me?"

"As a matter of fact, Michael, I do. To use your line, your waters run deep, very deep." His eyes twinkled like there were specks of mirrors in them.

One of the deckhands brought a tray filled with fruits of all kinds and plump boiled shrimp. Michael reached across her, picked up a shrimp by the tail, and put it to her mouth. "They're tasty. You looked like you needed one." She slowly parted her lips, looking him in the eye as her tongue toyed with the fruit of the sea. Teasing him was fun. He bought in so easily.

"Tres yum, Michael." Then, she fed him one. After a few nibbles, they both laid back, closed their eyes, and succumbed to a state of tranquility. "Maybe after a nap, we can take a swim. That is if it's safe out there and not shark-infested." Her voice dreamily faded into the wind.

He pulled her closer. "Shhh. Anything you want, now shhh." He was steadily falling asleep. She curled up next to him.

She wasn't sure how much time had passed, but she opened her eyes to beautiful blue skies with billowy cotton ball clouds. She could feel him looking at her. "Yes? May I help you?"

"You already have. I love watching you sleep. It's the one time you truly have no look of torment or sadness on your face, and you look totally at peace." He twirled her hair around his fingers.

"I have torment and sadness on my face? I don't feel it. Maybe sometimes, if I think of the past, I might get melancholy, but I'm at peace, Michael. You've brought a lot of peace into my life."

"Do you want to go for a swim?" He purposefully changed the subject, which was for the best.

"Sure, you're gonna go with me, right?"

"What do you think? Of course." He stood and reached for her hand, leading her to the stern. He spoke with the skipper. The boat started to slow down, and the sails began to sluff. "Give it a few minutes."

He went below and came up with fins and masks with snorkels. He handed them to Rainie. After donning the apparel, they sat on the side of the boat and rolled into the water. Looking through the mask, Rainie saw the creatures below were numerous and vivid in color. It looked like they were inches away instead of many feet beneath them. She grabbed his arm when she spotted a shark. He patted her hand as the shark ignored them and went about its way. The experience was frightening but exhilarating.

After a half-hour of being in the salty water with the sun beating down on them, her fair skin said it was time to get in some shade. They went down into their cabin. He rubbed her down with after-sun, and even though she had applied thick sunscreen, she'd pinked.

As he was applying the gel, he mentioned dinner was lobster, if that was okay. "You know when we were at your parents, Michael, and we looked at the stars? I bet it's going to be even more dazzling. You can tell me about the constellations again."

"And be your science-nerd husband? Wouldn't you rather me be suave and sexy instead of nerdy?" He swirled the cool gel on her shoulders.

She looked at him as he was capping the after-sun. "You're inspiring. Enlightening. I find it to be totally sexy." She tugged at his trunks. "Even though you're darker than me, it probably wouldn't hurt for me to apply some after-sun on you. Now get these swim trunks off and lay on the bed."

He started face down. Rainie straddled his hips. She rubbed the gel on the tops of his shoulders and down his back. She lifted and slapped his butt. "Roll over." He had a big smile on his face. "What's that smile about? Are you thinking you're going to get some somethin' somethin'? I want to make sure we take care of your skin." She put the gel on his face and upper chest. He caressed her breasts. "You're gelled enough." She climbed off.

"Really? That's it? What am I supposed to do with this?" He looked down at his body, which had come to full attention.

"What do *you want* to do with it?" she innocently but teasingly inquired. She had him with a lack of words. How dumfounding. She had thrown it right back at him, ever so coyly.

Michael closed his eyes and went somewhere in his mind. How bizarre, she thought, but when he took himself in hand and began stroking, she became undone. Rainie would've never expected this to be a turn-on, but her body and mind proved otherwise. She leaned over him and put him in her mouth, but he didn't stop. This whole scenario was like nothing she had ever been party to, and she didn't quite know what to think. She continued doing what she was doing while he did the heavy lifting. He removed his hand right before the finale. She firmly and quickly handled him, right in time to make it outstanding.

Odd as it was, and a first for her, it was titillating. She got hot watching. It made her want him in the worst kind of way, and dammit, she knew he knew it.

He opened his eyes. He knew the score. He knew he had floored her. She leaned over him, and with his thumb, he wiped some evidence from her bottom lip. She kissed him powerfully with intense passion. *Outstanding.*

Entwined in each other's arms, she began her never-ending stream of questions. "How do you come up with all your ideas for play? I mean, do you read books? You're like coitus extraordinaire. You could teach lovemaking. It would have to be *titled Advanced Sexual Techniques for the Adventurous Spirit.*"

He laughed. "How do you come up with so many questions? You act like our interaction is one-sided. Please take my word. It's not. Rainie, whatever we do is an equally shared adventure, including creativity. If I didn't know better, I'd have thought you had a lot more experience in the sack than you let on. I've been straightforward with you, I've been around the block a few times and knocked on almost every door, but for you, it's all-natural and part of your fiber. All it took was someone to let you love them and to love you right back." It was hard to tell where his legs started, and hers ended. They were completely entangled.

They had four full days and nights of basking in laziness, indulging in exotic fruits and a full spectrum of fish and seafood. They snorkeled, swam, and he even swung off lines into the water like a kid. She thought it looked like fun, but felt it best she refrained from swinging on ropes and dropping into the sea in her condition.

The staff was fantastic and met their every need. The nights were glorious, starting with breathtaking sunsets and turning to a vastness of shimmering stars. The moments were quiet, peaceful, and intimate. Playtime was different than ever before. Michael's skills and creativity in the boudoir never ceased to amaze and satisfy Rainie.

Time passed quickly, and before it seemed possible, they were driving back to the landing strip for the flight home. They had managed to find some huge shells while snorkeling and figured the boys would find them interesting.

On the flight home, they made a to-do list of things needing attention. Michael said the first thing was moving his stuff into their bedroom and turning the pool house into a proper party area with a pool table, ping pong, and wet bar.

Since they'd already done Christmas shopping before the wedding, they only had a few bits and bobs to pick up. He reminded Rainie to make an appointment with her doctor to know when they could expect their new little person to arrive. She was all about the efficiency of planning.

The flight seemed faster on the way back. "I loved our honeymoon, Michael. I can't believe it's going to be back to the daily grind. I've missed the boys and our home, but the trip was heavenly. How do you think it's going to go with the boys?"

"If we don't make it a huge deal, neither will they. It doesn't change who they are. They'll still be the same Thomas and Henry. I think if we do the big brother shirts as you mentioned, they'll get jazzed, but you know they're going to hope for a boy. Boys always do, but if the baby is a girl, I think they'll be just as excited. Boy, will she have a time of it. There will be many a cross to bear. Poor girl." He was beaming.

Rainie turned in her seat. "Will you be disappointed if we have a boy? You seem pretty sure the baby is a girl." She patted the top of his hand.

"Rainie, I have no idea if we're having a boy or a girl. It's a 50-50 shot, maybe even more leaning on the side of boy. The important thing is—you and the baby are fine. Amazingly, we had no idea. It wasn't on my radar. I guess because it wasn't an issue if it happened."

She became thoughtful. "I know when Mer asked me about protection, I felt stupid. It never entered my mind. I can't remember us using condoms, but I said, of course, we did. I didn't want to sound irresponsible or stupid. It was then that I had to think if we had ever used them."

Michael smiled. "I used them, at first, and I mean at very first. You were spontaneous; I never had any idea when things were going to happen. I've never had this much sex in all my life. I mean it, and definitely not like back-to-back-to-back. I didn't realize I still had it in me. It's not like I'm seventeen anymore with perpetual wood. The days of keeping condoms in my wallet, in case I got lucky, are long over. Before us, I pretty much knew the inevitable and was prepared, but with you, not so much."

She looked at him with a stern look. "Michael, were you a man whore before our relationship started?"

"No, I certainly was not. I've told you all my dirty little secrets, and yes, there was a time I was too promiscuous, but I've been totally open. Man-whore, the more I think about it, maybe." He faked a shocked look.

"I'm bustin' ya balls!" She laughed. "Whatever made you who you are today, I'm eternally grateful because I'm reaping the benefits, and then some." *Yes, and then some, indeed,* she thought.

The announcement came over the speaker that they were making the approach. She could feel the excitement mount at the prospect of seeing her boys.

# What's Next

All she could think about was getting back to the boys and seeing her parents.

They pulled up to her parents' home. As they approached the front door, she could see the smudge marks on the windows from the boys looking out.

They opened the front door. Rainie called out, "Anyone home?"

It couldn't be called a pitter-patter of little feet. It was more like a stampede coming their way.

"Mommy, Mommy!" Henry wrapped his arms around her. "I missed you."

Michael had crouched down for a hug. "We missed you guys too."

Thomas was happy to see them but didn't want to be as exuberant as Henry. "We have a surprise for you, but I'm not telling. You'll have to wait."

"A surprise? I can't wait to see it. Mimi and Poppy around?" Her parents were making their way to the front. It was good to see them, but they looked tired. "Momma, I'm happy to be home. How's it been here?" She gave her a tight hug.

"It's been fine. I know the boys are happy y'all are home, and we're happy to see you back in one piece. I'm sure y'all are dying to get home. Traveling always wears me out." *Very diplomatic, Mom.*

Michael had been quiet up until that point. "We are looking

forward to settling in, and I'm sure you're ready to have your home back to normal. Allie here?"

"She's at Stella," Rainie's dad said matter-of-factly. "She'll be happy to see you two."

Rainie found it odd Allie wasn't with the kids. She hoped she hadn't flaked because of the beau, Eric. Not that she had any objections to Eric, but to flake and shirk her responsibility onto her parents wouldn't have been cool.

"C'mon, guys," Michael encouraged, "let's get home." Those words sounded right. *Home.* Even though he'd been living there, Rainie knew he felt unsettled. He'd mentioned on several occasions how he was looking forward to sleeping in their bed, in their room, in their home. What was the new normal going to look like?

They loaded up and zipped home. *Yep,* she thought, *this is our home,* exactly as she had remembered it. They pulled into the driveway and went inside.

"Welcome home, y'all," Allie greeted. Rainie wanted to ask why she hadn't been at her parents' watching the kids but figured the answer would come eventually. She was sure there was a good explanation. "Go put your bags up. I have some soup on the stove for everyone. Boys, come help me if you would."

Rainie and Michael went upstairs. He dropped his bags and took hers and dropped them, then scooped her up and carried her across the threshold of their bedroom. "I know, not quite as romantic as the front door, but it would have been awkward with the boys."

"I can't believe you remembered." She gave him a quick kiss. "Before we left, I emptied the second closet. It's all yours now." He smiled and opened it, ready to put his one bag in. All his clothes were hanging in the closet, exactly as he'd had them at his French Quarter house before they bought the Stella Street house together, parlaying into him living in the pool house for the sake of propriety. He looked at her. "John," she said. "It was going to be Allie and Eric, but John said there might be some things in your closet of a personal nature. He moved it all, Michael."

"Wow. John did that? He said that? I owe him." Michael looked in the empty chest of drawers, and it, too, was neat and organized. He pulled out his phone to call John.

"Michael, first, I have a question. Does John have any idea of Pandora and the stuff?"

"Yeah. John does." He almost looked sheepish.

"Does he know we, um?"

"No. There's a story behind how John found out. Maybe tonight after we get everyone to bed. It's kind of amusing, but not."

The soup smelled good. A savory aroma filled the air. Rainie noticed everything in the house was clean and tidy. No signs of any wild parties or misbehaving. "Allie, soup smells awesome." She heard a male's voice.

"Glad you think so." Eric was standing at the stove. "Welcome home. It's chicken enchilada and tortilla soup. I hope that works."

Rainie was surprised. "I'm impressed. What is it with you doctors? Are you all full of surprises? I guess the starched white coats throw everyone off. Y'all come across so—"

Michael interjected. "Boring? That sums up residency, except those few breaks here and there, and then it's time to let go."

Eric agreed. "Pretty much. Cooking relaxes me. Sometimes the E.R. can get wild and scary. We have some real characters pass through our doors. You wouldn't believe the things people do and not only the crazy ones. People you think are humdrum ordinary people. Some of it is pretty freakin' funny and mind-blowing at the same time." He stirred the pot, "Mike, your brother came over and re-arranged your pool house and brought all your clothes from your other house."

"The pool house, too? I really owe him. Believe me. I won't hear the end of it."

"Michael, I think a thank you is all you need to do," Rainie said. "I bet, what is it, dollars to—"

"Donuts," he answered her.

Rainie continued, "He won't ever mention a thing. He said he'd rather me not tell you."

"Gonna call him." He pulled out his phone and dialed. "I know you're busy, wanted to thank you. No, I haven't been in the pool house yet. Just saw the closets and the drawers." He walked out of the room and continued to talk to John. There was a chuckle here and a laugh there. He was on the phone another five minutes, and as he walked back in, he told him, "Yeah, love you, too, and, by the way, it was most amazing. Words and pictures don't do it justice. You too. Later."

He walked by Rainie, kissed her, and then went out to the pool house. She followed. John had outdone himself. The pool table, ping pong table, totally stocked wet bar were all set up with a banner over the bar that read, "Here's to the happy couple, cheers!"

"Oh my, Michael. I can't believe he did all this. We're going to have to do something for him to say thank you."

He redialed his phone. "You busted your balls. Yes, I'm in the pool house."

Rainie grabbed the phone. "I'm in here, too. John, you did way too much, and we owe you, big time. You're such a dear. Love ya." She handed the phone back to Michael and went back into the house.

She wanted to get the skinny on the Eric-Allie thing. He seemed perfectly normal, but she wanted to make sure.

"Eric, what's your story?" Rainie leaned against the counter and got straight to the point.

Stirring the soup, he answered, "Like what do you mean, my story?"

"Where are you from, parents, siblings, school, growing up? Just being nosy, that's all. You spend a good bit of time in my house, and with my friend, so I'm curious. No judgment, merely info. For instance, I was born in New Orleans. I'm thirty-four. I went to LSU and, before that, went to the Academy of the Sacred Heart. I was married to Tom Todd, but he cheated on me; hence we divorced. As you know, Michael and I are married. I'm not athletic, but I try. I'm creative and have a good eye for color. I'm curious by nature and impatient, also by nature. I like to protect those I love, and Allie happens to be one of those people. So?" Her dissertation was fast and done.

He faced her and looked her dead in the eyes. "I recently turned twenty-six. I, too, was born in New Orleans. Grew up in the Lakefront, Lake Vista, to be exact. I went to St. Pius the tenth, then Jesuit, then Bama onto Tulane Medical School. Interned at Children's and now Residency at Baptist. I have an older sister, Lane, who's thirty. My dad is an engineer with Shell, and my mom stays at home and does whatever. I played football at Jesuit, but I wasn't stellar, at best average.

I'm not into working out, but I do some cardio. Let's see; I've never been married; I have no children. I have a condo in the warehouse district that I bought on my own, and I work my ass off. Oh, and I like to cook. That about sums me up."

Tapping her lips with her finger, she thought, then prodded. "How do you express your anger?"

He turned toward her, slightly shaking his head. "Are you really asking me these questions? I'm the shy kid that didn't date much. I've had sex with two people. I rarely get angry, and when I do, I pout, I guess. I'm told I have a good sense of humor, but I tend to be quiet. I have the occasional beer, and I don't smoke or use drugs. Anything else?"

"Just one more." Rainie looked at him with a squint. "What are your intentions with Allie?"

"Rainie!" Michael walked in on the last question. Allie was cracking up, and Eric had looked over at her from time to time during his dissertation. "Can't leave you for one minute without you misbehaving." Looking at Eric, he said, "I hope she wasn't too brutal."

"No, but very curious, I gotta say." Eric looked straight at Rainie. "I don't know what the future holds for me. Allie and I have a good thing going on right now. Could it be more? Yes, but maybe that's not what she wants. Now, good enough?" He didn't seem aggravated or annoyed. "Would you like some soup?" He punctuated the end of the interrogation.

"Brilliant. The perfect ending to your indulgence in my wife's curiosity." Michael walked behind Rainie and put his arms around her waist. "And, yes, she is always like this, before you ask." Michael kissed her cheek.

"No soup, right now, but can we save it for later? I'll make some grilled cheese to go with. Right now, I have to unpack and get the laundry on the go. Great chat, Eric." She winked at him with a smirk.

"Yes, ma'am." He watched as she and Michael walked out of the kitchen. He looked at Allie. "You said she could be intense, but wow, I didn't see that coming."

Allie laughed. "I've seen her do it with other people. She didn't with me, but the situation was different. She's extremely protective of her inner circle and loves me like a sister-daughter combo. I admire the hell out of her. One thing for sure, she'll never bullshit you, Eric."

Going up the stairs, Rainie tripped and started to fall. Michael caught her in his arms. "You're okay. I gotcha."

"Thanks. I wonder if this pregnancy thing has made me off balance, but I was fine on the boat. Maybe I'm just pooped." He followed her with his hands on her mid-back.

They walked into the bedroom and noticed one of the windows was open. Michael looked at her. "Why did you open the window? It's pretty cold outside."

"I didn't." She looked at him with curiosity.

"Well, I didn't either." They stood looking at each other with a concerned look.

Rainie, while watching Michael, called out, "Stella, you devilish soul, it's too cool for us to have the window open. Please don't open it again."

They started unpacking and pulled out their collection of shells for the boys. Almost everything in both bags went straight into the hamper. "Michael, y'all did a great job packing. Between you and Mer, I knew it'd be right."

Allie called up to Rainie. "When you get a chance, I need to show you some things in the office."

"Go do your thing, my beautiful lady." Michael turned her toward the door.

"I don't want to leave you. I don't want it to end." She hugged him.

He held her in his arms and kissed the top of her head. "Go, I'm gonna hang around here, maybe watch some tube, call my parents, and relax in our home. I love you. We'll be sleeping together every night in our bedroom. I know I've thought about this since we moved in, now get." He swatted her butt.

She raised her eyebrows and ran her tongue across her teeth. "Really? Too bad I have to go to work. Can't get away from work when the office is at home." She quickly kissed him. "Spank me later! Ciao, baby." Her laugh was contagious.

"I wanna do more than spank you, Rai. Maybe restrain you in tassels with a blindfold, play with the cat o-nines until that shiny clit of yours is like a beautiful pearl treasure waiting to be discovered and admired." He rolled his tongue like a purring kitten.

"Michael! You cheat!" He could hear her laugh all the way down the stairs.

He followed her down the steps and, as planned, watched the tube, spoke to his parents, and tasted the soup multiple times. He and Eric watched some mindless reality show and chatted here and there. Eric asked him, "Do *you* have concerns about my relationship with Allie?"

"No. Don't mind Rainie," he advised Eric.

Allie had the client files organized and prepared for Rainie to inspect. There were a couple more requests for bids, and it looked like everything was in order. "You've done a great job. I'm still on honeymoon time, and while I can have Michael, I'm seizing the opportunity. You know tomorrow when he's back in the office, our world will return to normal."

It was their first night in their own bed together as man and wife. The kids were down for the night, Allie was in her room, and Eric had gone. They were alone. "And here we are. Michael, I've been looking forward to this since we moved in." They faced each other. She lightly passed her hand along the side of his face. She leaned in and kissed him, nothing passionate, just a kiss.

"That'll never do." He rolled her on her back. His kisses became far more passionate and began with her neck down her throat and to her breasts. His hand moved evenly down her, stopping for a moment on her belly. He sat up whispered something to her belly, but she wasn't quite sure what he said because his other hand was firmly exploring below. He continued moving down.

He looked up at her face. There wasn't a sign of disapproval, so he continued. Intently, he stroked her with his tongue. He knew how to electrify her body. Every nerve ending was anticipating his touch, his kiss, and his penetration. He had her, but he wasn't going to stop until she was to the point where it was almost unbearable.

Between her deep breaths, she spoke. "Michael, I want you inside of me." He brought her ankles onto his shoulders, and as he rose, her body stretched upwards, making the penetration deeper. "Yes, Michael. Don't hold back." She ran her hands up his body, grasping at him.

They moved like rolling waves upon a shoreline, but the storm was not too far in the distance as the thunderous swells began to pound.

Her body glistened while beads of sweat rolled down his face. He pursued their pleasure to the fullest. She smiled up at him, "Welcome home? Just think, Michael, you could've been having this all the time if you would've moved into my bed in the beginning."

"Maybe so, but I think it was definitely worth the wait. You?" he asked through gasped breaths.

"Exhilarating!"

It was easy to sleep the night away after having total fulfillment.

The morning came, and with it the everyday hurry of getting the kids to school, Michael to work, and then the return to the office. The kids had a half-day, and then Christmas break began for the next two weeks. Allie would be with them, and she would field the odd call. Truth be told, Rainie and Mer had usually partially closed for the holidays.

She walked into the office. "Good morning, Allie."

"Heads up, Auntie M called, and she and Paul are at her OB. She wanted to let you know. I think something might be up."

Rainie called Mer immediately, and Paul answered. "What's up, Paul?"

"Babies are coming today. Everything is okay, but the doctor wants to make sure there isn't any distress. The babies sound good. If you want, you can meet us in a couple of hours at Baptist. Personally, I think he's more concerned about being called out on Christmas, but that's fine with us."

"See you there. Can't wait to meet these little rascals."

They hung up the phone. Allie was bubbling with enthusiasm. "I knew it. From the way she sounded, I thought today might be the day."

The impending birth of the twins had to be announced. Rainie called her mom and Michael. Everyone was on prayer alert. With everything taken care of at the office, she left for Baptist hospital.

By the time she made it there, Mer was hooked up to the monitors. Echoes of swishing baby heartbeats bounced off the walls. They had already decided to have the babies by Caesarean.

She hadn't seen Mer's parents in eons. They could catch up in the waiting room, and it would help make the time fly by.

Finally, the time came. The nurses rolled Mer into surgery, and Paul was in surgical attire. His eyes looked excited but filled with nervous tears. The babies were healthy and both in the six-pound range, which was significant for twins, but Mer and Paul were tall people.

Later in the afternoon, Michael came with a fistful of balloons. Rainie was holding one of the babies when Michael entered the room. He paused when he saw her. He made his round for kisses and handshakes. It was a joy-filled occasion with all coming through the event healthy. She could tell her friend was exhausted, so she and Michael begged off, which encouraged a couple of Mer's siblings to leave, as well.

By the time they got home, Allie had already fed the boys, and they were about ready for bed. They showed the boys pictures of the new babies and Auntie M.

"Mommy, why don't you have another baby?" Henry asked. "I think it would be fun to have a little brother. Thomas has me to pick on, then I'd have someone to pick on, but I wouldn't," he assured her.

"What if the baby was a girl and not a boy?" she asked. They were not going to tell the boys until after the doctor's visit, but it was a perfect time to get an idea of how it would roll.

"That'd be okay. It's not like I'd be playing house or dolls with her, but Thomas and I could teach her how to play outside games and video games."

"I suppose so," she answered.

Thomas teased Henry, "I bet I would catch you playing dolls with her." He laughed and then looked at his mom. "Why don't you and Daddy Mike have twins like Auntie M.?" Thomas looked perplexed. "It's okay if I call you that?" He looked at Michael.

"I think we need to make sure it's okay with Mom and your dad, first. It'll all work out, Thomas. It always does. Looking at my watch, I think it might be bedtime for you two boys."

Saturday was a blur, and Sunday was Mass and lunch. Things at the club were going swimmingly when her dad's phone rang. His face became stern. "Henry Williams here." Then began a series of "I see," "uh-huh," and a few "not sure." "Tonight will be fine. See you then." He glanced toward his wife.

"Everything okay, Dad?" Her dad never took calls on the weekend. *How strange.*

"Fine, Suga. Client with a problem."

"How odd to call you on a Sunday." She was inquisitive, "Anyone we know?" Her dad gave her the look of *not your business.* She knew the look and dropped the subject.

Lunch went back to normal, but she noticed her dad tried to move it along. It was time to leave. Her parents' goodbyes were unusually quick.

On the way home, Rainie speculated with Michael about the call. They were right behind her parents but turned off to their house.

In her parents' car, it was a whole different story. "I didn't want to say anything to Rainie, but it was Tom. He needs to talk about legal representation. He's gotten into quite a pickle."

"Oh my, Henry. Anything bad? You know Rainie thought something was fishy with him marrying the young girl from his office. She thought maybe she was expecting because it was all so rushed." She turned her head toward him.

"From what little we spoke, it could be quite serious. I'll know more when Tom gets to the house tonight." He had a pensive set to his jaw.

"It must be serious if he's coming to the house tonight. Will he be coming with his wife?" she asked, thinking of what she needed to prepare.

"No, dear. Just Tom."

He ended the conversation. They got home and continued with their Sunday routine until the doorbell rang. Henry got up to answer the door. It was Tom. He brought him straight into his study.

"Come on in, Tom."

Tom looked like a wreck. He had dark circles under his eyes, had lost weight, and looked exhausted. "Thank you for seeing me, Henry. I'm sure this is uncomfortable for you."

"Tom, it's business, and it's what I do. Tell me what's going on."

He began by telling him he'd only married Diane because she was blackmailing him and now demanding a child. He said he'd had to stop the lunacy and had told her he certainly would not produce a child to come into the world under the circumstances.

Tom explained. "Two years ago, we had an elderly client who gave one of the partners, Grayson, a tidy sum of money to hold for her. She died. He took the money, and I found out, he split it with me in exchange for silence. He didn't need to split it; I wouldn't have said one word to anyone. No one was going to be out money. It wasn't like it was going to family. Regardless, it was wrong, I know. Diane walked into my office as I was stashing it. I had been out with her a few times." Henry gave a disapproving look. Rainie had mastered it, and it was clear where she'd learned it.

"I know, another mistake. Anyway, Diane pursued me, and I really hadn't any interest in her. She made a point of reminding me of spousal privilege, and she'd hate to have to be called as a witness. No one had said anything about the whole thing. No one knew about me except her and Grayson, and I wasn't concerned. Then about eight months ago, I think, she presents a letter addressed to the bar citing my indiscretion. She once again reminded me of spousal privilege. Hence, the quick wedding, but I'll be damned if I'm going to bring a baby into this shit." He put his head down, running his hand through his hair.

"Henry, what do I do? I know if I tell her no, she'll pull the same shit. I want out of the marriage, but that ain't gonna happen."

Henry shook his head. He sat looking at Tom with his hands steepled as if he were praying, but he was thinking. "You're in a hot mess, but then again, you know it. Does Grayson know about what's going on? Diane know about Grayson?"

Tom was jittery in the chair. "Yes, Grayson knows, and no, she has no idea about Grayson. I know you think I'm an asshole, but there was no advantage to getting Grayson in the hot seat. Besides, Henry, no offense, he's older than you, and I doubt she'd have approached him. Maybe I should have. He's got a hell of a lot more money than I have, for sure. Grayson didn't give a damn about the blackmail or the circumstance. He didn't even flinch. He looked over the top of his glasses and said, 'interesting' when I told him. That was it." Tom was past nervous. His knee was bouncing up and down like a dribbling basketball.

"I thought you had a vasectomy after little Henry. Tom, I'm going to have to think about this, and I'll get back to you." As Tom talked, Henry had made a few notes but was mostly doodling as he thought.

"I told him on Friday. He's pissed but knows his neck isn't on the line yet. He finally gets the severity of it all. He has asked me if I had mentioned his name to Diane. I haven't. There's no point. I wouldn't have called you today, but she went nutso this afternoon. I need out. Henry, I'd appreciate it if you didn't mention this to Rainie." Tom had a look of pleading on his face.

"Tom, I respect attorney-client privilege. No dig intended. I take it—you're hiring me, correct?" Henry looked over the top of his bifocals.

"Yes, sir. I am." Tom sheepishly nodded.

"Get some sleep, and maybe you need to start going to Mass, but pick another church or service, please. It's going to take more than me to make you come out clean. Go home."

He walked him to the door and said he'd be in contact.

After the door shut, Leslie came from the back of the house. "Well, Henry?"

"Privilege, babe, but it's fair to say he's up shit's creek without a paddle. What's on the tube tonight?" He poured himself a stiff drink. "Les, you want something?"

"Wine would be nice. I'll turn on the box and see if there's anything."

# SAVE YOUR TEARS

Tom walked into his home. Someone had tossed the furniture around, knocked pictures from the wall, and there was broken glass everywhere. "What the fuck?" he yelled to Diane, but there was silence. He ran upstairs straight to their room. She was face down in a pool of blood. It looked like a direct shot to the back of her head.

He dialed 911. He was frantic. "My wife's been shot. The place is torn up, and she's dead. Send someone. Send someone, now." The operator told him to stay on the line with her that the police and paramedics had been dispatched. He was crazed, pacing the floor and sobbing.

He hysterically dialed Henry. "Leslie, it's Tom. I need to talk to Henry."

"Tom, I can barely understand you. Let me get Henry for you."

She covered the mouthpiece and said it was Tom and he was a basket case.

"I'm here. What's up?" Henry paused. "Crap. Don't touch anything and wait right where you are for the police. Yes, you'll probably be a suspect. The husband always is. Depending on her time of death, I may or may not be your alibi. You know the law as well as I do, Tom; keep your damn mouth shut."

Tom asked if he could call him if he needed him at the police station. Henry told him who to call, and because of their past relationship, it may be more prudent for someone else to be there if needed. Of course, he was an alibi if they put the time of death when he was at their house.

Leslie listened as Henry spoke to Tom. After the conversation, he looked at her, downed his drink, and poured himself another. "Shit! He's up a creek, alright. He got home from here to find his wife dead."

"Sweet Jesus. How?"

"He thinks she was shot. Says the house is all torn up. He wanted me to meet him at the police station if they brought him in. I wanted to say to him, 'Of course they're going to bring you in.' I gave him Sid's number. I better give Sid a head's up. I have a feeling this is going to be a long road ahead."

"Henry, you don't think Tom did it, do you?" Leslie was a ball of nerves.

"Babe, I don't know. I really don't know. It's too convenient. She got shot at the same time he was coming over here talking about a problem he was having with her and some legal issues he'd gotten into. I want to say, of course, he didn't, but something isn't right about this whole thing." He kissed her forehead and made his way to the study. "Calling Sid."

The phone rang a few times before Sid picked up. Henry started, "Good evening, sorry to call on the weekend, but wanted to warn you. You'll be getting a call from my ex-son-in-law, Tom Todd. It's going to be tricky, my friend. I can't be too close to it."

Henry continued, "Tom shows up at my house needing to talk. Problem one. He and she have some legal issues between the two of them, which I'm sure he will talk to you about. I can't for obvious reasons. Then, he leaves here, and the next thing he calls from his house where he's found his wife shot to death. Oh, and the house was tossed."

Henry listened for a few minutes, then replied, "I don't know. Since he was married to my daughter and is my grandchildren's father, I want to think not, but something's not right. Good luck. I have a feeling you're going to need it. Talk soon. Good night, Sid."

Tom sat on the stairs, waiting for the police. He couldn't believe the situation. It dumfounded him, and nothing made any sense. He knew enough to know he would be the prime suspect.

When he left the house, Diane had been in the bedroom, alive. When he hadn't folded on the baby issue, she'd gone wacko. She had threatened him with sending anonymous letters to the D.A., to the bar, and she'd tell Grayson. While she could no longer testify in a court of law about the stolen money, she could still do a lot of damage and make his life miserable.

He heard the police pull up. The crackle of their radios was unmistakable. He opened the door before they knocked. There were two officers.

"Someone called 911?"

"Yes, me." He was beside himself. "My wife is dead. She's dead. Somebody shot her."

"Are you injured, sir?" The officer tried controlling the situation.

"No, aren't you listening? It's my wife, my wife," he cried.

"Is there anyone else in the house?" Protocol was imperative.

"No. Just us."

"Where is she?" The officer remained calm, trying to calm Tom.

"In our bedroom, upstairs." He pointed to an open door at the top of the stairs. "You'll see, oh my God."

The officer nodded to the two other officers that had just arrived to go upstairs and check.

They went up. Then, the radios started going off.

It would only be a matter of a few minutes before a detective, the paramedics, and the crime lab would arrive. The officer led Tom out onto the porch.

Two officers began to roll out the yellow crime scene tape, locking down the area, keeping nosy onlookers at bay. One officer stood inside the door, checking credentials and taking the names of everyone entering the scene. The system was straightforward: control the crime scene, no breach of protocol, nothing that could compromise the investigation. Within ten minutes, the place looked like a scene from a TV crime and justice show.

Tom was unhinged, dazed, with glassed-over eyes. The first officer spoke to him. "Sir." Tom stared off into space. The officer spoke a bit louder, "Sir, I need to ask you a couple of questions."

"Okay." He was in a fog.

"I need you to step away from the house. Come with me," the officer coaxed.

"Like hell. This is my house."

"It's now a crime scene, and you need to come with me. Believe me. It's better for you to be out of your house, anyway." He walked him to one of the patrol cars. "I need you to listen to me." He read him his Miranda rights.

Tom was confused, "Wait, why are you reading me my rights? This is my house. That's my wife."

"Do you understand your rights as I have read them to you?"

"Yes, of course, I do. But—"

The officer continued. "Can you tell me what happened here tonight?"

Tom looked at the officer. "Someone killed my wife."

"Is there anything else you can tell me?" he asked.

Tom was out of it. "What?"

"Sir, were you here when it happened?"

"No. Do you think I'd let this happen? My wife's dead."

"Sir, I'm trying to get a picture of what happened, that's all," the policeman responded.

Tom raised his voice. "Somebody killed my fucking wife. That's what happened." He stopped realizing how he came across. "I have no idea what happened here."

Detective Marse had walked up as Tom started his outburst and what he heard was "fucking wife." He thought, who refers to their murdered spouse as "fucking wife?" Not a good sign. He walked up to the officer and called another over to stay with Mr. Todd. "Walk with me," he said to the first officer. He instructed the other officer to remain with Tom. As they entered the house, he flashed his credentials. There was really no need, everyone in the department knew or knew of Detective Marse, but it was all about the procedure. They started up the stairs. "Catch me up."

"Sir, Milton and I were the first to arrive. Mr. Todd let us in and pointed up the stairs. The victim, Mrs. Todd," the name rang a bell in the detective's head, "she was face down in the bedroom, one shot to the back of the head."

The detective interjected, "Execution."

"Yes." The officer nodded. "Haven't been able to get any information from the victim's spouse."

"I got it from here; thank you, Collins. Milton looks like he could use a hand. There are lots of nosy neighbors." Just then, the paramedics walked in, and behind them the coroner and crime lab. "Welcome to the party, guys," he said and went back downstairs.

The detective went outside to the car. "Mr. Todd?"

"Yes?" He was very weepy.

"I'm going to have an officer get you out of here. He'll take you to the P.D."

"But I haven't done anything wrong. I want to go back into my house."

"Until it's processed, it's my crime scene. It's better you get away from here anyway," Marse added, trying to show a bit more compassion.

The officer got in the unit, and off they went.

All Tom had on his person was his wallet and phone. He called the number Henry had given him.

"Mr. Sherman, this is Tom Todd. Henry Williams gave me your name." He listened. "Oh, he did. The police have asked me to go down to the station with them. Will you meet me there? Thank you, sir."

They pulled into the station. Tom had met Sid a few times at cocktail parties at Rainie's parents' home but wasn't sure he'd recognize him. As they walked in, he did recognize him. Sid was the one they'd always speculated was a linebacker in college. He was quite a specimen even at age sixty, maybe sixty-five. He had a presence, for damn sure.

The officer escorted them into a room.

After the policeman had walked away, Sid started talking.

"Henry gave me the gist, but what happened?"

"I don't know. We fought, I left the house angry, I went and had a beer to cool off and get my head together. I was there, maybe, a half-hour, then I called Henry again. I had spoken to him earlier. I went to his house, talked with him for about another twenty minutes, maybe half an hour. Then I went home. When I walked into the house, everything was torn up. I yelled for Diane and ran upstairs to find her on the floor. She had been shot. Look, I know they always suspect the husband first, but I didn't do it. I swear to you."

"How much time was it between when you left the house and got to Henry's?"

"I guess forty-five minutes." Tom was drained, and it showed as his shoulders slumped forward.

"Depending on the time of death, you may have to account for that time. Did anyone see you at the bar?" Sid was sitting facing him, trying to get a read on his client.

"Yes. The bartender knows me." Tom started wringing his hands, passing them through his hair, and nervously looking around.

"As long as the timeline works, I can't see where there will be an issue." They sat quietly for a few minutes. "They're going to ask you about your relationship with your wife."

"It wasn't good. I wanted a divorce. It's a long story."

Detective Marse came in.

"How are you doing, Mr. Todd?"

"Horribly." He looked at him with the look of *how the hell do you think I'm doing?*

"Any idea what happened or any information you can give me?" The detective had an expressionless face and appeared void of personality. "Where were you this evening?"

"I was at the home of Henry Williams." Tom sounded defeated.

Marse took a different route. "Tom, can I call you Tom?"

"Yes." Meanwhile, Sid sat there, not saying anything. While Tom was a lawyer, and a good one, he did corporate law, a whole different beast. He knew the basics, but he hadn't killed Diane; therefore, felt he could answer the man's questions. He had nothing to hide as far as this went.

"The whole time you were away from your home, you were at Mr. William's house?"

"No. I left my house and stopped at Fat Harry's for a beer."

"Oh."

"Diane and I had an—"

Sid cleared his throat.

"No, it's okay. I had nothing to do with Diane's—" He had to gain his composure. "Diane and I argued, and I went to cool off. We did not have a happy marriage. It was a mistake, and I had gone to talk to Henry regarding getting a divorce from Diane."

"I see. Seeing a lawyer about divorce on a Sunday night at his home seems a bit strange, but okay." Marse shrugged his shoulders.

"He's my ex-father-in-law from my first marriage. He knows me and is a voice of reason. I wanted some advice, and not from my mom. Diane's young and wanted kids, I already have two kids, and I don't want any more. That's it in a nutshell. I'm pretty sure she would have wanted to move on when she figured out, no kids meant no kids. The marriage was a mistake."

"Moving on." The detective seemed as though he understood the situation. "Do you know anyone who might want her dead? Or maybe want you dead? Or was it maybe a home invasion? Someone tore your place up good, almost like they were looking for something. Can you think what they might be looking for?"

Tom was exasperated. "Are you kidding me? Diane's a kid in her twenties. She's a cute girl. I made a mistake marrying her; what can I say? Anything I have is in plain view. The TV, sound system but anything else, my ex-wife has."

Marse was subtly pushing the buttons. Maybe this guy didn't kill his wife, but something about the whole thing wasn't right. He could feel it in his bones.

There was a knock on the door. The detective excused himself and left the room.

"Tom," Sid began, "you're talking way too much. My advice, and it is what you're paying me for, shut up. Untie my hands, and this can all stop for tonight. Nothing has been processed. It's too early in the game. Let's call it a night, how 'bout it?"

The detective came back into the room. He looked at Tom as he sat. "You have a gun?"

"No. No, I don't."

"Not any kind of gun? A lot of robberies are people looking for guns."

"No guns. I have nothing else to offer. I'm understandably exhausted. I want to leave."

"I understand, this has got to be tough, and I'm sure you have some strange feelings you're dealing with now." He sat back and looked at him again. He was going for another approach. "When I heard your name earlier, it rang a bell. You related to a Rai—"

"My ex."

"Oh, I see."

"You see what?" Tom asked.

"Just that you might not want to talk about the other Mrs. Todd."

"It's Mrs. Landry, now. We're friends, and she's the mother of my children. We have no bones to pick."

"Hm. We believe one of our officers might have found the murder weapon. They found a handgun near your house."

Sid spoke up. "Mr. Todd has been gracious enough to answer your questions, and unless there is anything else, we're leaving. Let's go, Tom."

Detective Marse handed both men his card. "Mr. Todd, this is the number I have for you." He showed Tom a form he didn't recall filling out, but Tom nodded anyway. "Do not leave the area."

Sid handed him his card. "If you want to talk to my client, this is the number you'll need to call." They walked out of the room and then out of the station. "Tom, you have your keys to your car? Your wallet?"

"My keys are at the house, but yes, I have my wallet and phone. Oh, and I do have a spare key to the car in one of those hide-a-key gizmos."

"The house is off-limits to you. I suggest you get a hotel room. Your car is not part of the crime scene. You can take it. Anything inside of the yellow tape is off-limits."

"I have no clothes."

"You can buy some tomorrow. Let me know if the police try to contact you. No more talking to them."

Sid dropped Tom off in the driveway.

As Tom drove away, thoughts rambled through his mind. He'd have to make the calls to family and Rainie before they saw it on the news. The first call was to his older brother. He offered Tom a bed, but that was in Pass Christian, so a no-go. His other brother lived across the country. There was minimal conversation regarding Diane's death or legal issues. He called his parents, and then he called her mother. It was the call he really didn't want to make.

Her mother was understandably hysterical with all kinds of questions he couldn't answer. He felt like a recording with the constant "I don't know." He wished he knew. This was horrible. Even though she had blackmailed him, she was just a kid.

It was time for Rainie's call. She might be able to break it to the boys easier than he could. She was better with such things—the important things. He listened as her phone rang. She always picked up by the third ring if she was going to pick up.

Out of breath, a male voice answered, "Hello." It was Mike. *Shit*, Tom thought. He obviously caught them at an inconvenient time.

"Mike, I'm sure this is a bad time, but I need to talk to Rainie." Michael could hear the exhaustion in Tom's voice.

"You okay, man?" he asked.

Out of nowhere, he broke down. "No. Mike. I'm anything but okay. Diane's dead. Shot dead in our house." Michael was waving vigorously at Rainie to come to the phone.

"Dear God, Tom. I'm so sorry. Is there anything we can do?" Tom thought, *Why does Mike have to be such a good guy all the time? Why hadn't he thrown out a "not my problem" comment?*

"Is Rainie around?"

"She'll be picking up in a sec. She's grabbing the other phone. Do you need to talk?"

Just then, Rainie picked up. "What's up, Tom?" She was a bit cooler than Michael.

He began to sob. "Diane's dead. She was shot in our house. The whole place is torn up. Oh my God. I know you know I didn't love her, you know me so well, but I wouldn't want anything bad to happen to her. Jesus. I don't know where to turn." He was steadily losing more and more composure.

Michael spoke, "Tom, come here and go straight to the pool house. We can talk in there without the boys."

Rainie jumped in, "Who found her? Where were you? Who would do this?"

"Rainie, let Tom get here, and then we can all talk."

"Okay." It was about all Tom could mutter.

They hung up the phone. Rainie looked at Michael. "Talk about bad timing for a phone call."

Michael was putting on his jeans and a tee. "I suggest you get something on. He'll be here in five, maybe ten minutes. And the hair?"

"Yeah, I know. Just fucked, right? It should be called almost-fucked hair!"

He waited a second then asked, "Where's your compassion? This is a horrible, horrible thing. He is distraught; anyone would be, right? Whether he loved her or not, no matter what the situation was, the girl didn't need to die." Michael gave her a scolding look.

"You're right. We better get to the pool house and be ready. Lemme grab some Kleenex." She quickly dressed, pulled her hair up, and grabbed a box of Kleenex.

They walked out to the pool house, turned on the lights, and got ready for Tom.

He lightly rapped on the door. Michael opened it. "Come on in, Tom. You want a drink?"

"Just water." He looked like hell. Rainie started with the questions, but Michael cut her off and told Tom they were there to listen and be supportive. It was like opening a dam. Tom sat at the table.

He started with the story of the old lady, the embezzled money, Diane, and the threats, and kept on going. He spoke non-stop for nearly an hour, it seemed, without taking a breath. When he mentioned calling her dad that afternoon, it was like a light bulb went off in her head. Tom was the call that had ended lunch.

He told them how she had pressured him for a baby. "Rainie, you know that's not my thing. Besides, I wanted a divorce. I never wanted to marry her in the first place."

She began to feel a little more sympathetic, just a little.

Holding his head in his hands, he wept some more. "After talking to your dad this evening at his house, I went home. The place was trashed, and she was lying on the bedroom floor, dead. I called 911. They took me to the police station, read me my rights. They didn't handcuff me, thank God. They think I had something to do with it."

Michael asked him if he had a lawyer, and he said yes, and told him about Sid. Rainie remembered him.

"Tom, does Grayson know about Diane and the blackmail?" Rainie, with her endless questions, sometimes completed the sketch. "I bet he thinks you told her about him." She leaned forward in her chair.

"I told him I didn't, and I wasn't going to. I see where you're going with this, but I don't think he could be involved in this. Not Grayson." Tom's fingers twitched nervously.

"Are you kidding me, Tom? I know you have some hero worship with him, but the guy is a sleazeball. He was constantly chasing my skirt. I also heard he's notorious for being unethical, like, um, taking a dead woman's money. Pretty slimy if you ask me," she said and shrugged her shoulders.

Tom dropped his jaw. "Rainie, you come up with some shit. The Tolbert, Thibeaux, Smith, and Todd law firm is reputable. No way in hell would Grayson Smith do anything that wasn't above board." Tom's face was dead serious, almost offended.

"Isn't that where the whole thing began? Hello, Tom, wake up." Her hands shot up in exclamation. "If you think for one second this is the first time he has pulled something like this, then you're a fucking moron. Oh, I don't think for an itsy-bitsy second he pulled the trigger. He doesn't have the balls for that. Oh no, he got one of his loser clients he got off on a technicality to do the deed. Y'all deal with the scum of the earth." She was heated. "And you better watch your ass because he won't think twice about turning on you. I don't know and don't want to know where the money is, but you better give it back. Regardless, he's gonna let you hang out to dry. His pockets are deep, and he can afford whatever he wants, pay off whoever he wants, but you don't stand a chance. Call him. Call him now, and tell him what happened, and see his reaction." She leaned back in her chair and crossed her legs.

"I don't think I can. I'm not strong enough right now."

"Oh, for the love, Tom. Call him." There wasn't an ounce of sympathy in her voice.

Tom took Mike up on the offer of a drink.

"Rainie's right. Call Smith. You'll be able to tell if something doesn't feel right. Get yourself together. Be calm, cool, and collected." It was easy for Mike to say, Tom thought, he was always in control.

Tom slugged back the drink and tapped the numbers. The call went through fast. "Grayson, it's Tom. I've had an incident at my house this evening. Someone broke in and killed Diane." The look on his face was one of horror. "That doesn't make anything better. They think I killed her or had something to do with it." He started pointing to the phone. "She was my wife. My wife. One of your employees. I feel for her mother. She was only in her twenties." Michael was signaling for him to get off the phone. "Yes, it is shocking. I'm sure you're right. I may be too close to the situation to understand the ramifications. Okay. I wanted to let you know and I won't be at work tomorrow. I have a funeral to arrange."

He hung up the phone. "What the hell? He wasn't bothered by the news at all, and he actually said, maybe, it was for the best in the long run. Who in the hell says a thing like that? When I told him they thought I had something to do with it; he said I did. After all, she was my wife. Besides, I had been sloppy about the money thing. I needed to be more cautious in the future." He got up and poured himself another drink. "The fucker was callous and matter-of-fact. Who do I talk to? Do I tell someone Grayson's involved in some kind of way?" He shook with agitation and anger.

Rainie turned her hands up. "Tom, I don't know anything about any of this kind of stuff. I do know someone at the NOPD that might listen to you and advise. My NOPD guy's a real straight shooter." She was point-blank with him.

Michael had to interject. "I don't know how wise it would be, Rainie. I know who you're talking about. Tom, ask your lawyer what he thinks of Rainie's idea." Michael was the tranquil sea in otherwise stormy conditions.

"Thanks, Mike. I can't go back to my place, y'all." Tom stood. "I'm getting a room at the Hilton downtown. Besides the details for a funeral, I have to pick up some clothes. I can't get back into the house until the police finish, and who knows when that'll be."

"I can lend you a pair of jeans and a couple of shirts if it'll help. I'd say our sizes are pretty close." Michael stood and walked toward Tom.

"Thanks, but that's okay. I'm gonna pick up a couple of things tomorrow. Thanks, y'all." Tom shook Mike's hand. "Rainie, I don't even know how to tell the boys or if I even should. They had just started to warm to her." He started to tear up. "I gotta go."

For once, she felt sorry for him. They turned off the lights and went into the house. "What a mess, Michael. I told you there was something with the rush wedding thing. I can't believe he took the money. I thought more of his integrity."

Michael looked at her like she was crazy. "Really? I'm not surprised, just maybe disappointed. I don't know what to think. One thing for sure. I don't want the boys with him until this is all over. I wouldn't be surprised if his partner doesn't or hasn't put a hit on Tom."

"Grayson, who was on the phone?"

Grayson looked at his wife of nearly thirty-five years. Their marriage had been one of pure convenience, and they'd stayed together after the kids were grown because it was easier. He walked to the liquor cabinet and poured a drink.

"Tom Todd."

"Oh, what did he want?" she said disgustedly.

"To tell me his wife was dead. Stupid bastard brought this all on himself."

She was even colder than he was. "I told you two years ago to get rid of him. He was a weak link. Then y'all made him a partner. Did you honestly think it would buy his loyalty or grow his balls? Tolbert was right from the beginning. He was too much of a pussy to get into your circle. What'd he think you were going to do with that piece of ass blackmailing him. Stupid girl. She should have stuck to spreading them and sucking dicks. And the asshole married her. I bet he had no idea y'all passed her around like a toy."

He ignored her crass comments. Who to call? It had to be someone different, and there were many in his debt, so he made a call. He spoke briefly into the phone, "Tom Todd. Chase his card. By morning. Ten grand." He hung up.

"Who'd you call?" she asked.

Once again, he ignored her. She left the room and went to her bedroom with a bottle of Scotch. Her young friend was putting her clothes back on. "Jeffrey's in the shower. Are you done with us?"

"You're a little premature," the woman said. "I'm nowhere near done, dear, not with you anyway. Jeffrey might want to check in with Grayson, though."

☙

Back in the squad room, Marse poured over his notes. He knew there was something big missing. The why. What was the motive? Todd was already planning on getting a divorce. When he looked him in the eye, he saw a scared, freaked-out man. Tom was totally out of his element. He looked like what he was, a corporate lawyer. A piece to the puzzle was missing.

One of the officers from the scene plopped in a chair in front of him. "You think the guy did it? I know they always say look to the spouse, but it doesn't ring true with me on this one."

"Nah, I'm not liking him for the crime. I need to get this wrapped up quickly, though. The deed was cold-blooded, and I think this Todd guy is next on the list. Don't know why I think that, but I do. We got a whole different kind of killer than one who commits a crime of passion. You figure he was out of the house for maybe an hour, two at the tops, and she gets whacked. This smells like a hit. Don't get me wrong, this guy is no angel; he's guilty of something, I'm not quite sure what, and what's more, I don't care."

# MERRY LITTLE CHRISTMAS

The morning came, and Rainie thought of Tom. She couldn't imagine having to go through the ordeal of funeral arrangements. She'd never had to. She didn't even remember Rand's funeral, but she knew there had been one, and the church had been packed. From the stories, Sacred Heart had been out in force, as well as her parents' friends and business acquaintances. Peculiar, she had no memory of it, and it wasn't like something where people would snap pictures. It truly was a blank.

In her head, she heard Rand say, "You, dear sister, were checked out. Wouldn't even look at me, but you were in the church—the back of the church being babysat."

"You're extremely thoughtful this morning." Michael came behind her, put his arms around her waist, and gave her a soft kiss on the neck, "Are you alright?"

"Yes. I'm feeling for Tom. Even though things were not the best with them, it's still got to be hard. Plus, I'm thinking about the discussion with the boys. What do I say to them? They aren't going to understand. I don't think either has known someone who's died. They have all their grandparents alive and kickin'." She was slow getting dressed. Her heart truly hurt for Tom.

"Ask God to give you the right words, and He will. Don't underestimate them; they're sharp and may very well get it. I wouldn't go into the how of it, only the result. We can do it together if you want.

Tell me when." He grabbed her as she walked by. "I'm here for you and the boys." Holding her close, he looked deep into her ice-blue eyes and wanted to take away her pain and the bad memories it conjured.

"Together would be better, in case I start to break down. I didn't know the girl, anything about her, yet I feel a pang of intense sadness." She had a blank expression on her face as though in disbelief.

"You know, Rainie, you put on a tough exterior sometimes, but you feel much more than you let yourself acknowledge. I think it may be a deep-seated something. You have let your guard down some, and as a result, you're experiencing your feelings differently. You yourself told me you felt like you'd never loved a man as you do me. It's because you've finally permitted yourself to take a chance." *Always wise words from Michael, like clockwork. Before you say anything, Rand, don't.*

It was almost time for Michael to leave for work. The kids were on Christmas break, so it wasn't the rush it usually was in the morning. "Let's talk to them now." To herself, she asked God to help her with the right words.

They could hear the boys stirring around in their room. At least they were already awake. Michael lightly tapped on the door frame.

"Hey guys, we gotta talk a minute." Both boys looked at her with a curious look. "I need to talk to you." She and Michael sat on their beds. "Mrs. Diane passed away last night, guys. Your dad is sad, and I know you may be, as well. It's perfectly normal."

Henry's bottom lip began to quiver. "Why? I, uh, we just got to know her. I know Daddy's gonna be sad. Poor Daddy." He slouched and brought his hands to his face.

Thomas was a little colder. "I'm sorry she died, Mom, but we only got to know her a little bit. It's not like we're going to miss her. I guess I feel sorry for Dad. He's gonna miss her a lot. I'm sorry I made fun of her now." He occupied himself with his iPad.

Henry rolled onto his side, face still covered, and began to sob. Rainie sat next to him. "It's okay to cry. It's sad for the people left behind when someone dies. All I can say is she's now in God's hands, boo." She hugged him tightly. "Just think, she's in heaven with Aunt Rand." He climbed up in her lap.

෨෦

Tom stayed in the hotel bed, not wanting to face the new day. He wasn't looking forward to being with Diane's mom.

Mrs. Albright was a nice enough lady, but she'd made her feelings known. She thought the marriage was premature. It wasn't about Tom, but her daughter. Growing up, in her mother's eyes, Diane had shown a questionable moral compass. Her husband had passed away when Diane was eleven, and she regarded her daughter's lack of moral fiber as a statement of her poor parenting. Diane was all she had. She either held on too tight or gave in too quickly. There was never a happy medium.

Tom looked over at the clock. It was 9:30. He had to get his ass out of bed and go pick up Diane's mom. All he had were the clothes from the night before until he could pick up more it was going to have to do. He jumped in the shower and then was quickly dressing when there was a knock on the door. "Shit, I told her I was picking her up. I shouldn't have told her where I was," he said under his breath.

He was tucking in his shirt when he opened the door. It happened too fast to slam the door closed. A man held out his arm and fired two rounds. There was no time for anything. His death had been instantaneous.

෨෦

Rainie kissed Michael goodbye. Having him next to her had made the talk more comfortable. His mere presence was reassuring. Henry had been quite tearful but managed through it.

They sat with Allie eating breakfast while Rainie was pulling out bowls and cookie sheets. "Y'all want to help me bake Christmas treats to bring to Poppa Jack and Missy's?"

Both boys looked at her as though she'd lost her mind. Thomas voiced his pass. They finished eating and went into the backyard to play.

Rainie and Mer generally shut down the office during Christmas and New Year's. There were never any bid requests at that time, and they had long stopped "decorating and maintaining" country clubs and businesses for the holidays. It became way too much physical labor and didn't pay near enough.

She and Allie were up to their elbows in baking when her mom called. She told Rainie to turn on the television. A young woman was reporting some sort of activity at the Riverside Hilton but had no details.

"Okay, I see it, Momma. They haven't said squat about what happened. It's New Orleans—nothing new around here. Crimes happen all the time, and you're watching way too much TV. Turn some Christmas music on or come over and help us bake Christmas treats."

"You're probably right. I get hooked on the scandal of it all. Good idea. Love you." They hung up.

Was it a good idea to listen to Christmas music or help bake? She'd know soon enough. It only took her mom a few minutes to get to her house. Rainie turned on her own Christmas music. It always added a festive touch.

While they baked, Rainie and Allie talked about the wedding and the honeymoon. She told Allie everything she could think of about the beauty of the place and the unique experience. The conversation turned to Michael's parents, and how they were going to celebrate Christmas at their house, and that her parents were going as well. Rainie couldn't quite figure out the dynamics of it all, but Michael said it worked. Nothing to fret about. She needed to roll with it and breathe.

Putting on her imitation of his voice, she said, "'Just breathe, Rainie.' He tells me all the time." She sifted the flour.

"Because you need to." Allie was as sweet as could be and elbow deep into baking. Rand echoed in her head, "Yeah, you need to. Even the girl knows." Rand snickered. Allie smiled as Rainie had that faraway look she often had. "Things have a way of working out, no matter what. It's much easier to ride with the flow than fight the current all the time." She flipped a batch of baked cookies onto a sheet of wax paper. "Eric and I are doing our own Christmas at his place. It's going to be weird, but then we'll go see my mom and dad and then end the night at his parents."

"Hm. Christmas together and parents' house—do I need to start looking for a new nanny?" Rainie smiled at her. "I'm glad you have someone special. I've wanted it for you."

With her hand on her hip, Allie looked at Rainie. "What? Absolutely not. If and when the time comes, I'll give you plenty of notice, but I don't see anything happening anytime too soon."

Allie saw Rainie's mom come in through the side gate. She tapped on the window to let her know the door was open. "Hi, Mrs. Williams."

"I love the smell of Christmas," she said as she peeled off her coat and propped her handbag in a chair. "Your house with its decorations could be on the cover of a magazine, Suga."

"Oh, Momma, come see the garland on the mantle. It looks especially festive." When they walked into the family room to look at the fireplace, there wasn't any garland on the mantle.

"That's odd. Would Mike have taken it down, or maybe the boys?" Her mom seemed surprised, but no more so than Rainie.

"I'm not sure." Rainie tapped her chin with a quizzical expression on her face. "I know the boys didn't. They know not to touch my decorations. Maybe Michael worried about fire. I'll have to ask him when he gets home." She knew damn well it hadn't been Michael. She and Stella, the decorating ghost, were going to have a conversation. "There are still too many cookies to make, and I want to make a happy birthday, Jesus cake. The boys need to understand the reason for the season. Michael made the comment we needed to read the Bible on Christmas Eve to the boys. The part where Mary—"

"Rainie, Suga, I get the picture." After a few hours, it was time for the boys to come in for lunch. Her mom prepared their lunch, and she took a moment to go to her room.

Rainie went in and shut the door. She looked around, and everything seemed in place. "Stella, we've been getting along fine since I moved in. We've never had any issues, and now you've taken my garland down. First, the window open and now the garland. I'd appreciate you putting the garland back. If we need to communicate, let me know. I know this was your house, and you loved it, but I must be able to do things and not have you thwart my efforts. I thought we had a good understanding." Rainie went back to the kitchen.

The boys were finishing lunch, and then an hour of quiet time would commence. She usually allowed them to play electronic games or watch TV.

"Mom," Thomas called out. "Dad's on TV."

She couldn't imagine why, but to appease the boys, she went into the den to see. It was a picture of him. It clicked fast enough she was able to get the TV off in time. She could hardly breathe. She could feel her hands trembling, her chest tightening, and her head started swimming. "Boys, no TV. Play your games instead."

"But Dad was on TV," Thomas argued.

"No, they had a picture of him on the television, that's all." She tried to hold it together but couldn't. "Oh my God." She started to cry.

The boys looked at her, completely confused.

Thomas was upset. "I'm sorry, Mom. I didn't mean to make you cry." His voice had a tremble as though he were about to cry.

She drew both boys to her and held them tight. "You didn't make me cry, Thomas." She swallowed hard. "I think maybe your dad was in an accident, and that's why his picture was on TV. I have to go find out, but y'all need to stay in here with Allie and Mimi." She called out to her mom.

It was difficult to concentrate, and she needed to be sensible and calm. *Breathe, Rainie*, she thought. She went back into her room and turned on the TV. She saw a gurney rolling out of the hotel, holding a body bag. Uncontrollable tears ran down her face. All she could think about was the conversation they'd had the night before. She called Michael. She told the receptionist it was an emergency. He was on in a dash. He listened and said he'd be on his way. "No, Michael, you need to see your patients. I wanted to tell you. Gotta go; I love you." Her voice cracked. She hung her head into her hands and sobbed.

The arm went around her shoulder in a comforting way. "Oh, Momma." She opened her eyes and saw the mist, no shape, only mist. It was like the mist when Rand visited her, but she could see Rand when that happened. She couldn't see a form in this mist, but she knew. "Thank you, Stella. He was my boys' dad. His name was Tom."

She could hear in her head, almost like a whisper, "Call Meredith."

Her heart was heavy, but she picked up the phone, sat on the bed while the phone rang.

"I was about to call you. What in the hell happened, Rainie?"

"Oh, Mer, so much has gone on since we got back from the honeymoon. Here it is Christmas Eve, and I have to tell the kids their dad is dead. So much for my blissful happily ever after." She drew her knees into her chest.

"Don't be like that. Why Tom, and what the hell was he doing at the Hilton?"

She laid back on the bed, "Yesterday Diane was killed, and now today Tom. Like we said with the rushed wedding, Tom was in trouble. He did something unethical. She caught him and blackmailed him. Now they're both dead, and I think I know who's behind it all. I'm not sure what I'm gonna do. I feel like I owe it to my boys to report what I know, but then maybe it would make it harder on them."

She could hear one baby crying in the background and the other one closer to the phone, making grunting sounds. "Rai, I'm on my way."

Why were things always so damn crazy? Did the rest of the world have shit all the time? It was one of those moments. *Breathe, oh, and pray. Yes, pray.* She dropped to her knees at the side of her bed and pleaded her case with God. She needed help and guidance and the right words to tell her boys. The prayers must have gone on for a while. There was a buzz going on downstairs.

Mer and the girls were there. Her boys were ecstatic, as were her mom and Allie. With all those willing hands, she and Mer could have time to talk. They went outside to the office.

Meredith paced for a few minutes, thinking. "Rainie, we have to strategize this. Handle it like you would a client. What are the advantages of taking the job? Do they outweigh the disadvantages? If you were to contact your detective guy, what's the advantage and the disadvantage? What kind of impact will it have on your family? Because my friend, that is number one. Could you maybe give the police the info and then be done with it? You don't have skin in the game, except you think you need to correct the wrong. Or you can always step away completely."

"Maybe I should talk to Michael." Rainie rocked back in her chair.

Mer plopped in the chair in front of Rainie's desk. "Or maybe you should do what you think is best. Mike will most certainly back your decision. Don't lose who you are because he's the knight in shining armor. You don't need rescuing. Don't get me wrong, it's great for you to have a man that wants to take care of you, but I'm watching you give your strength away, too. There's a healthy balance. Where's the feisty, Rai? Where?"

She had to sit back and think Mer's comment through. Had she lost her gumption? Did everything always have to defer to Michael? She was not some fucking damsel in distress. In her mind, she could hear an "Atta girl." Stella, Rand, or God?

"You're right. You're absolutely right." She got her purse, dug through it, and found Detective Marse's card, and without thinking or re-hashing it, she called.

He answered, "Marse."

"Hi Detective Marse, I don't know if you remember me or not, this is Rai—"

"I remember you. It's Mrs. Landry, right?"

"Yes. You know about the situation at the Hilton?" He said he did. "I think I know the why and the who."

"You have my attention. Lemme hear it."

She went on to tell him about the embezzlement thing with Grayson. She told him about the night before and the conversation in the pool house. There were no punches pulled when she described Tom's conversation with Grayson and the impression he was giving regarding his partner's cavalier attitude. He had come clean on all accounts.

"I don't want any more involvement," she told him.

"Mrs. Landry, thank you for calling, thank you for the information, and I hope I won't, but I might need to get your statement at some time, maybe."

Her heart sank. She didn't want Grayson to think she might know something. She conveyed the message to the detective.

"It probably won't come to it, but that's merely speculation. You did the right thing to call me."

"I think so, too. Bye."

Mer sat there listening to one side of the conversation.

"You did good, Rainie. I know it was hard. It's time for you to have a good cry, and I'm here for you, my friend."

Cry, she did. Mer sat still. It felt like hours, but perhaps it had been half an hour. She wanted to tell the boys with Michael, but she didn't need him. She was perfectly capable on her own. No, she wouldn't wait. It would happen after everyone had left. It'd be the three of them. Raw, open, and honest. She wasn't going to sugarcoat anything. They were bound to see or hear bits and pieces, and she wanted the truth, the whole truth coming from her—time to get back in the house.

Mer's babies were precious and tiny. The boys sat on the sofa, each one with a baby in their lap. Allie and her mom were standing close enough if needed.

"Mommy, look how little she is. You need to have a baby like this one." Henry was careful to be gentle, "Do you want to hold her?"

"Yes, Henry, I would." She sat next to him and held Baby Claire. "It looks like the babies might want their mommy. They're getting hungry." She looked at her friend. "Feed 'em here, friend, or you need to get going. They're getting fidgety."

The babies' things got packed up, and the friends embraced. "Merry Christmas, Mer."

"Merry Christmas, and I'll be thinking of you. You did good, my friend." She kissed her cheek. They loaded up the car with the plethora of things necessary to take a baby, let alone two, anywhere.

She asked Allie to pack the boys' bags for Christmas. Going to Michael's family for Christmas, especially with the chain of events, seemed like a good move. If there were any place in the world to help start mending those little hearts, it would be at Jack and Missy's. She hollered up to Allie to pack for more than a day or two.

The phone rang—it was Michael. "How are you doing? I've been thinking about you. Maybe it's a good thing we're going to Mom and Dad's. Their place makes even the worst of times feel better."

"Funny, I was thinking the same thing. Mer and the babies just left. Momma is heading out as well. It'll only be the boys and me. I have a lot to talk to them about. I love you, and I hope you don't mind—I'm gonna tell them before you get home."

"I'm here for you, Rai, but you have this. Don't doubt yourself for one second. I don't. I love you." He was there to support her if she wanted.

Allie went upstairs to pack the boys' bags. Rainie's mom was gone, and it was the three of them. They were back on the sofa with their games. She sat in between them.

"Guys put the games down. We need to talk without any distraction." She held their hands as she unfolded the nightmare of Tom's death. She was honest and started with Diane's death. She didn't go into what Tom had done or how Diane manipulated it, but she didn't sugarcoat how both their dad and Diane had crossed a line. And because they'd crossed it, both had been shot to death. There it was.

As expected, they were quiet and confused.

"Do you have any questions?" she asked them. Bubbles exploded in her stomach as her nerves raced to the edge.

"Is that why Dad was on TV and why you turned it off fast?" Perceptive Thomas, always a step ahead of the game. He looked her straight in the eyes.

"Yes. I didn't want you to hear about it on TV. I wanted you to hear it from me first so that we could talk about it."

Henry suddenly became perplexed. "Daddy's in heaven now? Will he still go to heaven even though he did a bad thing?" The tears started. "I won't be able to see him again? Ever? I don't like this, Mommy." He buried his head in her lap and broke down in sobs.

Thomas hung his head. She could see his shoulders shudder with held-back tears. "Thomas, it's okay to cry. You need to let it out." She tried to put her arm around his shoulder, but he jerked away.

"I'm mad at him. Why did he have to be bad?" The tears were coming from him too. "He and Miss Diane are stupid. I hate them. He always told us not to do bad things or else, but he was doing bad things. And now he's dead. He can't make it go away. I hate him. Why would he do that to me and Henry? He was supposed to be our dad and not do bad things, especially not really bad things, so that some bad guy would kill him. I hate him, and I hate Miss Diane."

It wasn't the time to stop the hate word; she had to allow his release of anger. The three of them sat in silence, holding hands. They all had the same blank stare of disbelief on their faces. Silence. She could hear the ticks from the clock in the hall. Pretty soon, it would chime. Any noise would be deafening right then. It was like the stillness could not be disturbed. Life would stand still if they stayed silent. At least for a moment.

What a horrible thing she'd had to do. It had been bad enough telling them about Diane, but Tom, it was crushing. And in some ways, Thomas was right. They were a special kind of stupid—they were greedy and selfish. She wondered if Tom had ever put the boys before himself. Probably not. He'd even admitted he wasn't a good father, but he wasn't a bad man. Neither of them had deserved to be murdered.

Allie put the boys' bags by the door. They were ready when the time came. Rainie still had to pack.

Michael had told her Christmas in the country was casual. Very casual, like hang out in lounge clothes all day kind of mellow. But, on Christmas Eve, everyone dressed to the nines. They would go to church soon after they got there, then dinner would be catered, but at the house and in the formal dining room. According to Michael, it was something to write home about. The itinerary was church, family pictures, dinner, and then Missy would read *The Night Before Christmas*. When he told her, he said, it had always been that way since he could remember.

As she packed, the boys entered her room with questions needing answers. They wanted to know how bad the bad thing was that Diane and their dad did. She explained that what their dad did wasn't right, but it hadn't hurt anyone. What Diane did hurt some people, not physically, but messed with their feelings. What she did was unkind and selfish, but that she was a young adult and maybe didn't know better. It seemed to suffice for the time being.

Michael made it home. The boys ran to him, not with their usual happy faces. He took both of them in his arms and hugged them. "I heard what happened, guys. I'm sorry. It's sad, and the sadness might hang around in your heart for a long time. My grandad's been in heaven for a lot of years, and still, sometimes I get sad missing him. I know your mom is going to be sad, too. She and your dad had some special memories. Like when you two were born and when you were wee babies." He held them close.

She watched them. Her heart filled, and Michael was right—she and Tom had special memories. Nothing could take that away, not even death. She knew she looked like a wreck. No doubt it had been a rough two days. "I'll get myself together," she told Michael. "While you pack, I'll get some concealer for these circles." She checked her reflection in the windowpane, patting her eyes.

"Not at all, you're gorgeous, and nothing's gonna change your beauty. You're sad, Rai, and you have every right." He hugged her tight, kissing the top of her head. "It's going to be okay. I'm glad we're going to the country."

They went up to their room, and as Michael packed, she told him the missing garland story. "I'll be interested to see what she does with the garland. I thought it looked nice how I did it, but I know it'll be outstanding when she does it. She even nudged me to call Mer after I found out about Tom." She went silent for a second, then asked, "We'll have time to change into dress clothes when we get there, right?"

"Yep, my ghost whisperer." He winked at her. "Ready, set, go. Let's head out. I'm going all back roads; the interstate will be a rolling parking lot. We'll have plenty of time to talk on the road."

They left Allie at the house, where she would wait for Eric. It was going to be a strange Christmas, and it sure didn't feel like Christmas Eve. The ho-ho-ho had gotten up and left.

# NAUGHTY OR NICE

D riving the back roads was scenic compared to the interstate. They chatted lightly, discussing just about anything to avoid talking about the elephant in the car. The conversation was all about the delicious cookies and Rice Crispy treats. The boys talked about the twins and brought up the baby discussion again.

"Have you made an appointment yet?" Michael whispered.

"I did first thing this morning. It's after the new year. Friday, January fourth, the first appointment of the day, which is 9 a.m. I thought it would be best for you." Brief silence again. "It was about an hour, maybe less, before Momma called about some hubbub at the Hilton. Little did I know...." Her voice trailed off.

The presents were already at his parents' house. Rainie had had them delivered there, and as they came in, Missy would call her, and Rainie would mark it off the list. Despite the sad situation, it was going to be a good Christmas. Since it was her and Michael's first actual Christmas together, she had gone a bit overboard, and given the circumstances now; she was glad she had.

"How long are we gonna stay at Poppa Jack's, Mom? Will I get a chance to ride, or is it too cold to ride the horses?" Thomas wanted to know.

"They love the cold air, kiddo. Maybe we can even go on the levee," Michael said. Rainie cleared her throat, looking at Michael with a spunky look, but he continued. He winked in the rearview mirror at Thomas. "Your mom loves the levee." Rainie grinned as she remembered the last time they were on the levee. The stars had glittered the sky, and then, oh yes *then*. She could feel her face pink and the nether regions tingle. This was not a time for her to be having thoughts along those lines. She felt guilty.

Michael could read her. He patted her hand, held it, bringing it up to his lips. "What has happened has happened, and has no bearing on a fun night on the levee. You're allowed to smile and laugh. It's not uncaring or disrespectful—it's human." He kissed her hand again.

"I know," she whispered.

He whispered back, "Permit yourself to laugh, to smile, to love. Concentrate on the happier times y'all had and remind those two of those times. You want them to have good memories. Can you get my mom on the phone?"

She passed the phone to him when she heard Missy answer. "Soon yes. Garcons papa a ete assassine ce matin, nous avons besoin d'un controls des degats passer le mot. Thanks Mom. Yes, Je t'aime, aussi. See ya soon."

She looked at him, bemused. "I didn't know you spoke French."

"Yep. Fluent in Italian, almost fluent in Spanish and a little German, but not enough to hold a conversation, but enough to read a menu and order," he laughed. "However, last time, I don't know where I messed up. I got a horrible plate of indescribable food. I will never live it down."

"Can you teach me French?" Thomas squirmed in the backseat.

"I thought you took French at school, no?" Michael inquired.

"Yes, but it's just saying the same words over and over again. How'd you learn?" Thomas was full of questions.

"My mom taught me when I was very young." They made eye contact in the rearview mirror.

Rainie jumped in, "I can see Wendy being multi-lingual, but John?"

"He speaks the most. He's got a knack for languages where he picks up on them fast. Not so much with me. Mom drilled me and wouldn't speak in English until I answered her properly in whatever language we were learning at the time." She noticed the corners of his mouth turn up in fond memory.

They were on River Road. The boys started getting antsy; they recognized where they were from Thanksgiving.

As the car turned into the driveway, Rainie opened the glove box and pressed the button. The gate opened. They could see Michael's mom standing by the fountain. When they got out of the car, Missy hugged Michael and whispered something to him, which he answered in French, then her attention went to the boys and Rainie.

"Let's get you settled. You know where to go, boys. Y'all are going to have to shower and dress in record time if we're going to get a seat." Rainie saw her parents' car so went looking for her mom. "Rainie, darling, your mom is in one of the guesthouses getting dressed. Now you scurry. We don't have much time."

Everyone went upstairs and rushed to get dressed. "Michael, what did you tell your mom on the phone? I knew it was something about the boys, and this morning, I remembered what little I studied in college." She, too, was moving quickly to get ready.

"I told her about Tom, the murder, and that we'd need some damage control, oh, and to pass the word. As you know, Mom is good with the boys."

Michael got the shower going and unpacked his things. As he waited for the steam, Rainie stripped her clothes off, and he watched with a growing smile. In no time, his clothes were off, and he followed her into the shower. "Hello in there. I love you," he whispered to her baby bump. He looked up at her and went to his knees. He skillfully maneuvered his tongue to all the right places. "I want to make you feel fabulous. Get that just been tasted glow."

She wrapped one of her legs around his shoulder. "You know what to do." He pulled her into him, following her request. "Feel free... anytime. Don't stop, not yet." He made the most of it, and while he aroused her, he let her know he was pleasuring himself, which turned her on. She watched and could tell his moment was imminent. "Oh, my God." Her body began to twitch, but she wanted to watch. It made her feel like she was a part of it. He nipped lightly. When she responded, he nibbled a little harder. Whatever it was, she felt better than good. There was no doubt she liked the rough stuff. Maybe after the baby and the six-week check-up, she'd ask him for a nasty romp. They were married; it was okay. Anything between husband and wife was within the rules, right? Especially a long, hard fuck.

They both rinsed off quickly and dressed in record time.

Since Allie wasn't with them, Rainie had to make sure the boys had it right. She popped into their room. They were playing with Sam and their cousins, and yes, they had gotten it right. The kids were laughing and playing.

"Y'all are going to smell like wet puppies if you don't settle down." Rainie gave each one a good look over. She straightened their snap-on ties, tucked shirts, and brushed hair. "Let's get downstairs. We're ready to face the grandparents." The boys ran down the stairs, sounding like a herd of buffalo.

Michael exited their room looking more than hot, wearing the bow tie from their honeymoon. It brought back fun memories, as he'd known it would. He could read her like a book.

☙❧

The decoration committee had done themselves proud, donning the church in Christmas splendor. Missy's house with its décor was out of a magazine, yet she took the time to compliment the ladies on their decorations for the celebration of the Savior's birth. The service was good, the kids behaved, and her parents seemed to enjoy the difference, which surprised Rainie, as they were devout Catholics.

The cars pulled up at the house following services, and the photographer was ready to start family pictures. Missy used the selected shot each year as the following year's Christmas card. She had done this since her kids were little and had a photo album specifically for the Christmas card photos.

When they entered the house, nothing could have prepared Rainie and her parents for the set-up in the formal dining room. Servers stood at the ready as though they were royalty and the food choices were exquisite – prime rib, chicken Marseille, or trout meuniere. The kids had chicken strips, shrimp, or grilled cheese. They started with turtle soup with the best French bread Rainie had ever consumed. For dessert, they served bananas foster, and what a presentation! At every place-setting was a Christmas cracker, an English tradition they had adopted.

Each person had their own, instead of the proper way of sharing. The kids started first. When they popped them, there was a loud clank at each place setting. Jack had had old-fashioned I.D. bracelets engraved. He showed the boys how he wore his. The women had Tiffany's signature bracelets. Rainie and her parents were awed. The whole thing felt like a scene from a storybook, sparkling with magical light from the chandeliers and gleeful sounds of yuletide joy.

It was then time to move into the Hearth. The kids all sat cross-legged on the rug, and the grown kids in chairs or propped on arms of chairs. It was intimate and beautiful, especially when Missy began reading the story. One could have heard a pin drop. Rainie had never listened to the story told with such exuberance. It was marvelous. Missy encouraged the whole room to say, "Merry Christmas to all and to all a good night."

Leslie took Missy's hand. "I have to tell you, I have never had such a beautiful and love-filled Christmas Eve as this evening has been. I cannot thank you enough for including us in the festivities."

It was time for the kids to go up to bed, and a few minutes later, Rainie checked on her boys. Henry was in bed with Thomas. While it was sweet, it was also highly unusual.

Henry was tearful. He snuggled next to Thomas. "Boys, do you want to sleep with me tonight? It's been a sad and strange day. It's okay." At first, Thomas said no, but then because Henry wanted to, he said he would. That way, Henry wouldn't feel like a baby in front of the cousins.

Michael was still downstairs with his parents, her parents, and John.

The kids followed and climbed in bed with her. The darkness of the room amplified the sound of sniffles. Henry was between her and Thomas. She held them tightly.

"Mommy, I'm being squished. You don't have to hug us so hard."

The three of them started to laugh. The laughter was through tears. It provided the perfect segue for questions.

"Anything you want to say?"

"Mom, there's nothing to say. I've already told you. I'm mad and sad all at the same time." Thomas was to the point, but she could hear a waver in his voice.

"That's normal, my love. It's something that happens sometimes." She felt his confusion. She was right there with him.

"Mommy, please don't do anything bad. I don't want you ever to die," Henry said. Her little guy began to sob.

"Henry, Mom doesn't do stupid things and never does bad things. Don't even think about that." Despite picking on Henry, Thomas was a good big brother.

Rainie kissed each boy's forehead. "Of course, I won't do anything bad. I love you. We need to try to have sweet dreams and go to sleep so Santa can come, right? Shut those eyes and go to sleep. Did y'all say prayers with your cousins?"

"Yes, Mom. Our cousins say out loud prayers every night. So, we did too. They were cool. Matthew prayed for Dad and our family. He started it, and everyone else copied him." She could hear the admiration in Thomas' voice.

"Good. I love you two. You're my boys forever and ever." She kissed them both again.

Downstairs, the rest of the grown-ups were having coffee. Unbeknownst to the kids, Michael, John, and Dave were setting the Santa scene. Wendy helped, but it was mostly the guys doing all the work.

"Remember those days, Henry?" Jack pointed to Mike, John, and Dave.

"It was always a very long night," he laughed, remembering Rainie and Rand and the Barbie dollhouses.

They talked about Tom and how shocking the whole ordeal was. Everyone expressed concern for the boys.

Michael piped in from across the room. "The boys will be okay. Kids are resilient. It's Rainie I'm concerned about. She holds things close and doesn't release."

Both Leslie and Henry agreed. They told them how she wouldn't acknowledge Rand's death for nearly a year and how at the funeral, she'd insisted on staying in the back. They'd had someone from the church remain with her. She didn't want to see anyone or talk to anyone. There were two people she would talk to, Mer and Sister Caire, besides them.

No one asked questions surrounding Tom's death, and Henry wouldn't have been able to say anyway. He'd made no bones about not liking Tom as a son-in-law. Henry had always had the feeling there was an underlying agenda. Nonetheless, this was a horrible thing to happen, and Tom hadn't deserved what he'd gotten.

The guys finished setting up the gifts. It looked like a toy store with a fancy window display. Then it was time to call it a night.

Leslie, once again, thanked Missy and Jack for such a magical evening.

Missy hugged her. "We're family, and that's what it's all about—coming together and celebrating the birth of our Savior. It just doesn't get any better. The day after New Year's Day, we begin planning for the next year. It's a Landry thing, what can I tell you? I love how our families have blended so beautifully." It was sweet and heartfelt. "I'm worried about Thomas and Henry. I know Michael and Rainie think it's a good distraction being here, but I'm not so sure."

"Mom," Michael said. "The boys are going to be okay. We wanted them away from the TV and all the bullshit. Tom did a number on them when he was alive, but I'll be damned if he'll do it from the grave. I was always cordial and polite. Never once did I utter a disparaging word or remark to anyone about him, including Rainie and especially the boys. My place is to listen, and I listen to her. Now, I'm heading to bed, and my beautiful wife and bid you all a very good night. See you for the mayhem in the morning. Merry Christmas."

He took the stairs two at a time. When he opened the door, he saw the three of them peacefully sleeping. His plans of romance went out the window, but their play could always wait, and this couldn't. He put on his pajama pants and crawled in next to them. The sound of their soft breathing put him right to sleep.

Peculiar dreams invaded his sleep. Tom, he, and Rainie were talking in the pool house. Tom told him he now needed to be the dad. The boys needed a steady hand. What could be better than a Christian surgeon, right? He said he should have stepped aside a long time ago. He hadn't been a good husband, and he was sorry. He said he'd miss them. And like a radio that is in between stations, the dream flickered in and out. Clear and then fuzzy. Tom got up and walked out the door, but before he did, he turned and smiled with a tear in his eye.

Michael sat upright in bed; his dream had been more than vivid, almost life-like. He rolled over but could not fall back to sleep; besides, go time was only an hour, maybe two away.

It gave him time to think about what the next Christmas would hold. There would be another child, maybe a boy or a girl. The miracle of conception and gestation had always amazed him. How could anyone not believe in God? Two cells come together, and this union, by fluke, makes a human being? Not in his world. It was all in the Creator's hands. He used the rest of the quiet time to talk with God. It was those early hours when he really could feel His presence and feel connected.

Henry was the first to start. "Is it Christmas yet? Did Santa come?"

"Let's whisper. We don't want to wake Mom or Thomas. Okay?"

"Yeah. I had a dream about my dad last night. He told me he was sorry, and he had made mistakes, but that you would be a good dad. He told me he loved me, looked at me, waved goodbye, and smiled. He was in our pool house. He talked to you, Mommy, me, and Thomas. I could see his lips moving but couldn't hear words when he was talking to y'all. He looked happy when he left. He's going to be with Jesus, huh?"

"I think so. I want you to know I love you, and I'll be here for you."

"I know, Doctor Mike, um—"

"We have time to figure that one out, buddy. Until then, Doctor Mike works fine."

It was still and quiet. Michael and Henry listened for any other voices.

Henry's eyes popped wide, and he stilled like a statue. "I think I heard Luke."

"You did," Thomas blurted.

Then Rainie jumped into the conversation.

Michael explained the deal. They, with the boys, would wait outside of the bedroom, as would Wendy, Dave, and their family and Uncle John. Sam would probably stand with John.

Thomas said, "You mean Big J?" He snickered. "That's what I call him. I hope it's okay."

"If he went along with Big J, then okay, I guess." Michael laughed.

They waited outside of the bedroom. The kids waved to each other. All of them were wound tight as tops and most fidgety. Michael mouthed 'Big J' to John. John gave two thumbs up.

First, they heard loud Christmas music. Then Poppa Jack called out, "Come on down, it looks like we've had good kiddos this year judging by what Santa left."

"It sure does," she hollered back. "Y'all come see what Santa brought for you."

The kids raced down the stairs in stampede form.

"Holy shit, Michael." Rainie was astonished.

Poppa Jack and Poppy had on Santa hats and were handing out presents—calling name after name. There was no separation as to who gave what to whom. The mayhem went on for over two hours. The kids were almost exhausted. Almost.

Missy and Mimi had elf aprons on. "Hot chocolate for everyone. Big kids, there's coffee and tea as well." Missy had the Hearth table stacked with donuts, cinnamon rolls, and pastries of every sort. Jack's rule was no cooking on Christmas Day. They all were still in loungewear and slippers. All the food for the entire day was finger food: paper plates, plasticware, just actual spoons for stirring hot chocolate and coffee.

Rainie couldn't believe her mom and dad would be at someone else's house in their PJs, but they were. Laughter and cheer filled the house. There was more loving going on than she'd ever seen. It felt good. All the kids thought Big J was the perfect name for Uncle John.

After the craziness had died down, everyone took the time to examine their gifts. Words of thanks bounced around the place. No one knew who had given what, and that was just the way it rolled at Jack and Missy's.

The three older boys had received minibikes. In their eyes, they were motorcycles. Sam did get a dirt bike, and Henry, Luke, and Little John had go-carts. Jack had converted an old paddock into a dirt track, complete with tiny mounds. Helmets were mandatory, and Jack told them that there would be big-time consequences if he found someone riding or driving without one. It was like a fantasy trip for kids.

As Michael, John, and Wendy had everything imaginable under the sun, their gifts were less exciting, except for a planned weekend trip to New York—great dinners and a play, but it was for adults only. While not overly extravagant, it was another opportunity to spend time with family. John had enough time to make himself available. He was given a note: 'No hookers or paid escorts, please.' He had three months to find a great date.

Michael pulled his mother to the side. "We don't know how far along Rainie is. She may not be able to travel."

"Honey, we will re-arrange if necessary, but I think she'll be fine. If she can't travel, we'll cross that bridge when we get to it. It's private, so we kind of control the situation." She winked.

John had a serious talk with his mom. She was as confident with John as she had been with Michael. What was there to worry about? If it came down to it, he could always ask Dominique, the girl from River Road. He tried to explain their friendship was not like that.

Missy spoke boldly. "John, I'm not saying you have to have sex with her. You could look at it as a travel companion. Y'all get along. She might like a trip to The Big Apple, but who knows. Let's worry about it when the time comes."

The kids played hard all day, which gave Michael and Rainie time for a nap. Michael asked, "How were the boys last night? I didn't expect them in the bed, but they were most welcome. I think it was good for you, too. You had some just-you time to snuggle with them." He wasn't sure if he should tell her about his dream. Maybe he should wait.

She had something in her eyes. Like she wanted to say something but was unsure. She closed her eyes. "I had a weird dream about Tom last night."

"As did I and Henry. The little guy told me all about it. I'm sure he'll tell you." They discussed the three dreams. They were similar scenarios. "See if Thomas had it too. I bet he did." The messages had been slightly different, but each message was customized and pertained to their relationship with Tom.

"Today has been amazing. Is it like this every year?" she asked.

"Close, but there were five more people, so it added to the fun. I hope your parents come every year. I don't know why Wendy's in-laws don't come. Come to think of it, they've never come. They're lovely people, but maybe we're not sophisticated enough for them, being country folks. Maybe they can't afford it, but it doesn't seem as though that's the case. Who knows?"

They snuggled and relaxed amid a sea of thoughts.

She broke the silence. "Michael, what is your favorite kind of sex? Ya know, oral, va-jay-jay, forget anal not gonna happen, dominance, self-gratification?"

He smiled big with a snort. "You really don't like the word masturbation." Their bodies molded like spoons in a drawer. "It depends on the circumstance. There's no better or worse. It's all great, as long as I'm with you. I love it all." He rolled on his back and peered beneath the blanket. "Now, look what you've done to me."

"Christmas sex has to be wholesome, family-style," she laughed.

"I sure as hell am not inviting the family to our private time." He had a deep belly laugh straight from his core. "I know what you mean." He had to laugh again. "Let's start with a kiss." He kissed her. He touched her. He slowly made love to her. It was gentle, romantic. It was definitely her idea of Christmas sex. Afterward, he inquired, "And your favorite?"

"Oh, that's easy. Hard, rough, and raw, nothing sweet." She burst out laughing.

"You're fucking hilarious. I wanna know, did you set me up from the get-go? Cause if so, I bought in hook, line, and sinker." He was still laughing.

"No, I didn't. It just came out. Like you, it depends on the situation. I love it all emotionally, but I think I like it rougher from an orgasmic point of view. But just now, I felt immensely loved. I know this is going to sound horrible coming from an expectant mom, but sometimes I like being your whore."

He looked shocked. "I would never treat you like a whore. Where did that come from? Oh my God, I love you. I hope I don't make you feel—"

"Don't be so serious, Michael. It's like sometimes I want it playful, sometimes sweet, sometimes down and dirty. I want to please you. I've even been thinking about after the baby, never mind." She wrapped her ankles around his and stammered in an attempt to avoid the question.

"No, ma'am, you started this. Honesty is our thing. You'll never get judgment from me. You can tell me anything."

"After the baby, I've fantasized about going into your Pandora den of pleasure, and I want you to do to me what you've done to other people. I know we did what we did, but I'm sure there's more. I know it would be different with me since I'm your wife, but I wanna try it out. Curiosity, I guess."

The silence was deafening. She knew Michael was thinking of the best answer.

"We'll see. I was in a very dark place, and I never want to get there again. I love you any way I can have you, even if it's snuggling. I think this whole conversation was ignited by my self-gratification, as you put it, but it's different than lying in bed thinking of you and jerking off. It's an us thing. Admittedly, before we were together, there were quite a few nights when I let my mind go to your face, your smile, you in general, and I self-gratified." He laughed. "It's nowhere near the same. Like you claim you never have, um, yet you seem to go for it and enjoy when we're together. Does that clarify things for you?"

She started getting antsy. "It does, and I do get it. We've been up here for a while, and there'll be little people looking for us." They got out of bed and got dressed back in their PJs.

At the door, he grabbed her. "My crazy, gorgeous wife, I love you. I almost forgot I have something I wanted to give you alone." He reached into a drawer and pulled out a slender box. Her eyes sparkled as she opened the box.

"Wow. It's beautiful." A tennis bracelet of sapphires and diamonds glistened against the black velvet tuft of fabric inside the box.

"It's to match your engagement ring."

"Oh my gosh, it does," she said with a glint in her eyes. "Michael, we agreed on little gifts."

"Thank you would have just worked as well, and for your information, this is a little gift." She gave him the squinty, you're-in-trouble eyes. They went down to the Hearth.

Jack looked out the window, watching the kids play. Michael stood next to him. His dad put his arm around him. "I sure wish I could bottle their energy. I'd make a mint. I used to say the same thing when y'all were kids. Next year, Mike, there'll be another stocking to hang for old St. Nick."

"Yes, sir. I'm excited." The melodic rhythm of his voice and puffed chest expressed way more than excitement.

Sam entered the room. "Where's Miss Rainie?"

Michael pulled him over quickly. "Call her Aunt Rai, Sam. The miss thing sounds old to some people. I learned my lesson years ago. You need her?"

Sam was holding her cell phone. "This thing has been going off a bunch. I reckoned she might wanna know. That's all, sir." Sam was a bit skittish.

Michael took the phone and found Rainie in the kitchen with the two moms. "Your phone has been going off, according to Sam."

"I don't even remember where I put it. It should have been in my bag. I put it away when I come here." She cocked her head with a look of curiosity.

"Do you? Well, maybe Sam can tell us where he found it." Michael looked perplexed as well.

Sam told Jack, John, and Michael he'd been coming from Neverland, his room, and heard the phone going off like crazy. He'd followed the noise and found it, figuring it must be important for someone to call on Christmas Day. The fact that he'd gone into their room sent up a red flag even though his motive was well-intentioned. It would be a discussion for another time.

"I hope everything's okay. It's gotta be Allie or Mer." Rainie looked at the missed calls. She felt her stomach drop as she thought, *shit, I didn't tell Michael about Detective Marse.* "Michael, can we go outside for a minute?" Once out the door, she continued, "I totally forgot to tell you." She explained about the call and the conversation with Marse. "He's the one who has blown up my phone."

"You what?" He was not happy. They moved further from the house. "How could you forget to tell me? I'd say that's pretty important information. I wish you hadn't, but what's done is done. I'm right here with you. One hundred percent. Damn." She could tell he was pissed.

"I'm sorry if I pissed you off." She placed her hands on his as he gently held the sides of her face.

"No one can get pissed on Christmas, so I'm not pissed. I will be tomorrow, however. What did you tell him?" Michael looked down, gazing directly into her eyes.

She told him everything she had said and made sure to mention the part regarding not testifying.

"Call him back. Let's get it over with." Yep, he was pissed. He rarely got angry, but had it not been Christmas, she probably would have had an earful. Michael looked toward the floor, listening, but distracted with anger, he controlled so well.

She called. "Detective Marse, I see I've missed a few calls from you. I was away from my phone since it's Christmas." He apologized but thought she should know. They had spoken briefly with Grayson Smith. His gut said her feelings of concern were warranted.

Rainie put the phone on speaker. Michael let him know he was in the room. "Dr. and Mrs. Landry, I know this is time with your family, and I didn't want to make the call, but Mrs. Landry, you seemed quite concerned, and I think with due cause. I wanted to let you know, and also I need to know—do you think Grayson knew y'all had spoken to Mr. Todd?"

"No," Rainie answered with certainty. "The only time he and I spoke was when we transferred the boys from one car to another, and it wasn't overly civil. I think everybody in town knew things had not gone well. I'll tell you, Michael and I are disturbed and sad about the whole thing. Nobody deserves what either of them got." She looked at Michael, clearly trying for an apologetic expression.

"Thank you for the information, and I'll do my best to keep you out of court. Have a good rest of your day, and Merry Christmas."

"You, too, Merry Christmas, detective," Michael replied. They hung up. He looked at Rainie. "Anything else I should know?"

"Nope," she said. "We'll more than likely see Grayson at the funeral. Not that we need to talk now, but what about the boys? I don't think they should go, you?"

They looked at each other, trying to read between the lines of silence. Rainie could see the argument both ways. Yes, it was their dad, but did she want them to have sadness as their last memory?

"I don't think so, but it's your call," Michael said. "I think it would be better for the boys to remember him as they do rather than lying in a box. I'm not sure how disfigured he might be, and you don't want that to be the last memory of their dad. Up to you, though." He held her hands in his, raising them to his lips. "Your call, Rai."

Deep in thought, they were both startled by another voice.

"Suga, there you are. I was wondering where you two had gone. Momma and I would have left this evening, but Missy convinced your momma to stay until morning. I guess we will. Michael, this has surely been one of the loveliest Christmases I can recall. Leslie and I feel blessed as our two families have come together as one. Your parents are very special people." Her dad put his arm around Michael's shoulder.

"Yes, sir. I think so, too. I'm blessed to have them and to have you and your wife, as well." He turned his head with a smile.

The three of them joined the group in the Hearth. The discussion was about what family game they could all play after dinner.

There was nothing special for dinner, just the leftovers from the night before and remnants of the Jesus birthday cake. Then they went to bed.

Prayers had been said, teeth had been brushed, and the tribe of boys were tucked into bed. Rainie whispered to Henry, "Do you want to sleep with us again? It's okay." He shook his head.

Michael got into their bed and watched as she took off her loungewear from the day. She turned to him. "Do you think your parents would mind if we stayed a couple more days?"

Still watching her every move, he answered, "Not at all, but I can't. I have a sizeable patient load this week because school is out another week. You and the boys would be more than welcome, though, and Wendy's group won't fly out until January second. I can always come back and get y'all whenever you want. We'll do New Year's Eve here. Warning, my dad likes fireworks as much as any kid. We need to find out from Tom's parents when the service will be; you'll have to put on your big girl panties."

She adjusted her posture to a more defensive pose. Shoulders squared off, and no sign of a smile anywhere to be found. "That's not nice to say, Michael."

"No, it's a fact. It's not nice at all. I know how you feel about these sort of things." He was articulate and made it known it wasn't up for discussion.

She threw on a tee shirt and climbed into bed. "Whatever. I'm beat, Michael. Hug me to sleep."

He pulled her in next to him. It was a peaceful night's sleep. No messages from the dead. No scary bad guys. All the turmoil had brought up the same weird feelings she had experienced with the break-in earlier in the year, but she had her shit way more together.

Michael's self-confidence was contagious. He had managed to break through the walls she had craftily created, insulating her feelings from being hurt. It wasn't that she was weak, just that she had built so many walls she had become numb and hadn't given a fuck about anybody or anything except her two boys, her parents, and Mer. Until Michael.

She may have acted like a ball-buster to some, but those who really knew her knew the truth. Inside she had deep feelings and loved like there was no tomorrow. Yes, she was a strong woman. Yes, she had been through a hell of a lot, but there were many, many people out there with it far worse. She didn't go in for pity parties; it wasn't her style.

The next day, Michael was up way before she was and had already spoken to his parents about Rainie staying. It was agreed, if she or the boys wanted to go home before he came back the morning of New Year's Eve, his dad would provide the ride.

He tip-toed into the room. The sun came through the windows as though announcing a new and wonderful day. He leaned over and kissed her. "Good morning, sleepyhead. I'm getting ready to head out. I have appointments starting at eleven today. I thought everyone deserved a lie-in after the Christmas high. Mom and Dad know you're staying here, and it's fine. They're ecstatic. I'll be back the morning of

New Year's Eve. If for any reason you or the boys want to come home earlier, my dad will bring you home, or I'll come get you."

"I don't want to be away from you that long," she pouted. "But I thought the boys would like it here with Wendy's kids and Sam." She pulled him down to the bed.

"Baby, I can't. You're deliciously tempting, but I have appointments." He tried to hold a serious face.

"I'm not wearing any panties. FYI," she flirted.

He slid his hand under the sheets between her legs. She was wet and welcoming. The more he touched her, the more of a temptation she was and the weaker his resolve. She threw her head back and arched. Her body was begging for his. He turned her sideways in the bed, pulling her to the edge of the mattress. He dropped his trousers and took her with force. She fueled his drive and welcomed his intensity.

He had known rough, and if that's what she thought she wanted, he'd make sure she had it. The wilder it got, the more she desired. She seemed to get off on the rawness of it. He'd brought her to the point of no return. She started gasping, to which he responded, "Oh no, baby, this is what you wanted. I'm taking it all the way." She grabbed his hips and held on for the end of the ride.

Rainie was rapturous, and having caved to her wanton lust, Michael was disheveled, sweaty, and in dire need of a shower. He was going to be late, something way out of his norm. What would he say? Traffic was terrible, or my wife and I were having a fucking good time, literally?

"Woman, you're insatiable. I'm spent. Hopefully, the ride into the city will get me back on my game."

As he came out from his quick shower, she smirked playfully. "Doctor Landry, your game can't get any better. Do you mind me staying here?"

"I love you staying here. I know Wendy and my family do too."

She walked him to the car in her Christmas PJs. It was a quick bon voyage. She watched as he went out of the gate and took off on River Road. He'd been gone for maybe twenty minutes when her phone rang. She answered with a smile on her face.

"I miss you already, Rainie. All I can think about is our morning escapade. You are an amazing temptress."

Lounging in the bed, she was free to tease him and, in her sassiest tone, said, "Oh, I don't think so; you, my friend, still like it rowdy. Let's just say I'm glad my doc appointment isn't for another week. He might think a wild animal had attacked me if it was today. I have bite marks on my inner thighs, bad boy!"

"Yeah, maybe, but it's no longer about dominance and submission. Baby, it's all mutual and equal. You control as much as I do what happens and what doesn't. Did I cross any lines?" Silence. "Didn't think so."

She lazily stretched. "Not yet, but don't worry, I'll let you know in a heartbeat. The thing is, Michael, I love it all with you. The romantic, sweet, slow, almost melodic way we make love and the downright hardcore animalistic rawness of a hard fuck. It's all great, my love. You keep it interesting. Now drive carefully and stop thinking about it or you'll have some explaining to do when your patients see you come in with a bulge in your pants," she laughed.

She threw on some leggings, an oversized sweater, and fluffy socks. Padding into the kitchen, she helped herself to some orange juice.

Missy, sitting in her chair, smiled at her. "You already miss him. I see it on your face." Rainie nodded and got a little choked up. "It's okay, dear. A lot of it is the pregnancy, but y'all have had quite a roller coaster ride as of late. The wedding, the honeymoon, then getting back to the Diane and Tom thing. I would have understood if you had wanted to cancel and have us come to town. Come sit by me."

"I wouldn't have missed this for the world. Y'all's Christmas blew my parents away." She grabbed one of the kids' donuts. "Missy, do you believe in paranormal interaction?" Rainie curled up in the chair next to her mother-in-law.

Missy was quick to answer. "Heavens, yes. We have a couple of souls still around here. I think one is Jack's grandad. He resented the aging process and not being able to climb the steps to go to his bedroom. I see him walking around the property sometimes. I say hi. I never knew him, but I'm pretty sure he knows me."

"Do you think Michael ever saw him?"

"If he did, I didn't know about it. I think women are more inclined, but maybe not. There was a child that died on the plantation some hundred plus years ago. Wendy came in one day from playing. She must have been ten at the time and told me there was a little boy who looked lost wandering around the property. Nobody else saw him, and she had been playing with John and Michael. I haven't seen him, but I have seen Jack's grandad. I hear you're called the Ghost Whisperer." Her eyes glittered as she spoke.

"I can't believe he told you. Has he told you I communicate with Rand? It's like she's always with me." Rand's voice rattled in her ears, "You got a problem with that, Rainie?"

Missy's eyes widened for a quick second. "There's very little he doesn't tell me. Coming from Michael, nothing shocks me. He's deep and has always been a smidge different. John, he's a lumbering, what-you-see-is-what-you-get kinda guy. He opens his mouth before he thinks, but that's who he is. Wendy is my thinker. She talks a lot too, but her words are all chosen, even if she acts silly. All three of them love deeply. In that, they're identical. They're the same at the core, but then again, it's Jack's and my way as well. We're a family of truth-tellers, lovers, caretakers, and loyal to a fault. It's who we are, and I think you fit right in, my dear." The corners of her mouth turned up.

Rainie sipped her orange juice as she swallowed the last bite of the donut. "Our house is haunted by a woman who was killed by her husband. The house is hers, no doubt. I found out she'd been one of New Orleans' best interior decorators. If you were anyone, she did your house or office. She's fantastic. I notice small changes here and there. Like I might put a plant in one place, and the next morning it's been moved. It's pleasant, and I think she likes us. I hope she's happy. I always thought spirits were trapped between two worlds and were unhappy, but Michael seems to think it might be dimensional, and they can pass back and forth."

Wendy entered and pulled up another chair close to the conversation.

Missy patted next to her on the chair. "I have room here for you, my darling." Then turning back to Rainie, she continued, "Who knows? We all will find out one day," Missy smiled and looked at Wendy, who was sipping a tumbler of juice. "We're talking about communicating with or seeing ghosts."

Rainie looked at both her new family members. "It's odd, the night

Tom was killed, Michael, Henry, and I had similar dreams. They all ended with him waving goodbye with a smile on his face. I don't know if Thomas had the dream or not, and I'm not sure how to ask him without making him feel bad if he didn't."

"Don't worry yourself about that. Thomas will process in his own way. Can you girls check on Jack? He's painting in the barn."

"Sure."

With their glasses of orange juice topped up, Rainie and Wendy headed to the barn. Wendy called up to Jack. No answer. So, they went up the spiral staircase, but he wasn't in there. Rainie glanced around at his newer pieces. One caught her attention. Even though it was impressionistic, there was no doubt it was from the wedding. The painting emanated love. She and Michael were facing each other. It was when he was putting the wedding band on her hand. Even with the blurry edges, he'd captured the love. It brought tears to her eyes. She could have stood there and cherished it for hours, but she was on a finding-Jack mission.

Wendy sniffled. "Dad's paintings are wonderful. Don't you think?"

"Absolutely."

They heard him coming up the stairs. "What're you doing up there, Rainie girl, oh, and my precious lady?"

"Mom sent us to find you, Dad."

Rainie was still misty. "I saw the painting from the wedding. It's spectacular, Jack. It filled my heart. So beautiful." She hugged him.

"I think it will look great in your family room, but that's a decision for you to make. It's yours. I'll bring it in when I finish. I have some touches to add."

"It's perfect as it is."

"Have y'all checked the kids out on the dirt track? You need to see them in action, but don't be alarmed. They're doing well."

She and Wendy started toward the track. Now she knew why Jack said not to be alarmed. The slight mounds and dips didn't look scary until she saw the boys on their minibikes flying over them. Thomas looked over and waved.

"Two hands, two hands. Look where you're going!" Rainie yelled. He went around again, then pulled off and rode to her.

"Mom, maybe you should stay inside and not watch. We're having fun and playing by Poppa Jack's rules. Aunt Wendy, you tell her, she's such a worrywart." Wendy laughed and said she was going back to the house to visit her mom.

Rainie warned him to be careful but to have fun, then walked back to the stable. She called up to Jack, and this time he answered. He was an interesting man to talk to with all his life experiences, the places he'd seen, and the people he'd met. She and Jack shot the bull for an hour, but her stomach growled, drawing her back to the house and the kitchen.

She made a plate and moseyed into the Hearth. Missy had her nose in a book. She recognized the cover; it was the one her friend had given her, *Fifty Shades of Grey*. Trying to keep her eyes off the book, Rainie smiled and asked if Missy wanted anything from the kitchen.

"Rainie, have you read this book?"

"Yes, I have. Where's—"

"Upstairs with Dave," she answered and continued. "It's a sweet love story. The guy is head over heels for her." She closed the book. "The sex is pretty out there, but I guess whatever floats your boat. Jack laughs and tells me I'm reading smut. I told him hardly. Some of the other books I've read make it look like a nighttime story. Of course, I would never tell him; he'd be horrified. Men can be silly. By the way, the boy I told you about, he comes around a lot when the kids are here, so don't be surprised, Mrs. Ghost Whisperer." Rainie tried to keep her mind as blank as possible, given the topic and the book.

Rainie sat, sandwich in hand. "Hopefully," Missy continued, "with time, he'll talk to you. I'd love to know his story. I've always had the 'gift,' as they call it. I don't know about it being a gift though. Jack believes me, but it doesn't happen to him, so he doesn't truly understand. Usually, they don't talk to me like they do you, but I wonder if your lady spirit would talk to me." *Fascinating.* Rainie had a lot in common with Michael's mom.

"I don't know. Maybe next time y'all visit, we'll try to talk to Stella in my bedroom. Michael isn't bothered by it, but I know he thinks it's weird. He's seen her do things like open doors and windows. She's never tried to communicate with him, to my knowledge. I figure she didn't like my garland and took it down."

"Rainie, you didn't worry about fire?"

"No. It wasn't hanging down low enough to catch fire," she answered.

"I bet your Stella moved it because she worried about fire. Does she know you're expecting?"

"I would imagine. Michael and I talked about it."

Here they were, she and her mother-in-law talking about the paranormal. She started feeling funny about it. Missy cocked her head, looking at Rainie.

"What's on your mind, Rainie? I just got an odd vibe. Does it make you uncomfortable talking about this with me?"

*Fuck, she read my mind.*

In her head, she thought she heard; *It's part of the gift.*

*Oh shit.*

Missy giggled. "I censor them, dear. I always knew what the kids were up to, but as I said, I censor. I don't want to know what people are thinking, and I can't hear everyone's thoughts. It's strange. We all have our gifts. Yours may be you communicate with those who've passed on. I've only seen them but never spoken. Grandpa salutes me or winks." She giggled again.

"Maybe. It started with Rand. When I think about my teenage years, I used to feel like she was looking back from the mirror at me. I had extremely vivid dreams about her, but I was a bit freaked when I thought I felt her presence. Seeing the mist and feeling her next to me was a total mind fuck. Sorry but that's the only way I can express it." Rainie put her fingers to her lips.

"I've heard the word. Remember, I had two boys and my husband worked the river. Never use it toward anyone, I think."

"I don't."

"I didn't think you did. I have a good book you might want to read. It's a bit racy, but I'm sure you can handle it." She handed Rainie a book by C.D. Reiss. "She's a wonderful storyteller."

They sat quietly in the Hearth and read. Missy had been right; it was saucy, but the pace of the book was fast, and the characters popped off the page.

Michael's drive back to NOLA was uneventful. His mind turned back to the morning, then pondered how Rainie had held her sensuality dormant for as long as she had was a mystery. Any man would have totally fallen for her wicked abilities. Whatever had awoken inside of her, it was blowing him away. He felt he was a blessed man. She thought it was all him, but that was far from reality.

Even with the playtime in the morning, he was only fifteen minutes late to the office. The girls at the office oohed and cooed over the wedding and wanted to hear about the honeymoon and family Christmas.

The examining rooms were business as usual, but a few patients noticed the wedding band and congratulated him. His appointments kept him busy until the day finally came to an end. When he pulled into his driveway, he suddenly felt alone. He knew the feeling all too well and didn't want to experience it ever again.

He went into the house, unloaded all the Christmas gifts, packed a bag, and got back on the road. The trek was familiar and went by fast, but not fast enough. By the time he got there, it was dark.

The gate opened, and he pulled in. His mom and Rainie were by the fountain waiting. He jumped out, bag in hand.

Rainie ran up to him and wrapped her arms around him. "I can't believe you drove back. I've missed you."

The corners of Michael's lip twitched upward. "Why do you think I drove back? The house was empty without you and the boys. All the packages are at home. I got to see my patients and hear all the girls' yakking about the wedding and questions about the honeymoon. I have an early case tomorrow, so I'll have to leave extra early." He looked directly into her eyes, looking for confirmation.

"Message acknowledged and understood." She blushed.

His mom put her arm around his waist, and the three of them walked toward the house. "Michael, you're right in time for dinner. I had Dominique prepare dinner. I wish John would pay closer attention to her. She's adorable and so nice."

Michael looked at his mom and said, "And *that* is precisely why he doesn't pay more attention to her. I don't think he's looking for adorable and nice."

Ignoring Michael's comment, Missy continued, "I happen to think he might have changed his attitude since your engagement, and especially now that you have a baby on the way."

Rainie's phone buzzed. "Hey, Allie. What's up?" She listened for a few moments. "How'd you find that out? His parents left a message at the office? How bizarre. Thanks for the heads up. Of course, I'll be there. See you tomorrow." She looked at Michael. "Tomorrow night's the wake, and then Thursday's the funeral. Odd, Tom's parents left a message at the office and didn't call me. My country holiday will need to be cut short."

They went into the Hearth. Everyone was sitting at the table waiting. The men stood up as soon as Missy entered the room. Wendy's kids knew to stand. It didn't take long for her boys to pick up on the protocol. They promptly jumped to their feet as well. Missy told everyone to take a seat. She invited Dominique to join them.

Jack and Michael gave each other a look like, 'She didn't really do that?' Dominque declined the invitation. "Mebbe some other time, but t'anks." She looked at John and smiled. Michael caught the wink from John to the woman.

The boys told their glorious tales of dirt track riding and kept the conversation going throughout dinner. Soon after dinner, John excused himself and took off. Missy pursed her lips. "Jack, I told you. Y'all don't listen to me. A mom knows her kids."

"I'm not arguing, but you don't know where he's going." He sipped his coffee.

"Bet I do, but that's talk for another time." Missy was smug. She knew John was meeting up with Dominique, no doubt.

The grown-ups exchanged looks for a few moments and then went back to listening to the tales of the day.

Michael and Rainie had agreed it was best for the boys not to attend the funeral but didn't ever want them to resent not being told. Seated on the bed, they called the boys into their room and told them about the wake and the funeral. They also explained the option of staying with Missy and Jack but that she and Michael would be leaving for the city very early in the morning.

Thomas was emphatic about staying and not going to the service. "Everybody's going to be crying, and I want to think about Dad at Disney and at my games. We know he's in heaven now with Aunt Rand and Miss Diane. Dad will be happier now. He wasn't happy a lot. He's gonna get to see Jesus, Mom," he said with animation.

"So, you guys are sure? I don't want you to be upset later." She held Henry close on her lap.

"Mommy, I'm still very sad. Knowing I won't see him again for a long, long, long time hurts right here." Henry pointed to his chest. "When I think about Daddy, my throat squeezes, too."

Thomas patted Henry's leg and glanced into Rainie's eyes. "Maybe you'll have a dream like I did. Dad was in the pool house talking with us. He told me to make the most of my skills but to be kind. Dad said he was sorry but that he'd be watching me and that his spirit would be cheering me on. Then as he walked out the door, he turned, looked at us, waved, and smiled. I know he's okay." Thomas nodded. "He's okay, little guy."

Henry perked up. "I had that dream, too, and so did Dr. Mike and Mommy. He's okay. He smiled."

There it was—everyone had been allowed a final goodbye. That was good of Tom, she thought. It had been settled.

# HOLD ON

The morning came too fast, and soon they were flying down the interstate, both trapped in their own whirlwind of thoughts. She knew the next couple of days were going to feel weird. She had been able to arrange with her parents a time to meet at the wake. There was no reason she'd have to stay the whole time.

It was still early when Michael dropped her off. As she leaned across the car and kissed him goodbye, he asked, "Rainie, you okay? I know this has to be hard on you."

Rainie turned sideways in the seat, watching him behind the wheel. Even his profile was perfect. "It's really not. Do I sound horrible? I'm concentrating on the good times because I want to feel good about him rather than have bad feelings. Bad feelings would only lead to guilt, even though I have nothing to feel guilty about." *I bet I sound like a cold-hearted bitch.*

He put his hand gently to the side of her face. His eyes full of love for her, he said, "You're one amazing lady, and to think you're *my* lady."

"That I am, Dr. Landry, and if you don't get going, you'll be late. Now kiss me. I'll see you this evening." The hand he had so gently traced along her cheek slid to the back of her neck, and he pulled her in for a hard, deep kiss. "Ooh, Michael, I think I'm gonna swoon. What a kiss!"

Her heart rate sped up, and all she wanted to do was say, *take me now.* "Michael, you need to leave now, or you *will* be late for your surgery. I'm a horny mess, thank you very much." She giggled as she exited the car.

"Oh, you'll thank me later tonight. That's a promise, and you know I always keep my promises." He laughed teasingly. Her eyes lit up, knowing he was thinking about the last time he had warned about not threatening but promising. *He blushed. He actually blushed. My goodness, Michael.*

Standing by the driver's side, she leaned in to kiss him sweetly and give him a great view down her shirt. "Have a great day, my love. Later."

She waved as he backed out. The house felt empty and had a bit of a chill to it. What was needed was a fire to take the dampness out. The mantle looked beautiful. Stella had arranged the garland, so it was built up a bit more, and she put a bit more flounce in it. Perhaps Missy had been right, and Stella had worried it was too close and might catch fire. "It's gorgeous. Thank you, Stella." She got the fire going and put some decaf to brew. She pondered as she walked around the house, turning on her wax warmers. *Ghost Whisperer.* She giggled. *I'm sure there are lots of people that have the same experiences. I get Rand, but Stella feels just plain weird.* Rand piped in, "Well, I'm glad you get me. Ever think Stella is lonely?"

Calls to Mer, Allie, and her mom took about an hour. She lounged on the sofa in front of the fire. She opened the book Missy had given her. The more she read it, the more sexually aroused she became. At this rate, she'd be panting by the time Michael got home. She heard the kitchen door open. It was Allie. *Perfect.*

"Glad you're home. Have I got stuff to show you! First, how was Christmas with the new in-laws?" She plopped next to Rainie on the couch, full of smiles.

Feet crossed on the ottoman holding tight to the book; she turned to face Allie, who seemed dazzlingly happy. "Enchanting, magical, love-filled are a few words that come to mind. Like a fairy tale Allie, but I've been thinking of you and the new beau."

"It was great, and I'll tell you all about it, but I gotta show you some crazy shit in the office." She pulled Rainie's hand.

They took a quick few steps outside to the office, and Allie held up a file folder from the stack on Rainie's desk. She had an expression of excitement but also a leeriness.

"These are the files you found in Stella's study drawers. Out of curiosity, I glanced through briefly. She was meticulous with notes and progress. Everything was detailed. Anyone could pick up the file and know what was going on. We need to implement some of her practices. When Mer comes back, she can feel in the loop, but when I found this one, I knew you had to see it."

Allie handed the file to Rainie, who began reading at once. "You've got to be kidding me. She did the decorating for Momma at the house before we moved in. Look at this." There were notes about Rainie's mom and then circled; there was a big note about Rand's death and the sister. Stella had also written that she had recommended Dr. Poche to her client for her daughter. Rainie laughed; he'd been her first shrink. *That's where Momma got the shrink's name, hm.* Nobody knew, but Rainie had played the game. There was nothing or no one on earth able to help her get through Rand's death. It was going to be her way and her terms, but she'd played the game well. Rainie showed the right progress, so had graduated from psychiatrist to psychologist to counselor. What a wicked web she spun.

She picked up the phone, punching in the numbers. "Hey Momma, want to hear something bizarre? Do you remember the name of the decorator you used for Northline?"

"Sure, hon, Stella Saunders. She was excellent. We hit it off from the beginning. I think she retired a while ago. Why do you ask?"

"No, Momma, she didn't retire, she was killed, and I'm living in her house. Coincidence? You really didn't know?" She walked around her desk, put her feet up, and rocked back in the chair.

"Suga, I'm positive the family was not the Saunders. It was something like Richards or Richardson, definitely not Saunders."

"I'm holding a file about the renovations on our house before we moved in. There are notes about Rand, you, and Daddy. She even has the name of my first shrink. I guess she recommended Dr. Poche to you."

The hesitation on the other end was like three lanes of traffic flowing into one, but the wheels were turning. "Come to think of it, Suga, she did. Dear heavens. What a small world. I guess she went by her maiden name for the business. She had been an interior decorator for years and years."

"Weird, huh?"

"Rainie, don't read too much into any of that hocus pocus stuff. Talk later."

Rainie fingered through the file, contemplating whether Stella already knew she had been the teenager from the house on Northline or if it would be a shock to her as well.

Allie understood the gist of the conversation. "Freaky. What is it with you and dead people?"

Rainie heard an exasperated Rand say, "What a rude thing to say!"

"Dunno. Maybe my link with Rand opened up the ghost world. Who knows? Spirits are roaming the grounds at Michael's parents' place. And you want freaky? His mom can hear some people's thoughts." *I wonder how much she knows about Michael's and my, shit, nix the thought.*

Allie began straightening the piles of papers on her desk. "I wouldn't like that. I wouldn't want her knowing my thoughts or hearing what other people think. That's creepy. You better keep your mind clean and not do too much fantasizing about Doctor Mike and you. It's one thing for Mer and me to hear your flirty talk, but his mom?" Allie laughed. "How embarrassing."

Wow. Rainie did a quick search through her mind of thoughts she may or may not have had since meeting Missy and Jack. It boggled her mind. *Oh well, it is what it is*, she thought.

At present and in the forefront of her mind was communicating with Stella. She'd leave the file in the study with a note on it. There had been several times when the drawers had been left ajar or the chair turned. Rainie knew Stella frequented the study. Maybe they could communicate better in writing. She'd have to research other people's experiences with paranormal interaction.

Jotting a quick note, she stuck it on the file. It said:

*"Stella, I don't know if we can communicate better this way or not. Are you aware you decorated my parents' house on*

*Northline twenty years ago? It's curious, isn't it?"*

She went directly into the house with the file in hand and put it on the study desk. It would be, if nothing else, an interesting experiment. Maybe she should start documenting all her paranormal encounters.

Her phone buzzed, diverting her attention. It was Tom's mother, and she inquired about the boys and their attendance at the service.

"It was a hard decision, but I want the boys to remember Tom as he was, not in a box," Rainie said. "They're only six and eight. Thomas might be able to handle it, but I know Henry can't." She felt guilty about her decision but thought it best.

As expected, and understandably, his mother thought it was disrespectful. She was shocked the boys would not be in attendance. What would people think?

Rainie, being herself, said she didn't care what people thought. Her boys came first. She wanted to smooth any bad feelings his mom might have, so she told his mother about the boys' dreams and that they loved their daddy very much. Wouldn't she rather them remember him laughing and playing with them than be in a crowd of people giving them sad stares, sizing them up, and then to see a big box and know their dad was inside? Whether convinced or not, his mother said she understood. Rainie said it was absolutely not any disrespect intended, but quite the opposite.

Glancing at the clock, she figured she better eat something. The evening was going to be weird, and she didn't know when she'd be able to eat. She fixed a plate for Allie and herself and headed back to the office. At the risk of looking like a whack job, she told Allie about her thoughts on communicating with Stella.

Allie swallowed a bite down. "Had I not personally had an up-close experience with your sister, I'd probably think you were cray-cray. Time with you has been eye-opening in many ways. It's been over a year since my Rand encounter. Does she still visit you?" Their eyes locked as they both nibbled on their food.

"Her voice is in my head almost constantly, mostly bitching at me. I think I see her in the mirror sometimes, but instead of turning away, I now try to look deeper. I've done a little research, and most spirits get locked in one spot, like a house or building. I think Rand is locked inside me, maybe. Because it doesn't matter where I am, she connects with me. Nonetheless, I'm experimenting with Stella. I want to learn more about after-life and stuck in-between if that's even true. Maybe like Michael says, they drift back and forth through dimensions."

Allie said she wasn't so sure trying to commune with the dead was a good idea. What if it brought bad stuff, too? Maybe Rainie needed to leave well enough alone. At least, Allie requested, she should give it some thought. Mer might be a source of good advice.

Rainie knew she would see Mer at the wake. She'd toss the idea at her then. One thing was sure, Mer was black and white, and either she'd say yes or hell to the no! But, then again, who better than her sister?

It was time to look over the profit-and-loss statements. They'd made out well on the living room-dining room job. They had a few things queued up for the end of January and the first week of February, but then it was Mardi Gras, and once again, the city would come to a grinding halt. The day flew by too quickly.

Before long, Michael pulled into the driveway. The workday was over, and it was time to get ready for the wake. They had their usual hug, kiss, back and forth daily banter about the day, but something was lacking, and both could feel it. When they got to their bedroom, he took her in his arms. Her body was stiff, and she knew her face would be painted with apprehension. "Are you okay?" He stepped back and took her face gently with both hands.

"I'm not looking forward to this. I'm sure Grayson's going to be there. You know I don't hide my feelings well. I don't want to be involved in this whole mess. I'm not, and I shouldn't be. Tom should've never told us anything." A single tear rolled down her cheek. Her heart felt heavy. It was time to get over herself.

Michael watched as she got ready. He could see she was working herself up, and that wasn't good for anyone. She turned for a zip. He obliged, then wrapped his arms around her waist and kissed her neck. "Breathe, my love. Just breathe. You'll do fine." His breath on her neck was comforting, but the nerves still rattled inside, and there would be nothing she could do to get rid of it completely.

She told him about Tom's mother calling her and how the

conversation had gone down. He told her she'd handled it beautifully; he'd be by her side, and there was nothing she couldn't handle. He had one hundred percent confidence in her.

Her chest tightened even more, and her breaths were shallow. She looked at Michael with pleading eyes. "It worries me because I know he killed them or had them killed. How can I act as though nothing happened?"

He looked at her squarely. "You can, and you will. You've got so much more to talk about. We recently got married, and we're having a baby, the new house. When you talk about our growing baby, your eyes dance. It'll be all he sees. I'm pretty sure he knows you and Tom were not on the best of terms. Breathe, my love." He pulled her close, studying the pools of beauty in her eyes. He smiled at her, gently moving in for slight wisps of kisses. She held him tight. "Remember yesterday morning?"

She smiled. "I most certainly do." Her energy level was waning. Even the usual sexual revelry he so easily engaged her in was being tested. She smiled weakly. He kissed her neck and whispered his love for her and want for her body. Hopefully, he could distract her. Her pulse quickened, and a wave of warmth rolled through her body. He could feel the tension leaving her and tranquility taking over. "Michael, you are temptation on two legs. Could you be any sexier? I felt lethargic, so sad it was paralyzing, then you woke my heart. How could I forget yesterday morning?" She lightened a little, and the more she thought about their pleasurable moments, the more lively she became.

"Keep that thought on your mind, and nobody will have any idea of what you're thinking. You've surprised me in so many ways, sexy lady." She could feel him starting to become aroused. "Are we going to eat before or after?"

She gave him a knowing smile. "Most definitely after."

The funeral parlor was fifteen to twenty minutes away. The crowd had already started getting thick, and parking was limited. Michael held her hand as they entered. She stopped and chatted with Tom's mother, who apologized for their call earlier. Rainie said it was a stressful time for everyone and to call if she needed a listening ear. Tom's dad and brothers seemed in much better shape, and the conversations centered on how good she looked and the pleasure of meeting Michael. They inquired after the boys and expressed they hoped she would bring them around—all polite but superficial—forced funeral talk.

Outside of the parlor, a background of voices came together as a low reverberation, while inside was a sea of mournful faces glancing toward the casket. There was a beautiful floral blanket on the closed casket. Wreaths and sprays of flowers formed a horseshoe around the room—from traditional carnations to lovely, exotic designs. Rainie wondered how bad Tom looked. It must've been bad if they had to keep the casket closed. She and Michael made the rounds. Meredith and Paul arrived, which gave her even more stability.

"We had a helluva time finding parking. Y'all?" Mer stood back and gave her the once-over, "Rai, you look good. When's your doctor's appointment?"

Their conversation was interrupted by a familiar but unwelcome voice. It was Grayson Smith and his wife. She wondered if the wife had any idea of the monster of a man she had married. No bad thoughts. What had Michael promised for later? Her smile returned.

"Rainie, I'm sorry for your loss. How are the boys?" Grayson put on his most sincere look of sadness and concern. *Are you kidding me? Wipe that sad sack look off your face. Murderer.*

"Nice to see you, Grayson, sorry it's for such an occasion. The boys are resilient. They're obviously devastated, but we're keeping it positive, which on my end can be challenging. Have you met my husband, Michael Landry? We married a couple of weeks before Christmas and honeymooned in the Caribbean." She was doing well thus far.

Grayson rocked forward and said with an almost whisper, "I can't imagine who would do something like this." He tested the water. "It's horrible." She could tell he was watching her closely to see any reaction. *Oh please.*

She took a breath. She imagined Michael in many different sexploits. *Wow! What a great diversion, far better than imagining people in their underwear.* "I'm glad we were out of town, or the police may have been knocking on my door.

"As you know, things had been a bit rough between Tom and me. Not to speak ill of the dead, but everyone knows we had issues and didn't talk. We tried to be civil in front of the boys, but that was the extent of our relationship.

"Regardless, I'm glad we were not around." She imagined her and Michael's plans for the night. A brief laugh came out. *Fuck! Could I have been more inappropriate,* she thought, quickly putting on a more somber face.

*Need to recover, fast,* she thought. "The boys are dealing and keeping good memories; it's why we didn't bring them. I imagine things will be difficult for y'all at the office. What a blow." He looked a bit startled. "On a brighter note, I'm expecting." Her eyes glittered as she looked at Michael.

"I guess congratulations are in order," the monster of a man replied.

"Oh, yes. We're surprised but thrilled. While Tom and I had our differences, I hope they get the son-of-a-bitch responsible." She shot a look at him. "If you would excuse us, my parents just arrived."

The four of them, Michael, Paul, and Mer followed her to greet her parents. Mer was doing the best she could not to giggle. They had a brief hello with her parents and moved to the receiving line.

Mer stood close and looked at her. "What the fuck was that, Rai? You almost laughed in Mr. Smith's face. What's wrong with you?"

"Long story, but brilliant. I'll tell you later." She linked arms with Mer. Out of the corner of her eye, she could see Michael looking at her. She glanced over and winked at him. He had a look of amusement on his face as he approached. He maneuvered past Mer and then behind her. As he passed, she felt his erection move across the back of her. Yeah, he knew exactly what she was doing.

"Are you feeling hungry, my love?" he asked her.

She flashed her eyes at him. "I am, thank you."

"Paul, Mer, we're gonna grab a bite to eat. Would y'all like to join us for dinner?" *What?*

Mer quickly answered, "If I don't get out of here, I'm going to leak on my dress. It's almost feeding time. We'll have to take a pass on the offer, but thanks. We planned to pop in here for only a minute, and it's time to go."

"Are you going to the service tomorrow?" Rainie asked.

Mer looked shocked. "No. I'm not going to pretend I was a fan when I wasn't. I'm sorry for him and your boys, but I don't have to play charades. I came tonight for you, my friend, but you seem to be doing fine. We'll talk tomorrow. Come by in the morning after Michael goes to the office." They kissed cheeks. She whispered, "You're something else. Tomorrow."

Mer pulled Paul by the hand and went for the door. They stopped to sign the guest book and were out of there.

☙☞

Michael whispered in her ear. "I want to know what images went through your mind." She had a tickle emanating from all the right places. "I know you don't do caskets. Let's bug out, too."

"Michael, we have to sign the book and get something to eat." She led him to the book. They signed and split.

As they were walking to the car, he let out a belly laugh. "You laughed in the guy's face. Naughty, nasty Rainie. I can't wait to hear this." He held her hand tightly. "Too much." He laughed again.

"What a great distraction. Oh my gosh. I had always heard 'imagine people in their underwear,' but imagining you doing, you know, takes the cake. Michael, I must have feel-a-vision."

"I told you I wanted to—don't I keep my promises?" *Wow, how does he do this to me?*

With a flirtatious flutter of her eyes and a quick pass of her tongue across her lip, she said, "I'm counting on it. All my sinful thoughts would have been for naught."

He stopped abruptly, pulled her into him, and kissed her deeply. The bulge in his pants was hot. She could feel the heat through their clothes. It was going to be intense, and she couldn't wait. He opened her car door.

On the way to the house, he turned into the café by the railroad tracks. She looked at him with curiosity. "Really, Michael?"

"You need to eat. Lack of food isn't good for you or the baby."

They grabbed a table.

"Your mom and I had some interesting conversations." She grinned. "She can kind of read my mind. Freaked me out at first." Her eyes widened, and she could feel a slight flush to her face.

"Only if you're in an in-depth conversation with her. Sometimes she can, and sometimes she can't. Like all moms, she would say she had eyes in the back of her head. I think all moms have spidey senses to some degree. When I was at my lowest, she would say things seemingly appropriate for what I was thinking. I think she knew about my sexual predilection, but she never said anything specific."

Rainie looked at him through her lashes. "Do you get embarrassed she might know?"

He looked a little confused. "No. Mom didn't and doesn't judge. At least, if she does, I don't know about it. She had always taught us not to judge people unless we had walked in their shoes." He laughed. "However, she was a fervent prayer warrior. At different times in all of our lives, she had motherly concerns, but she prayed us through those times."

The server approached them and quickly took their order. Rainie paused a moment, volleying the idea of sharing her thoughts with her practical, sensible Michael. She took his hand, glossing over his wedding ring with her thumb. "I'm reaching out to Stella." It was a matter-of-fact, not up for a discussion.

He looked her dead in the eyes, almost like an order rather than a helpful, caring suggestion. *Really,* she thought, *well, that cinches it.* "I don't know about that. Your sister is one thing, and the occasional directive you give aloud is okay, but I don't know if I'd try to get her as my BFF. You need to back away from that thought."

"I'm curious about communication between the living and the dead. There's a connection there, don't you think?" she said, totally ignoring Michael's directive to cease and desist.

*No choice here, Michael,* she thought. *I'm merely humoring you.*

"I'll sleep on it? Not saying you need my approval," Michael said. *Damn Skippy, I don't.* "It doesn't seem to sit right, that's all."

Dinner lasted for a couple of hours. What they planned as a quick bite for caloric value on their way home to play all night turned into a deep conversation regarding the living and the dead.

☙☙

In a gravel-sounding whisper, Grayson's wife said, "She knows or at least suspects, Grayson. How'd y'all let this get so out of hand? It should have been dealt with two years ago." She feigned a sad smile in the direction of Tom's brothers.

"Shut up, Marguerite. It was obvious she and Tom were not on good terms. Think about it; he made a complete fool out of her with all his overt playing around. She bought into the whole marriage thing, and he broke her heart. She's into the new husband. Unlike some people," he looked at her, "she's into the marriage thing."

Marguerite was indignant, throwing her shoulders back as though taunting him. "Excuse me? You were the first one to break our marriage vows with the young man from the bank, or are you conveniently forgetting that exploit?" She held her face taut, but her eyes had deep resentment.

"Maybe so, but you certainly didn't complain when I brought him home for both of us, oh and not to forget his lesbian friend. You took to her, my dear, like a duck to water."

She glared at him with a bristling look. "No need to sling mud at me; we both have plenty of misdeeds. What's important is the problem at hand. We need to give our condolences and get out of here."

They started to walk toward the family. All the partners from the firm were there, and if one were to watch the room, they'd see all the shifty eyes. They were all guilty, guilty as hell. None of them had done the deed, but they were all culpable.

Tolbert called. They agreed to meet at a restaurant down the street.

☙☙

They sent their wives home, and the three of them, Bob Thibeaux, Randolph Tolbert, and Grayson Smith, met at a local favorite for dinner. It was nothing out of the ordinary—given the current event, it would be expected. To any onlookers watching, it wouldn't have any air of impropriety.

Little did they know; the investigation had begun, and all three were under heavy scrutiny. The officers, too, took a table. If one were to look at the young couple, there was no indication of them being police—they looked like sales reps. From all appearances, it seemed they had spent their time waiting for a table at the bar and had an apparent buzz going, but it was all for show. They blended right into the rest of the crowd.

After they placed their order, Thibeaux started, "I'm freaking out. This whole thing is fucked up. I had no idea anyone was going to be killed. First Diane and then Tom? Y'all have put me in an uncomfortable place; not saying I can't handle myself or it poses a problem. But we need to get this cleaned up." It started to cross his mind; if he didn't shut up, he would be next on the hit list.

"You knew exactly what the deal was," Tolbert corrected. "Diane was a troubled young woman. I wish it would've looked more like a suicide than homicide. I told her on several occasions, what happens at the office stays at the office. I reminded her about the confidentiality clause in her contract. I failed to mention about blowjobs or handys." The three of them had a chuckle, but Thibeaux was merely going along.

Tolbert continued as he shoved a piece of French bread in his mouth, "She let me do things to her my wife would never do, all for a five-buck-an-hour raise. She thought she was controlling the situation with her not-so-great pussy, but I have to admit fucking her up the ass was worth every one of the five dollars. It was like having a hooker without the high price, risk of disease, being mugged, or crazy pimp."

Smith re-focused the meeting. "Let's get back on track. We have to act shocked, cooperative, and fucking squeaky clean. Whatever baggage we have lying around, it needs to go. This guy Marse from the NOPD has a real hard-on for this investigation. As he said, he's going to 'connect the dots.' He was talking about finding the person responsible for the homicides, but I felt some underlying current. Take no chances. Get your side of the street clean." Smith was definitely the person in charge and the mastermind behind all of their nefarious activities. He was also rumored to be the most perverse in sexual exploitation, although no one had confirmed any of the gossip.

By the time their dinner arrived, it had been decided that they would frame Tom as the one with the blemished persona. Hidden in his office would be ten grand in cash and an ounce of cocaine. Thus, his murder and the murder of Diane could have all been part of some horrible drug deal gone wrong. They would rebut the accusation saying they knew Tom to be an upright man. They'd known him for years, etcetera. They would play the concerned partner role. The dead guy would be the patsy, and life would return to normal. They needed to find another Diane who would do anything for more money and a bit of a promotion. Like Diane, the girl would never learn each of the men knew about the others, and it was just a seedy plan to get their jollies.

Both of the young officers wore an earpiece designed to amplify conversations from a distance. It was for the elderly but worked like a charm for hearing details from two tables away. What they had heard was sickening, and it was obvious who was in charge. They couldn't wait to report to Marse.

❧

Rainie rolled onto her side, facing her husband. "You're soaking wet, Michael. I don't think I've ever seen you this sweaty. I hope you aren't coming down with anything." She felt his forehead.

"I'm not sick; you've worn me out. I can't get enough of you. I think I'm starting to have a problem," he snickered. "Seriously, as I told you earlier, I have never had this much sex in all my life. I hope all this rough stuff is okay with the sleeping one." He gently stroked her belly.

"I'm sure the sleeping one is fine, and the sex? For crying out loud, we're newlyweds; we're supposed to be like dogs in heat, right?" She got out of the bed and turned on the shower. "Michael, come get in the shower with me. I promise to keep my hands off."

He walked into the bathroom, ready to jump into the shower. "You're a jackass. Have I told you that? You better not keep your hands off me."

"I have questions." She took his hand and brought him into the shower with her.

"I'm shocked. You, questions? God forbid." He held her close. "What do you want to know?" His smile dripped with playful sarcasm.

"You said John knew about Pandora, and you said no one had ever visited your house or spent the night. I was the first. But, you did have people play with you in Pandora, yes?"

He sat on the bench and kissed her belly. "Firstly, I'm going to answer you, but I have an observation about the first comment. One. No one has been to my house except workers. Two. No one has ever spent the night, not even in Pandora. Yes, a select few know about Pandora. They came down the side of the house to the back from the gate. Remember, the house was a construction site; all entering and leaving was down the walkway. Does that answer that?" He cupped her belly with his hands.

"Yes, thank you. I'm tired. I can hear the John story at another time." She kissed the top of his head and turned off the water.

"But I need to tell you my observation. Tom's partner Grayson, I've seen him before, and it bugged me where and then it dawned on me. I saw him the night I saw John at the club." He looked up at her face then stood.

"You saw John at the sex club? Oh my gosh, how weird, huh? Okay, I'm listening." She was still hanging on his every word. *This is gonna be good.*

"Nothing much to tell." He grabbed a towel and started drying her off. "John had gone to the club with some woman he knew, and I happened to be there with my friend. We came out of different areas and almost ran right into each other. We both got a laugh out of it. I was a little high. He didn't know that part. He would have kicked my ass, but anyway, I told him to find me when he was leaving. I wanted to grab a drink with him. It was during the drink that I told him about Pandora, and he wanted to see it. We went back to my place, and I showed them."

"Oh my gosh, what did he say?" Her eyes were wide with curiosity. "Awkward." She raised her voice to a higher pitch.

"Nothing in front of his friend, but later he told me he couldn't believe how twisted I had become and did I go to those kinds of clubs often? It was his first and only time, as he said, 'not his bag.' We had a long talk about where I was mentally and emotionally. He told me I needed to get my shit together.

"He was right, but more importantly, I've seen Grayson there, and he's into some serious things with noticeably young men. He was pretty blotto whenever he was there. When we saw him tonight, I could tell there wasn't any of the 'I know I know this guy, but from where?' when we met. Rainie, he's one twisted fuck. I don't pass judgment on people's sexual escapades, it'd be the pot calling the kettle black, but this is different. He wanted to hurt people, not control, but really hurt. I think he got thrown out of there, if I'm not mistaken." He took her hand and led her into the bedroom.

"Gross. Sounds horrific." She thought for a moment, "I hope Detective Marse gets him and nails his ass. He belongs in prison."

☜☞

When Marguerite got home, she went straight to her bedroom. Her young piece was still squirming in the bed. Both wrists were rubbed raw from the restraints. At one point in her life, Marguerite had been a cute girl with a curvy body. Regardless of the appearance of her well-respected family, she'd had a strange upbringing. Her parents had been made aware of the actions of her uncle on numerous occasions.

Every chance he had, his hands would go up her skirt or down her shirt. When she tried to talk to her mother about her uncle, she was told people didn't talk about those kinds of things in their circles. Certainly, Marguerite was confused. Her mother cut off the conversation right there.

Marguerite was damaged goods, at best. She figured if nobody would help her, she'd use the situation to her advantage, as her uncle was even wealthier than her parents. She milked him with threats of telling, and he lavished her with gifts for her silence.

"Missed me?" she growled at the girl.

"Fuck you, bitch." The girl was pissed off. "I can't believe you left me cuffed."

"Honey, you have no idea, I get what I pay for, and if you think the last session was rough, you haven't seen anything yet. You'll start to enjoy it if you let go, but there are lessons you need to learn. For starters, it's my way, I'm the customer, and the customer is always right. I expect results, and thus far, girlie, nadda. It's going to be a thrilling experience for you. Pay attention."

The girl thrashed, trying to break the restraints, but Marguerite had her securely immobilized. As she watched the girl, she began to disrobe. Rummaging through her drawer, she pulled out an extra-large dildo and greased it with lubricant, rubbing the shaft. She saw the girl shake her head. "Do not touch me with that thing."

"Shhh. Nothing you've done has given me the slightest hint of pleasure, but your struggle *is* arousing," Marguerite laughed, rubbing the greased jumbo between her own breasts. She leaned into the girl, biting her thighs, then plunged the rubber monster into her. "That's it; let me know how bad it hurts." The girl pleaded with her to stop.

The doorbell rang. Marguerite's eyes lit up, and she smiled, threw on her silk robe, and went to answer the door. The girl could hear laughing, heading back to the room. It was hard to distinguish if the conversation was between two women or if the new guest was a man.

Even after seeing the person, it was still hard to tell. The woman made Marguerite look like a dainty damsel instead of a twisted freak. The newcomer took off her outer garments. The sight was almost frightening. She had clamps on her nipples and piercings on her oddly shaped breasts, but down below was perhaps the longest and thickest cock she'd ever seen. He or she ripped Marguerite's robe off her body and slammed her on the bed.

This new person was barking commands as he rode Marguerite hard. He scolded her. By this time, the young hooker was utterly bewildered. He picked up the rubber monster, close to the same size as his dick, and shoved it up Marguerite's ass. The craziness continued for what seemed an eternity. He orchestrated the show. He pulled himself out of her captor and straddled the shoulders of the young girl. He rubbed himself on her face.

She stared into his eyes. There was more crazy there than she'd ever seen. He was wild. He shoved himself into her mouth, bucking in and out. She couldn't even gag; he was so big. He backed off a bit, giving enough space to put his hands around her neck. He began to strangle her. She could feel herself losing consciousness. At the moment she started blacking out, he let go and exploded down her throat. His release came at the same time as her very life breath.

He jumped off her and untied her wrists and ankles, but she didn't want to get up. She watched as he serviced Marguerite, obviously awakening what had otherwise seemed lifeless. No matter what trick she knew from her profession, nothing had worked. Her client had seemed bored with everything until the newcomer arrived and turned on the insanity, and then she'd come alive. She watched her cry like a little girl, beg like a victim, but then reel out of control with delight.

The man saw the door open and grinned over his shoulder. Her husband had come home. Grayson had leather chaps on with his flaccid dick dangling. It wasn't until he started whipping the man that it began to get erect. She had heard of some of the things her captor's husband was doing to the man but had never witnessed it before, and it was ugly, sick, and a total nightmare.

The older woman looked at her. "I'm done with you, now. For a first time with us, you caught on. Your money's on my dresser, dearie." The girl quickly got the hell out of there. At least they paid well. Her take for the four hours was two grand.

❧

Michael pulled Rainie close to him. He loved the smell of her hair, the softness of her skin, and all that made her the beautiful person she was. He also knew the next day was going to be strange for her. Rainie had no choice. She had to go to the services, and he knew how averse she was to anything dealing with death. He wished he could quiet her pain but knew it would always be there under the surface. He couldn't imagine the pain of losing a sibling, let alone a twin. They'd started life together; it had to feel like a void aching as a perpetual reminder. He prayed as he did every morning and night for her relief from her tortured soul.

❧

"Marse," the detective answered the phone.

"It's Connors, sir."

"What you got, Jimmy?"

"You ain't gonna believe this shit. You were right; Mr. Smith is the ringleader. I'm following him right now but will outline it all for you, sir. He called the hit, no doubt."

"Stay tight on him. I've got a team going with me to the office tomorrow. Getting the warrant signed first thing in the morning to search Mr. Todd's office."

"Sir, they'll be more than accommodating. In Mr. Todd's office, y'all are gonna find an ounce of cocaine and ten grand planted by Smith himself." His radio crackled in the background.

"Oh, I'm looking forward to your notes."

"Ten-four."

Connors pulled his car a few doors down from the Smith residence about the same time as a cab pulled up to the house, dropping off a huge woman or drag queen. With the exaggerated swish in the walk, he pegged the person as a drag queen. Connors saw the door open, and Mrs. Smith, wearing what appeared to be a nightgown, scurry her visitor quickly inside. He managed to get a couple of pictures even at his distance. Grayson Smith had already pulled into his garage. He doubted the man even saw their visitor get dropped off.

Sergeant Connors glanced over his notepad. When he read the bit about Diane being the office play toy, it disgusted him. They were not only pompous assholes, but they were pigs. Obviously, the girl had been troubled, but shame on them for the abuse. He liked a good blowjob just as much as the next guy but knowing they were all getting a piece of the pie and laughing about it disgusted him.

He wondered if the guest was an overnight thing or if some big battle was going on inside. It had been a good forty-five minutes since the cab had dropped off the visitor. The front door opened, and a young girl came running out of the house. She literally ran toward the corner. He could tell she was on the phone. Fifteen minutes later, a blue Camaro picked her up. Whatever was going on inside the Smith residence, he was damn sure it wasn't pretty. Two hours later, a cab pulled up, and Ms. Swish-swish came prancing out, got in the cab, and off they went. The night dragged on, and all was quiet. Morning came, the garage door opened, Smith backed out and took off.

Slowly Connors pulled out and followed the white BMW as it headed downtown. Once he made sure Smith was in the office building, he could go home for some shut-eye. From all accounts, this looked like it was going to be a lengthy investigation, which meant many more sleepless nights.

෨෩

The Hilton had already sent the tapes, and they had been reviewed. The shooter had worn a hoodie and sunglasses, but like most dumb criminals, he hadn't put his gloves on until he was in the hallway outside of Mr. Todd's room. His prints were all over the elevator button to the fifth floor. The cleaning crew had already done the elevators; therefore, the only print on the button was a punk with a long record of burglaries, car theft, and public intoxication, yet he'd managed to get off on technicalities courtesy of his attorney, Grayson Smith. Coincidence? Marse was pretty dang sure it wasn't. The trick was getting Desmond Cruz to flip on Smith. He wondered how many other nefarious acts he had performed at the instruction of Mr. Smith?

The Todd home had been examined top to bottom in search of any clue as to the killer behind Diane's murder. Up to this point, nothing had turned up. He'd have to check the records to see how many and who were the names of Smith's clients who'd been released on technicalities. The man-hours it would take probably wouldn't be approved by the chief, but maybe.

# LIKE A PRAYER

The morning plan was Michael would go to his office, and Rainie would visit with Mer. He offered to pick her up from Mer's and take her to the funeral. Michael left first, but Rainie wasn't too far behind.

It looked like Mer was home alone. Rainie liked Paul a lot but needed time alone with her friend. So much had happened, and she needed to unload.

The door was unlocked, she went in. "I'm here," she shouted. She heard Mer call to her from the nursery with the girls. As she walked into the room, Mer passed her a baby. There were two gliders in the room, one for Mer and one for Paul. Rainie sat in Paul's. Mer looked tired.

"Are you sleep-deprived? It won't last forever, I promise but make sure you put them on your schedule, not let them dictate the schedule. You'll have a few hard weeks, and you obviously can't do it for another couple of weeks, but trust me on this one. The boys were sleeping midnight to five at eight weeks. Of course, I didn't have two at the same time, but Momma was the one with the advice for me, so it must have worked with us." It felt good to hold the baby. *Soon I'll be cradling my own. Not in my wildest dreams did I think I'd have another. God surely has a sense of humor.*

Mer glided back and forth. She looked totally spent. "I need a laugh. What in the hell was going on with you last night? You laughed in Grayson's face, Rainie."

Rainie told her about Michael's strategy. "You know I can't conceal my feelings. It's like they're printed on my forehead in neon. I know Grayson had something to do with Diane and Tom's murders, maybe all the partners, who knows? I don't want any of them thinking I think it was them. It would put me next on the hit list. It worked better than the underwear thing we've used for years." Rainie grinned like the Cheshire cat.

"Yeah, I'd say it worked. You had an odd smile on your face almost the whole time you spoke to Mr. Smith. What's up with his wife? She's one hard-looking woman. I bet she was something to look at when she was younger, but her face has a resting bitch scowl, plus she seemed like a real bitch." They put the babies back in their cribs.

Walking downstairs to the kitchen, Rainie was to the point. "She never was warm and fuzzy for sure. I think she's miserable. Michael told me he had heard rumors; evidently, Grayson is a twisted individual. Big time into sadism, like real twisted. He gets off on hurting people and young guys at that."

Mer pulled out some green liquid concoction and poured two glasses. "It's better than it looks. Who'd have thought such a pudgy little man even had sex. Looking at her, she's absolutely miserable. I never understood the hurting thing. I love getting wild in bed with Paul, and it gets intense, but never more than being sore for a day or two." She laughed. "Probably more info than you needed."

"Nah. On a different subject, I wonder how the police are gonna catch Grayson, or if they'll even be able to." Rainie sipped her vegetable beverage; then they went back upstairs to the nursery.

They rocked the babies and talked about their own hypotheses of the situation. While they agreed they were probably right, the question was how the police would prove it. They both jumped when they heard a knock on the door. It was Michael.

Rainie loved watching him hold one of the babies. "Meredith, they're absolutely perfect. Y'all are going to have a couple of blondies, I think." Michael looked like a natural. Bubbles popped in her stomach up to her throat at the thought of Michael holding their baby. It tickled down deep. They told him about their thoughts on the murders and wondering how the police would prove it.

Michael cleared his throat. "Detective Marse is a smart guy. I believe he'll get to the bottom of it. Y'all don't need to play detective." He looked at Rainie. "Promise me, Meredith, if she starts talking about checking into things, call me. As you know, she can be hard-headed." *Really, Michael,* Rainie thought, but she knew already, he could be over the top sometimes.

It was time to go. She blew a kiss to Meredith as they were leaving.

The ride to the funeral was silent. Michael figured if Rainie needed to talk, she would. The crowd at the funeral home was substantial, which Rainie imagined made Tom's mom feel good. To think he had touched as many lives had to be heartwarming. His brothers and dad were attentive to her. His mom seemed out of it and wore a dazed look. Rainie couldn't help but think she'd had to be medicated. If it were one of her boys, they'd have to bury her too. It made her stomach churn like she was about to vomit.

Michael put his hand to the small of her back and moved her along. They took a seat. Grayson and his bitch wife stopped to greet them but then moved on quickly. Randy Tolbert and his wife passed by without a glance. As people passed, Rainie told Michael who was who. Toward the latter part of arrivals, Bob Thibeaux and his wife stopped.

"Rainie, I'm sorry. Tom was a good guy. I know y'all had your awkward times, but he loved the boys. This is surreal. It's going to be a great loss at the firm." His eyes were almost teary, and he had a genuinely apologetic look on his face. She made a mental note to tell Marse. Thibeaux may be the perfect weak link—the only one with a conscience.

"Thank you, Bob. It was quite a shock, and for the boys' sake, I hope they catch the people responsible for this." She watched for any reaction. He stared blankly and nodded.

Thibeaux and his wife walked away to find a seat.

"Michael, did he seem strange to you? I'm going to let Marse know he might know something. His condolence came across like he was apologizing for something."

He patted her hand and looked her squarely in the eyes. "Yes, I saw something, but I don't think you should get involved in anything to do with this. Rainie, be a mom. You certainly don't need to be the sleuth. I worry you're going to get hurt, and then I'd have to kill someone." He had a dead serious look to him—something she had never seen in him.

"Sounds a bit dramatic, Michael," she said, trying to make light of it.

He turned to face her. "Make no mistake. You are my wife carrying our child, and if anyone tried or even implied they were going to hurt you, I. Will. Kill. Them. Not being dramatic, my love. A matter of fact, but it's not going to be needed, right?" *OMG*, she thought, and Rand had to weigh in as well. "He's right. Stay out of it, Rainie."

The music began, signaling the service was about to begin. She took a deep breath.

Midway through the service, Rainie excused herself to the ladies room. Michael looked at her carefully. Had he been a betting man, he'd bet there was something up. She could be extremely headstrong.

On her way to the ladies room, she called Marse. "Detective Marse, this is Rainie Landry. Against all advice, I'm calling you to tell you about a feeling I have. I'm at Tom's funeral right now, and I think Bob Thibeaux might be a weak link for you. He seemed very disturbed about Tom's death. I saw it in his eyes."

Marse listened, and it was certainly an avenue to pursue. He was interviewing them all anyway, but Mrs. Landry had been perceptive before; he'd be sure to follow up.

"One thing, too, detective—if we could keep this call between the two of us." *Please. And for God's sake, I hope he doesn't tell Michael.*

"Ma'am, I've already told you I would do what I can to keep you out of it, but if you keep calling me, I'm going to have a hard time doing that. I'm not discouraging your suspicions, but I'm sure you understand. We found the identity of the man hired to kill Diane and Tom. I think we have all we need to slam dunk our investigation. Okay?"

"Yes, sir. Good day," she said and hung up.

She took her seat next to Michael. He held her hand, "What did Detective Marse have to say?" he whispered.

"What?" She had an overly animated, questioning look.

"You heard me. It was written all over your face. Rai, please stay out of it. Promise me?" he asked.

"I'll try; I can't help it. If an observation I have opens a door for the police, then the risk would have been worth it, right?" she tried to reason with him.

"Wrong. Rainie. Wrong on so many levels. For your sake and the sake of our baby, stay clear of this, okay?" His voice was stern and demanding.

She could tell Michael was aggravated with her, but too bad. She understood exactly what he was saying, and these people obviously had no conscience or hesitation. They eliminated anyone who might spoil their good time.

The service ended, and they followed the processional to the cemetery. It was brief, and now she knew where to take the boys later on. The ride there was quiet—no words were spoken between them at all, and it appeared the ride to Mer's would be just as silent. He was totally pissed.

She broke the silence. "Michael, I'm sorry if I upset you."

"You have." Silence. No facial expression as he glared at the road in front of them.

"Can we talk about it? I don't like you being angry with me. It upsets me." She tried to pacify him. She reached for his hand, but he pulled it away.

"It upsets me, too." He had never been this short with her. This was something new, and she had to break the wall down. Her eyes welled with tears, and she desperately tried to swallow the thick lump in her throat.

He brought her back to Meredith's. She leaned over and kissed him, but he was stone cold. "Michael, I love you."

"I love you too, Rainie. But right now, I can't say I want to talk to you. Just get out of the car. I have to get back to work." He didn't even look at her. She could see his jaw pulse as he held back his anger.

☙❧

She quietly got out of the car and walked toward Mer's. She turned back to wave; she could feel him watching her. His face looked angry and sad all at the same time. She could feel the tears trickling down her cheeks.

She opened the door, and he pulled away. Mer called from the kitchen, "How was it?"

Rainie walked in as Mer loaded the last cup in the dishwasher. Tears, by this time, were flowing in a steady stream as her breath hitched in sobs.

"Oh gosh, Rai, it was that hard? I'm sorry."

"No, it's not about the funeral. I fucked up, and Michael's angry with me, angrier than he's ever been since I've known him, but he doesn't understand I had to call." She leaned against the counter.

"Call who? What happened? You know he won't stay angry with you for long." Mer took both her elbows, looking her in the eyes.

Rainie told Mer about Bob Thibeaux and how peculiar he had been, and then about the discussion with Michael and then her calling Detective Marse.

"Yeah, I'd say you fucked up. Mike's insanely in love and devoted to you and the kids, and now with a baby—he's a passionate guy. And I don't doubt for one second he wouldn't hesitate to kill anyone venturing near you or the kids in a harmful way." She started to say something else but held the thought back. They sat at the kitchen table. "Want more of the vegetable drink?"

"No. What were you going to say?" Rainie pressured her, an intense look on her face.

"Did he ever tell you about a fight he got in back in med school?"

"No."

"Oh shit. Swear to me you won't tell him I told you. He was almost falling down drunk when he told me about it. I'm not sure he would even remember telling me." Mer kept stalling. She fixed herself a glass of the green liquid. "Need crackers or anything?"

"Okay, okay, I swear, but I'll get him to tell me so then I can know and won't let on you told me, okay? So he got in a fight, what of it?" Rainie massaged her temples as they pounded with each beat of her heart.

"He was walking from the hospital through one of the high-rise parking lots to his car. He hears this girl screaming and some scuffling.

He ran to help. One of the girls in his class had been grabbed by some guy. He had knocked her down. She was fighting him, but he was trying to rape her." She paused.

"And?" Rainie asked, palms upturned with annoyance.

"And Mike beat him to within an inch of his life, left him for dead or almost dead, and took the girl to the E.R. He's got this weird thing about women. Not saying any guy wouldn't have done the same thing, but Mike was cold and matter-of-fact about the whole thing with the guy. He was torn up over the girl and went through the 'what if I hadn't been there' and all those scenarios. I asked if the guy lived or was hurt badly. It was as if I asked him what he had for lunch. He had no idea, and what was more, he didn't care—at all. I know it doesn't sound like compassionate Mike, but he was as serious as a heart attack. He's never told you about that?"

Rainie shook her head. "Nope."

"I guess it's a moment he's not proud of." Mer shrugged her shoulders.

"He saved the girl from a creep. He should feel good about it."

They talked for a while longer, Rainie giving in to the green glop, but she was lost in her thoughts. Mer let it go and figured she was having a Rainie moment. She'd been known to space out and go somewhere in her mind mid-conversation.

Rainie's phone rang, bringing her out of her thoughts. It was Michael.

"Rainie, I love you, and I don't like to be at odds with you. There'll be very few things I ask. Staying away from those people and the whole fucked-up mess is something I must insist upon. I can't be distracted wondering what you're up to or if you're okay. It's not a control thing, it's a real thing, and I'm not being dramatic or macho. Taking care of my family is as essential to my life as breathing. You know me, and you know how I was raised. If John or my Dad thought for a second you were in trouble; they'd be side by side with me killing the fucker." She could hear the intensity in his voice and could actually form a picture in her mind.

"I promise, Michael, I will not call or contact anyone else again about this matter. I'm sorry. I felt compelled at the time, but seeing and hearing how upset you are, I give you my word. I will never do anything again if you ask me not to, no matter what. Forgive me?"

"Yes, and I understand why you did it, but let's make these decisions together in the future. Can we agree?" he asked her brokenly. She could tell he was still pissed and was trying to fight the feeling.

"Yes, Michael, I can and will," she mustered as much sincerity as she could.

❧

Detective Marse and his investigative team had subpoenas to search Tom's office. It included cabinets and any cases he was currently working on. Marse knew there'd be a fight about attorney-client privilege, but he'd try his hand at it. The new mandates that had been handed down fell in favor of the attorney-client privilege. In his heart, he knew it had nothing to do with Mr. Todd's clients. It was something internal between the partners. At least that was what his gut told him. He looked forward to the conversation with Connors.

As predicted earlier by Sgt. Connors, the law office was most cordial and compliant. The partners arrived about half an hour after the police. They had provided the necessary paperwork to the office manager and been escorted to Mr. Todd's office. During the search, the police found $10,000 cash, an ounce of cocaine, prescription bottles for Adderall, Xanax, and oxycodone.

One by one, each of the partners entered the office to speak with the police. They seemed overly cooperative and interested in the findings. When the three of them saw the cash and cocaine, they took to the stage with performances of surprise and alarm. They were most insistent they had no idea and couldn't fathom Tom as such a sort of fellow.

Rainie had been right, Marse thought. Thibeaux would fold quite easily. He could've probably cracked him right then and there, but he wanted the one who'd ordered the hit. While Tolbert was an arrogant asshole, feigning to be helpful and upset over the whole incident, he was complicit but clearly not the one in charge. On the other hand, there was no soul in Smith's eyes. He was a scary kind of sick but extremely polished in his act of propriety and eagerness to assist.

Smith could have won an Oscar for his performance when he saw the money and the drugs. They were clearly planted, not truly hidden away. Marse was curious where the big money had gone. Had it all been spent? The influx of cash into Tom's account could be traced and was legit. He had been bought out in cash by his ex for the house on Nashville Avenue. He had a mortgage on the love nest he kept in the Garden District, and he drove a nice car, but it was run through the firm. The money had to be hidden somewhere

When the tech team arrived, things started to become interesting. Smith seemed particularly surprised. As expected, the techs confiscated Tom's computer. Tolbert and Thibeaux raised their eyebrows upon the discovery of the discreetly hidden cameras. They were shitting on themselves, imagining there were cameras in their offices. Cameras were in each of the partners' offices and the offices of the whole cast of underlings. The hidden eyes were in the reception area, in the file storage room or, as they called it, the vault, and in the kitchen. The hallways were monitored by cameras placed in the exit signs.

Marse called in for a search warrant for the entire office and everything in it when they found the first camera. The warrant included all computers and electronic devices. He couldn't wait to see what the eyes in the sky had captured. His meeting with Connors was set for 3 p.m. He had another lieutenant from the investigations team come to the office to oversee. Everything was by the book—documented when the first truckload left the office and signed off in the property room. It would take countless hours and personnel to weed through the recordings.

Before Marse left, Smith cornered him. "Detective Marse, I feel it necessary to inform you there may be some compromising situations of a personal nature captured in the recordings. I certainly hope you will use your discretion."

"We will do our job, Mr. Smith. Our interest at present is connecting the dots on the two murders. Your cooperation is appreciated." He could feel the apprehension from Smith, who had been relatively smug up until the finding of the camera. As Marse began to walk off, he turned around. "One question, Mr. Smith. I couldn't help but notice there are no cameras in your office. I find that odd, you?"

He could see Smith begin to bristle. "Over the years, I have become heavily invested in the firm. Being a prudent man, I keep watch over my investment. Nothing happens in this firm without my knowledge. The personal indiscretions are of no concern to me. Hours billed are a different matter, and I care a great deal about that. You will also note I don't have recording devices hidden in the conference rooms. I'm sure you might find this all a bit strange, but I take loyalty to the firm very seriously, and everything I have done here is within legal boundaries."

Marse stood there with a poker face. "Just a question, Mr. Smith, it was just a question." He turned back around, continuing his trek to the car and his meeting with Connors.

He called Connors. "You're gonna shit when you hear what went down here. See you in a few."

The men met in a quiet café in Mid-City. Given the hour, they had the place to themselves. Connors started the conversation. "Grayson Smith is one cold-hearted son-of-a-bitch. Pure ice runs through his veins. Tolbert is full of himself. Thibeaux is freaked the fuck out. I know people bring things on themselves, but I was disgusted. They were all doin' her, or she was doin' them. It was all a big joke to them. She was what, fuckin' twenty-six at most? She was trying to get ahead, and she figured the only way required sexual favors. I think Todd was the only one oblivious to his partners' exploits with her. Smith called the shots. He ordered and paid for the hit on both murders. He's a real sicko bastard."

Marse drank his iced tea and waited as the server brought their food. He thanked her, and she trotted off to the back. "Search was routine until tech found cameras throughout the office except in—"

"Let me guess, Smith's office?" Connors had a shit-eating grin on his face. "What an asshole."

"You got it. Until then, Smith was cool as a cucumber. As I left, he felt it necessary to let me know there may be some personal matters on the recordings, and he didn't care. It was all about timekeeping. He got a little shaken when I mentioned his was the only office without a camera.

"I had to hear how he watches his investment, and that's why the cameras. I'm looking forward to seeing them. I wonder if it's going to show him putting the coke and money in Todd's office." They finished their meal. Connors went into more detail about what he overheard, then about the strange drag queen, the missus answering the door in her nightgown, and the young girl running out of the house.

"Boy, would I love to be a fly on the wall. No, I take that back. I couldn't handle it. I bet it's one freak show after another," Marse said in a disgusted tone. Connors handed Marse his camera and showed him the pictures.

"That's one big queen. I've seen him. Before you start your tail on Smith, stop in with Vice or Street. I'm betting both the young girl and the big queen are working girls." He looked closer at the young girl. "What is she, sixteen? She seems drugged or something. Besides being an asshole, Tolbert seems normal, and Thibeaux is in way over his head."

Connors had to agree with his boss. Thibeaux was out of their league when it came to fucked-up, but said Tolbert was pretty callous and foul. All he could comment on regarding Diane was blowjobs and anal sex. His missus didn't go for up the butt.

They parted company, Connors planning on checking out the girls with Vice and Marse following up about Smith's punk killer, Desmond Cruz.

❧☙

Rainie was lonely at home without Michael, especially since the fight. She busied herself with laundry. There was very little food in the house, so she had picked up something to cook for dinner on the way home. It was during these quiet, lonely times she couldn't stop thinking about Rand. She wondered if she'd ever appear to her again like she did that night. Maybe it would be better if she went back to be with her boys at Jack and Missy's. Her head was swimming with thoughts.

Rainie felt the temperature dropping to icy in the room. Rand's voice was audible, not just in her head. "Please listen to Michael, Rainie. Don't get all hard-headed. You always have to prove a point, stretch the boundary, and then bam, you've gotten yourself in deep. One day it may be too deep to get out. You have it all. Stop being so dang stupid." Rainie hung her head in her hands. Rand was right.

Michael was right. "Get out of your funk, go see your girl, Allie." The atmosphere returned to normal, and Rainie did as advised.

Rainie left the kitchen and went outside to the office to see Allie, who was excited to see her and began babbling at once. "I've been out of it. This has been one helluva a year, don't you think? I can't wait for the new year and things to get back to normal. Will there even be a normal? I hate it when y'all are away, Rainie."

They shared a sandwich and visited, catching up on the Eric relationship, the funeral, and missing the boys, then Rainie went back to the house and as she started to prepare dinner, it dawned on her she had never checked the study to see if Stella had responded to her note. Atop the file was a message, and even from the doorway, she could see the writing.

> *Rainie. Yes, I remembered your mother the first time she came to check out the house with you. I hear you when you speak to me and communicate when I feel it necessary. It makes me feel alive to see the life and love in this house. It's been dreadful for such a long time. My home was meant to be yours. Forever, Stella*

Rainie quickly jotted another message down.

> *Stella, this will be the last time, just one question...do you know my sister Rand? Can she communicate like this to me?*

Rainie stood, watching the note, waiting to see if she would answer her right then, but nothing. She didn't know how fast she would get the message or if she was willing to answer her. Stella was the one holding the cards; it would have to be on her terms. She let it go for then.

After she'd gotten dinner ready to go in the oven later in the evening, she joined Allie back in the office again. She hadn't noticed before, but it felt almost sterile, lifeless. It didn't have the buzz it once had. She wondered if R&M had run its course.

Allie cleared her throat. "I wanted to let you know I have decided to sit for the LSAT. I tossed around going for my master's, but I think

I might want law. A girl I know from class is interning at a law office this semester."

"Oh." Rainie seemed sad. "Would you be giving up working here? You know Mer's coming back, and life will get normal again, not that I'm discouraging law school, by no means. You should talk to my dad." She busied herself looking at the newest files.

"Good idea. The girl from my class, Stephanie, is interning, or going to intern, at Mr. Todd's." Allie became suddenly quiet. "I'm sorry. I can't believe he's gone. I know he wasn't the best husband or dad in the world, but it's still sad. Even though Eric didn't know Mr. Todd, he went with me." Rainie sat, consumed by her thoughts. While she was looking at a file, she hadn't read one word.

Rainie snapped out of it. "I'm sorry. I didn't see you at the service. Tom's death has been like a nightmare. You did a great job straightening the office, thank you. It's gonna be weird; I'd venture to say, for some time. Warn your friend to watch out for the partners. If she's cute, they'll hunt her down. They're all pigs."

They spoke back and forth about the girl she knew. Allie said they weren't friends; she barely knew her and only talked to her on occasion. According to Allie, the girl "worked" her way through college, as in "working girl." Allie wasn't sitting in judgment; people did what they had to do to make it. She felt lucky to have found a family.

"She'll fit right in, then. I think they're all sleazy. I know Tom used to hit on every new girl they hired to work there, and I'm sure the other partners do the same. You stay away from there."

☜☞

Marse could hear laughter coming out of the tech room. As he entered the room, they all put on a straight face. "What y'all got?"

"Look for yourself, and this is just the beginning." On several screens were shots of different young girls bent over desks or down on their knees. "This has more sex in it than the last porno I saw. There's one," the tech said, and he hit rewind then stopped. "You can only see the back of this guy, but from all accounts, he's giving it to her while she blows the other guy. The guy getting the blowjob is Randolph

Tolbert, unsure who the mystery guest is or the chick. This is her debut footage. She doesn't seem to be having a good time if you ask me."

Marse asked the tech to get a closer shot of the guy's hands. The guy had a grip on her that drew blood. He was pile driving her, and when finished, she left, upset. Tolbert reminded her of a confidentiality agreement as she walked out of the room. Then he started to laugh when they heard the door close. The mystery man spoke only in very faint whispers, while Tolbert was his usual boisterous self. His comments were crude. The other man managed to walk out of the office without showing his face.

"I know we didn't get his mug, but there's no doubt, that was Smith. Anybody else notice the blood? He must have dug his nails into her skin or something. I want to catch this guy doing something illegal and not just disgustingly immoral. Other than the fuck fests, let me know if you come up with something important and for crying out loud, keep it down to a low roar. There better not be any of these recordings missing or copied." Marse walked out, disgusted by the recordings.

His team pored over the footage for hours. What started as amusing became boring as it was an endless stream of deplorable behavior and sexual abuse. The acts ran the gambit. Then Tom showed up in the recording. He entered his office with a green gym bag, placed it on his desk, and took stacks of cash out of the bag. He turned his back to the door, unlocked a file drawer, shoving all the files to the front, and started stashing the money. He suddenly stopped and looked to the door. They saw Diane walk in, constantly turning to watch the door.

"You can't traipse in here anytime you want," Tom barked at her.

She very coyly responded, "You usually enjoy my impromptu visits, but I can see you're busy. Looks like a lot of cash, Tom."

"I'm holding it in keeping for a client. I'll buzz you when I'm done." He stood, towering over her, trying to intimidate her, unsuccessfully. She was ballsy.

"No. I don't think so. I don't think you're holding anything for anybody but yourself. None of my business, pass a little my way, and I don't have to mention it to anyone. Your secret is safe with me," she almost cooed. She sat on the bag with the rest of the money in it, pulled up the front of her dress, and spread her legs. "Now, Tom, you take care of me like I've been doing for you these past months." She snapped her fingers at him.

"I don't have time for this, Diane." She didn't move.

"I imagine some of your partners might like a piece of that action. Should I buzz them for you? Oh, Tom-Tom, do it like you want it. Just like you tell me, make it count; we don't have much time. Get to it."

"This is not a good time, Diane." He stood up, grabbed an envelope, put a wad of cash in it, and handed it to her.

"Drinks and dinner at Windsor Court, after work. And Tom, bring your best game. I'm a needy, needy girl." She got off his desk, adjusted her skirt, took the envelope, and left his office.

"What the fuck? I can't believe this," Tom said to himself. He stashed the rest of the money, locked the drawer, and left his office.

"This one looks different to the rest of the recordings," one of the techs noticed.

The other ran it back. "It's because it was three-plus years ago. Crap, I wonder when the recordings started."

The techs pulled footage of the hallway. It had the date and the time, which made it easy to match up with the office encounter. The camera showed Tom coming out of the office, knocking on Grayson's door, and entering the office. About a half-hour later, Tom returned to his office. The scowl on his face was indicative all had not gone well.

He got into his office and started mumbling. "What a bastard." In a menacing voice, he imitated Grayson, "'Well, Tommy-boy, looks like you got yourself a girlfriend.' He's right. She's going to bleed me dry. How the shit am I gonna get out of this?" He sat and thought for the next couple of hours.

The techs noted all the details calling Marse into the room. He scanned through the jotted details, put the pad down with a sigh. "I want footage of Grayson planting the cocaine and money. Also, find out where Tom ended up putting the old lady's money. I want Smith and bad."

"Yes, sir. We'll be on the lookout."

Michael pulled into their driveway. Allie had gone to Eric's, an event that was getting more frequent, and Rainie had dinner in the oven. She ran out to meet him.

"How'd your day turn out?" She wanted to take the temperature since their earlier parting had been disastrous.

"Okay, but I've been down all day. I'm still really pissed, Rainie."

She put her arms around his waist and kissed him. "I love you, Michael. You have every right to be angry with me for not talking with you further about it, but I felt compelled to call Marse. Maybe I shouldn't have done it behind your back after you asked me not to, sorry. She changed the subject. "I cooked dinner for us."

"I look forward to it." He held the door open for her and followed her into the house. "I'm gonna shower and change. Maybe it'll give me a fresh start and improve my disposition." She followed him upstairs. There was no invitation to join him. "Give me some time and space, Rainie." She desperately wanted to talk and followed him upstairs.

"Allie's going to take the LSAT. I told her I'd check with my dad."

"Why don't you go check on the food?"

"The food is fine. It's just the two of us tonight, by the way." As he was taking his clothes off, she began taking off hers. "Can I shower with you?"

"I need space right now. Not trying to be a dick, but I'm trying to work through my anger, and right now, I need to be alone." His entire demeanor was not the usual, Michael. He was calm, but he seemed done, tired.

"Michael, are we okay? You seem strange to me. You still love me?"

"God, yes. I love you. It rattled me today when I realized I wouldn't always be able to protect you. You're who you are, and I wouldn't change that for a second, but with it comes heart-filled but sometimes reckless decisions. It makes me feel inadequate." He stood under the showerhead and escaped into the feel of the water. She watched him and felt terrible for the pain she had caused him.

She wasn't going to be able to fix this. It had to run its course.

With a towel wrapped around his waist, he laid down on the bed, staring at the ceiling. "Rainie, there's something I want to share with you. I had forgotten about it until today. I struggled with this for some time. You know when I said I would kill someone? It wasn't bravado speaking. I may or may not have killed a man when I was in med school."

She listened to him as he began to unpack his story, the one Mer had already told her. As he finished talking about the girl being attacked and his actions to stop him, he paused. "I know my motives were right at the time, and I would do it again in a heartbeat, but it's frightening to think the potential to harm another human being is inside of me. They say it lives inside all people, but I saw it come out in me, and it's scary. I don't know if the guy lived or not, or had permanent damage, or what. Something came over me, is all I can say. I kicked the guy in the throat. It could have crushed his trachea or a host of many things. You mean more to me than anyone; God knows what I'd be capable of. My parents raised John and me to be masters of emotional control. For someone like us, it's devastating to lose control, and I felt those feelings all over again today. I have to digest it."

She laid next to him in silence with her arm around his chest. It was time to take dinner out of the oven. She lightly kissed him, changed into a nightgown, and went downstairs. She stopped in the study. There hadn't been any more writing on the paper.

Once dinner was on the table, she called up to Michael to come down. He went straight to her, took her face in both hands, and kissed her passionately. "I love you. Thank you for loving me."

It was a quiet night of dinner and lounging on the sofa watching some horrible reality program, but at least there was some interaction with him, and she could feel the walls coming down. They fell asleep. Around two in the morning, she woke him, and they went upstairs to bed.

They had one more day, and then they'd be back with the boys at his parents' house. They were both ready.

"Run it back again. I think you got Smith." The two techs had been working through the night. They'd found an oddity in the footage taken before the close of business the night of the wake. It showed a man walking down the hall toward Tom's office. It looked like he might have had something inside his jacket. He barely opened the door to the office, partially leaned in, then shut the door and locked it. They compared it to the time stamp from inside the office. A shadow could be seen of what might have been a man's arm with something in hand, but it was unclear. If they hadn't looked for the shadow, it would have gone unnoticed.

They looked at the crime lab photos taken from the office. Next to the door was a hat rack with a trench coat, a green gym bag, a blazer, a tie, and a large potted plant. They looked through the notes and found that the cocaine had been in a coat pocket and the cash buried in the planter. Judging from the photos, it was debatable as to whether someone of Smith's size would have been able to reach the plant. The coat rack was dead easy, but the plant might be arguably too far of a reach.

The techs had secured all phone records and turned them over to Marse. Two numbers stood out because both had only been called once. All the other numbers had been called repeatedly. One of the unknown calls was on the day of Diane's murder, and the other later that night, the night before Tom was killed.

When pinged, one of the numbers showed an address a block off Claiborne Avenue. Marse had two uniforms dispatched to the address. It was an old run-down shotgun sandwiched between another shotgun and a big house, probably condemned from the look of it.

One of the officers knocked on the door while the other looked down the side of the house. The door was ajar. He called to his partner, and they called for backup before entering the property. Two minutes later, the other car arrived. Three of them entered the house while the fourth one kept watch down the side.

All appearances indicated there was nobody home until they got closer to the last room. The stench hit them like a wall. There was a man slumped over a small kitchen table. From what they could see, he'd been shot in the back of the head, execution-style. They called the coroner and crime lab. It was one of eleven shootings needing to be processed from the day. Preservation of the crime scene was the most critical task at hand; besides, the sooner they could get out of the room, the better. It was one of those smells that stuck in the nostrils and was hard to shake. Three officers stood outside, and one waited for the detective at the front door. They cordoned off the property. There were no onlookers, and it looked more like an area of desolation. The other officer knocked on the surrounding doors.

The occupant of the neighboring house was an elderly man with a head of white fleece, and he was the only other resident living on the block. It didn't take a brain surgeon to see he would be a dead end. The only information they could obtain was the deceased had lived there only a month, and the man had only seen him once. Had it not been of such a serious nature, the conversation with the neighbor would have been nothing short of funny due to his extreme hearing loss. It was a "who's on first" kind of moment. The officer thanked him for his time. A message went out to Marse, letting him know the suspect in the Todd murder was dead.

☙

Marse punched in the numbers. "Teddy? Marse here." The usual courtesies started to ensue, but he cut them off. "I got a question. Are you familiar with the name Grayson Smith of—"

Teddy interrupted, "Rick, you caught me at a bad time, heading out to lunch at Mother's, gotta get there before the crowds, later." He hung up.

Marse was a bit baffled about the call, but he decided he would gamble and go to Mother's. The conversation felt strange, to say the least.

When he arrived at Mother's, there was already a line going out of the door, as usual. He spotted Teddy, Rick's Fed contact, a block away. It wasn't unusual to know half a dozen people waiting in line or seated at a table.

A few people approached him, exchanging niceties. The line moved slowly. Teddy finally made it, joining the end of the line. Rick Marse had been with the force twenty years, developing a shrewdness and no-nonsense approach, but was liked and respected by most. He knew a lot of people, and a lot of people knew him. When he got his food order, he noticed a table with three men winding up their lunch.

"Mind if I sit, gentlemen?" They glanced at his shield worn at his waist.

"Take a seat, officer. We're almost finished." The men made small talk for a second and said goodbye.

Teddy walked up. "Hey Rick, mind if I take a seat? The place is jammed to the gills."

"Jammed every day. Did I read you right?" Marse took a bite of his sandwich.

"Yes, sir. Our friend is on the Mateo Moreno payroll. He runs interference, gets things thrown out before they reach court. He's a smart man, finds all the loopholes. Proceed with caution." The conversation seemed cordial and light to any onlookers.

"This common knowledge?"

"Yep." Teddy took a swig from his iced tea.

"Possible to get a list of thugs he's helped walk?"

"Yep. Not on our phones. Mateo has some of your compadres on his payroll. Never know who." Teddy was nonchalant in his manner and tone.

After swallowing a quick bite, Rick commented, "Mateo is a fed problem, above my pay rate. I'm gunning for Smith. He thinks his social standing makes him above the law, just the kind of prick I like to get."

"I drop my little girl at dance class around three-thirty," Teddy said. "It's in Metairie on Vets, the name's Metairie Academy of Dance." He continued to eat as Marse got up. People were waiting to take his place.

Marse didn't really feel like going to Metairie in school traffic, but he'd like to look at the list. He was impressed by Teddy's expediency. Rick found it interesting that Tom's killer had already been whacked. It was like a chain. There would always be someone looking over their shoulder. He was glad someone else had caught the call; his plate was more than full.

He mulled the whole situation over. He had breadcrumbs all around Smith, but there was always a degree of separation. Checking the list was a step. Diane's killer had to stay alive. He was a direct link to Smith.

Next on the list of things to do was interview all the partners individually. If Rainie had been correct, he should be able to break Thibeaux. Tolbert would be more difficult. He had to keep Smith feeling confident. With Grayson's arrogance, it might be easier than expected. The ducks had to be lined up just right. He'd need to offer a plea to get a confession from the killer. There wasn't usually much loyalty between thug killers and the people who ordered the hit, in his experience.

# ICE, ICE, BABY

The more Marguerite thought about it, the more she thought Tom had told Rainie. Perhaps if Grayson had played the compassion card with Tom during the call, it'd be different, but being such a hard-ass only confirmed any fear or suspicion Tom might have had. She'd like to speak with the sassy redhead.

She let her mind drift and wondered what it would be like to have her. She'd find out if she was a natural redhead or not. She needed to shelve those thoughts. If she could get the latest young whore to come back again, she'd dye her hair red and let the fun begin. She was sure if she could get her hands on Rainie, she would, for sure, be crying with her little vanilla self. The substitute would have to do a good job of acting to fit the bill, and Grayson would need to be there for her own selfish punishment after the whore left. She'd have to pay even more for tears.

She picked up the phone. Grayson answered, "What is it, Marguerite?"

"I think Tom spilled to his ex."

"I don't. Are you obsessing over Tom's ex now? Your addiction is getting worse—keep it up, and I'll put you away. Last week alone was over eight grand. That's absurd, even for you. You need to learn how to take care of yourself, Marguerite." He had zero tolerance for her and rarely showed any genuine affection.

"I'm pouting now, Grayson. You know it's not good to let me

pout." She slammed the phone down and got on the phone to Hot Babe. She had wickedly dark and active demons. The last time he'd dismissed her, it wasn't pretty.

He knew better than to deny her. She knew everything about him. He needed to remember; she had been the one to introduce him to Mateo.

∞

Marguerite met the Colombian teen when she was young and traveling with her parents long before he became a powerful man. He worked at the hotel where they stayed. She'd go to the pool in her bikini, displaying all her curves. She was quite an eyeful. She watched him watch her through her sunglasses. To get his attention, she ordered fruity drinks with little umbrellas and cherries just to flirt. The broken English was intriguing; he made her name sound glamourous with the rolled "r." His olive skin begged to be touched. She fantasized about the two of them making love. Little did she know, he was a virgin. She would be his first kiss and his first for everything she had learned from her perverted uncle. She quickly became his obsession. When her family left, she gave him her number and got his number and address. They kept in touch, and she would occasionally fly down to see him on her uncle's dime.

On her final trip to see him, she found a much different Mateo. At twenty-one, he had entered the world of the cartel and moved up the ranks quickly. He was no longer the youthful lover she'd dominated. He had hardened, and he wanted her for his woman. He scared her a little, which she found exhilarating.

The romance with Mateo came to an end when she met Grayson. He was what her parents expected. At first, he got into her peculiar tastes, but he was nowhere near the lover Mateo had been. He didn't have an ounce of masculinity and nothing that ignited her, but they married with all the pomp and circumstance someone from their circle would expect. They were country club members, had two children, and lived a normal, well-heeled life from all appearances.

It wasn't until after the children were in college that they began intense experimentation with other couples of the same sexual preference. It evolved to membership in an elite club with like-minded people. Marguerite's need to be brutalized grew, as did Grayson's propensity for inflicting pain. His preference was large, rough men who could take it or young first-timers to teach the ropes with his heavy hand. One night he took things too far, the establishment asked him to leave, and their membership was canceled.

What love they may have had at one time was long gone. Their marriage was one of convenience and appearances. From time to time, Mateo needed an attorney for one of the young men working for him; and Marguerite suggested Grayson. Mateo hired Grayson with a monthly cash retainer. Hence the large amount of cash he had been caught stashing.

෯෯

Lounging on the settee, she picked up the phone. "I hope I'm not catching you at a bad time, Mateo. This is Marguerite."

"My beautiful friend, your voice is one I will always recognize. What can I do for you? Are you alright?" He was hard and all business to the world. His responsibility was immense. He didn't have time for friends and very little for his wife, but he still had a spot for his Marguerite; she was his one weakness. His accent was not nearly as broken as when he was young but always felt like a song to her ears.

She began to whimper, "I'm miserable. Grayson is horrible to me. One of his law partners was killed, and I think the partner told his ex-wife company business before he died. Gray thinks I'm crazy; he says I'm saying this because I want her. I only want to talk to her, that's all. I'll be able to tell if she knows anything. He says the most horrible things to me, Mateo." She whined and acted the part of an abused wife.

"Come see me. Grayson cannot help but feel intimidated by you. It is why he acts as he does. He is not a man, as I have told you before. No real man would be held on strings like a puppet. Are you sure about this woman?" His voice was soft as velvet.

"He used the old lady story to his partner when he saw him with cash from you. At the wake, there was something uneasy in her voice.

She knows, and the only way is he told her something. First, the partner's wife was killed, then they killed him. She knows. What if she goes to the police accusing Grayson of these deeds? He thinks I'm saying it because I want to have her."

There was silence for a few seconds. "Do you? Would you rather have her than come to see me? Maybe after a visit with me, you will forget all about the woman and, if not, then I'll get her for you. Tell me when to have the car at the airport."

"You're so good to me," she cried. "I'll book a ticket for tomorrow."

"Yes, my love, come see me. I will make all your sorrows disappear. You will see."

⚘

Traffic going into Metairie was a bitch, but it would be worth it if it helped Marse catch Diane's killer. He pulled up to the dance studio. Teddy was waiting for him.

Rick went to Teddy. "The list wasn't as long as I thought it would be, but they're all frequent flyers. One thing in common is they've all walked one way or another. Good luck, Rick. I hope you get him before he's on a slab."

"Yeah, me too. Thank you. Your list saves me time and aggravation." They shook hands; Marse went back to his car, only to go back through the traffic he had just fought.

Marse called the tech team, checking on the money trail. "Mr. Todd has come and gone with his gym bag every Tuesday and Thursday," one of the techs said. "We only saw him put some money in the bag one time, but it wasn't even close to all of it. Even though the guy was a total douche, boss, he put his hours in and seems like he was a good attorney. The only thing he got out of the drawer were files, and that was when he was on the phone with a client."

"Look closer. If he didn't take the bulk of the money out, then where is it, and wouldn't we have seen him move it to another hiding place? I know we went over the office thoroughly. Could we have missed it? I don't think so. Also, take a good look at the footage. Run it to the end."

After examining the newly acquired list, they found a correlation to a name. To Marse, it seemed a long shot, but they had the address of the man. Diego St. Marten picked up for car theft. Jumping from car theft to murder for hire was a considerable leap and unlikely, but the number matched up. On a hunch, he called a connection he had with the DEA.

"Long time, no hear. How goes it, Rick?"

"Good. Working a case that's gotten under my skin. You have Diego St. Marten on your radar?" His squishy stress relief ball was starting to split. He couldn't help but think how appropriate it was; it was exactly how he felt.

"Not him, but his old lady. St. Marten does mechanic work for a car ring part of the Mateo Moreno organization. He's small, small potatoes. Now, Delores Moreno, she's a piece of work. She runs drugs as well as oversees the car ring. You'd never suspect her to look at her. She's a head-turner, but from what I gather, she'd slit her own mother's throat if the price were right. If you're looking for someone for something big, it's got to be the woman. Wait until you see her. She's hot. Watch it; she can put on the wiles with her sweet smile and perfect jugs. The girl can work it."

"Got the picture. Thanks." He called out the address he had to see if it was current, and it was. It was time to pay a visit to Diego St. Marten. Hopefully, the woman would be there as well.

He grabbed his brand-new sidekick, a kid two years out of the academy from California. By the female officers' reaction, he was as much a heartthrob as Bradley Cooper or Channing Tatum. He had been assigned to Marse, supposedly to learn from the best. Did they not think he knew they were blowing smoke up his ass? The kid wasn't half-bad, though, and was a quick learner. He was a chick magnet. Thus far, it had worked in the NOPD's favor; Marse didn't mind when they re-assigned him to be his sidekick. It couldn't hurt.

When they arrived at the house, it was a lot more upper class than expected. He rang the bell. She came to the door in yoga wear, which left little to the imagination, and the description had been dead-on-balls accurate. She had enchanting eyes and a winning smile. There was no way this sweet young woman could be the killer his DEA connection had portrayed—and herein lay her advantage.

If she had knocked on Diane's door, pretending to be broken down and without her phone, he could easily see where Diane would have let her in. Her accent was almost undetectable.

He let the side-kick ask for Diego. She was full of questions but was quick to call him into the foyer. Diego was a good-looking guy, but it was easy to tell who wore the pants in the relationship. They read him his rights and ushered him to the car. All the while, she pled with them not to take him and asked what they were accusing him of, assuring them that they were certainly mistaken.

"Don't worry, Diego, I'll call for you," she promised.

She appeared distraught, as any normal wife or girlfriend would be if their partner had just been hauled out in handcuffs. Marse was pretty sure the act was for their benefit. It was a little too practiced.

❧

Once Delores was inside, she grabbed the phone. "It's me. Diego got popped. On his way now. I know, I know."

Mateo reminded her of a conversation they'd had just days before. "I told you our pretty boy didn't have the balls for anything of importance. Had he been a man, Delores, he would have insisted on making the hit, but he let you."

"I know, but I love him, Mateo."

Scolding her, "No, Delores, you love his cock and pretty face; that is what you love. They are a dime a dozen. I do not want you to call Smith. I will call another, a young attorney who has wanted my business. Smith has pushed the matter too far."

"Now, who's making decisions for the wrong reasons, brother? When is your American lover coming to you?"

"You lay low. Make sure nothing is missing from the puzzle." He covered all the bases.

"No. Nothing." She knew he was asking about the gun. So many people on a job tossed their weapons in the first dumpster they came to. No, she kept it for herself. Nobody would ever find it. Instead, she threw another gun belonging to the man responsible for Tom Todd's murder, and she had already tied that one up. It would seem the case had been solved. Done.

This whole thing had been a mess from the beginning, and it was all for his American love interest. She must have had a solid gold pussy or something. Mateo could have any woman he wanted. His wife was beautiful and good to him and the children. The American was brash and worn-out looking. She had fucked everyone from the water boy to a senator and whoever else in between.

❧

Once Diego was in interrogation, Marse was ready for him. He observed him, getting a clearer picture of the man he would be interrogating. It would be a fun day; he had both Diego and later Robert Thibeaux to interview.

He had all his props, the coffee mug in one hand, a file with Diego's mugshot attached, and his glasses halfway down his nose so he could peer above them. Marse had his own style. He came across matter-of-factly and straight to the point but always civil, almost polite. It was go-time.

"Mr. St. Marten, do you know why you are here?" He watched him squirm, trying to come up with an answer. "Apparently not. Interesting. According to our information, you shot and murdered Mrs. Diane Todd in cold blood. My question would be, why? What would be the motive?" Marse adjusted the file, making sure Diego would catch a glimpse of his mug shot as he made a note. He stared at the suspect like he was staring through him.

Diego started shifting in the chair. He cleared his throat, "You got some water?"

Marse leaned back in his chair and tapped the glass behind him. Then he went back to staring at him. "Why? What was she to you? Maybe a customer, you fixed her car?"

An officer brought a cup of water to him. "I want my lawyer."

"That ends our conversation. An innocent man would not be screaming lawyer. I already know you did the deed, Mr. St. Marten. I thought we could make it simple; maybe the courts might be more lenient." He shoved his chair back and stood up. "I'll see you again when your lawyer arrives."

Nearly half an hour later, a disheveled young man came in asking to see his client, Diego St. Marten. He was brought to him.

Diego looked at him, confused. "Who are you?"

"I'm Joseph Perez, your attorney." He shifted his briefcase to shake Diego's hand, but his client declined the overture.

"You're not my attorney. Where's Smith?"

"I don't know any Smith. I only know a call came into my office asking I come here to help." The attorney turned both his hands up. "You want representation or not?"

The two men whispered back and forth.

Marse entered the room and sat. The lawyer looked up. "Detective Marse, my client, says you are falsely accusing him of murder."

Marse smiled, "Mr. Perez, in all my twenty-plus years, I can't tell you how many people claiming innocence have sat in that very chair. In my experience, not one of them has been innocent." He looked at Diego. "Did someone else pay you to kill Mrs. Todd?"

"I'm telling you, I did not kill anyone." His lawyer told him not to speak, but it fell upon deaf ears. "If someone asked me to do such a thing, I would say no."

"Did anyone ask you to kill her, but you refused? Maybe they're trying to make it look like it was you, framing you." Marse was still looking at St. Marten.

Perez counseled him, "Don't say a word. If they had anything on you, they'd have arrested you already." The new attorney had his tablet out, ready to take notes.

"Let's say," Marse continued, "for grins, someone called you, and you said no, then whatever evidence we have would pertain to someone else, even though it's pointing straight to you. Sounds like B.S. to me, just saying. Who would do that and why? Back to the why question, Mr. St. Marten." He leaned back and tapped the window again.

"If you have something, then arrest my client, or we're leaving." It appeared the new lawyer had grown a set, but they were baby balls.

Marse smiled. "I just tapped the window. That was their cue, gentlemen."

"W-wait, hold on. Someone did call me, but I didn't kill no one, mister."

Marse had an amused look on his face; he almost chuckled. "Okay, I'll play. Who allegedly called you, Mr. St. Marten?"

"I don't know," he quickly responded.

"How convenient. Some person you don't know calls you and asks you to kill someone. Can you see where I might find this whole scenario made up? No one called you. For some reason, I know not why, yet, you shot a young woman, only in her twenties, to death. You murdered her in cold blood. Do you know what they do to people that do that? You, sir, are going to get the big bon voyage." He looked at his watch and tapped on the window again.

"No, I did no such thing. Alright, I know who called me, but I can't say they'll kill me."

"Diego, you are trying my patience. Now you say someone you know did call you, but you, a cold-blooded murderer, are afraid." He slammed his hand on the table. Diego and his attorney, who hadn't said another word, jumped with the loud bang on the metal table. "I'm done."

"Smith, it was Smith, Mr. Grayson Smith."

"You expect me to believe a person of Grayson Smith's esteem called you? You're a real piece of work. Isn't Smith your attorney, usually?"

Diego was manic. "You see, you see. That is why he didn't come today, but I didn't kill no one."

"If that were the case, you're aware you have to testify in a court of law? You'd have to say exactly what you told me."

"Yes, yes I will." Diego looked him pleadingly in the eyes. Marse pushed a pad toward him.

"Write it down. The whole thing, don't skip any details. Did anyone witness you taking the call?"

"My wife." Diego's hand was shaking to the point he could barely hold the pen.

"Sorry, but that won't stand up. Your wife can't be your witness, by law."

Bingo, he'd gotten what he wanted. The next one on the chopping block was Thibeaux. It was like shooting fish in a barrel.

Now that it was all falling into place, Marse would concentrate on flipping someone in the office to get to Smith. Tom's murderer had gotten his justice. His goal was focused; he wanted to prove Grayson Smith had orchestrated and paid for the hit. He wanted his ass in jail.

Everything about Smith rubbed him the wrong way. No matter his class, he was sleazy to the core. The way he invaded his employees' offices, the debauchery he allowed, encouraged, and participated in was enough to turn anyone's stomach.

∽

Because of all the hours out of the office, Michael's schedule had been more than hectic. The girls in the office were able to get patients shuffled around, but it made for a long day. Rainie didn't play the role of the little woman well. Cooking, cleaning, and all the other domestic crap wasn't her forte. She had someone to clean, and Allie helped with the kids. For the past few years, she and Mer had worked in the office. Even though it was downtime, they'd still pop in. There was always some party or luncheon to go to, but neither seemed to be in the mood anymore.

Although she'd never been known to be domestic, Rainie had found herself planning and preparing meals for Michael during the past few days. Part of it was that she wasn't running around with the kids, so she needed to fill space, or she'd start thinking, which usually spelled trouble. Something about idle hands. She could see where someone might find enjoyment and relaxation in cooking. The novelty would wear off soon, no doubt.

She heard Michael pull up. She missed him. Since the wedding, they'd spent most weeks together, and any time they were apart for any length of time, she missed him. He came in with his usual bounce and compliment on the aromas from the stove.

"This smells great. If I didn't know better, I'd swear you were enjoying your time away from the hustle and bustle." He came up behind her. "You smell good." He kissed the back of her neck, "Where's Allie?" he whispered against her neck.

"At Eric's. We won't see her until after the New Year when the boys come home. It gets lonely around here without anyone to play with.

Mer's tied up with the girls, Allie's domestic with Eric," she sighed. "I miss you. I take it all is forgiven."

She turned around in his arms. They were face to face. "But not forgotten, Rainie. Just let it go. I have. So back to what I was about to say." He cleared his throat. "Sorry, my love, my schedule has been wild and the hours long, but it's only for a couple of days. We go to my parents' house in two days. We have tonight, tomorrow, and tomorrow night and then it's kid time. You'll yearn for this solitude when the madness is back in force. Enjoy. Go get your nails done, have a massage, or shop." He massaged her neck in between kisses.

"All good options to consider. I'm used to fitting things in between a tight schedule. Don't do well by myself with nothin' to do. I've been reading the book your mom gave me." She could feel her face heat up.

"You mean the smut?" he teased. "It must be sizzling because you're blushing. I can't believe my mom reads erotica but with Dad home all the time, who knows with them."

"I'm going to find out how she deals with getting hot and bothered. I can't read too much. I get frustrated." She hadn't taken her eyes off him. He backed her up to the kitchen table. He lifted her onto the table. "Michael, this is where we eat."

"Precisely." He raised an eyebrow. He scooted her jeans down, not once breaking eye contact, and as he pulled them off her legs, he began kissing her ankles and up the inside of her leg. He did one then the other, slowly—still looking into her eyes. "What do you do when you get hot and bothered? Maybe if you closed your eyes and did what came naturally, you wouldn't be out on the lurch, oh, but you don't do that." He devilishly smiled as he tugged at her panties. There was little holding them on. He ripped them off her. "Now there, that's more like it." He moved his hands over and into her body with precision, making sure he hit all the highlights. "Almost."

The table provided the perfect height to take her. Sitting on such a hard surface, she felt slightly different on the inside. "Better?" he asked as he pushed himself into her. She wrapped her legs around him. He thrust harder as he increased the motion.

"Oh, this feels different but oh so good."

"How bad have you wanted this today?" He picked up his pace.

She watched as he ran his tongue over his teeth. His breathing intensified.

"Oh, God, Michael. I have wanted you beyond bad."

He pulled her even closer, almost raising her body off the table, thrusting faster. "Come on, baby." She felt his pulsing as her body raged. She grabbed his hips as they both hit the pinnacle.

"Shower time?" he asked.

She let go of him. He picked her up off the table and set her down. "Yes, Michael, shower time. But first, turn off oven time. I'll turn it off while you wipe off the table. Am I going to get hot and bothered when I look at our kitchen table? Probably."

They went upstairs and showered, continuing their conversation about the day, the boys, and New Year's Eve without skipping a beat.

"What a welcome home surprise, Rai. The boys will be home in a couple of days, no more novelty table talk." He tossed his clothes in the hamper.

"Probably not, but we can lock the study sometimes, or you could come home for a nooner. I take lunch breaks and can't think of anything better than you to quench my appetite."

"No calls from Marse?" he asked, raising an eyebrow.

"Nope. I told you I'd tell you, and then you can talk to Marse. We need to dry off and get dressed so that you can taste my new recipe." She was excited about the adventure in the kitchen but more so about putting distance between them and any Marse talk.

Her meal was tasty; they did the dishes and sat on the sofa. She loved being with him. They turned on an old movie and cuddled. Rainie felt happy and content like she didn't have a care in the world.

☙❧

Grayson came in with a scowl on his face and went straight to the bar. He poured more than usual into the glass. Marguerite hadn't acknowledged him getting home. She was probably still pouting from earlier in the day.

"Marguerite, I'm here," he shouted in the direction of her bedroom. The last time she went on a tirade, she'd ripped the sheets and pillows and shredded a bedside chair. It had been a nice chair with the perfect seat for easy-access blowjobs. It even had a matching pillow, but she had ruined it all. He walked to her bedroom. The door was shut. He knocked, "Marguerite?"

"Come in," she said without inflection. It was more like a drone.

He walked in; she was packing a suitcase. "What're you doing?"

"Grayson, what does it look like I'm doing?" The sarcasm was thick. "I'm going to Cartagena tomorrow."

"Oh, for God's sake, why on earth would you go there? Are you going to see Mateo? I have enough bullshit going on around here. I don't need you running to your beloved Mateo. He certainly doesn't have what you want," he responded in a condescending manner.

"He's my friend, and right now, I seem to be finding myself short on friends." She continued to pack, ignoring his presence.

"You don't want a friend. You want to punish me for not giving you Rainie Todd. She's off-limits. I swear, you go near her, and they'll find you with a bullet to the head. Do I make myself clear? She doesn't know anything. Listen to me. She's into her new life and new husband." He turned to walk out of the room.

"All I wanted to do was talk to her," she responded with indifference.

"My ass. I could hear it in your voice. You wanted to tie her to your bed and strip her of her dignity with one of your strap-ons or punishment toys. You can't get her twat out of your mind. For shock value, Marguerite? She isn't your type, and you sure as hell aren't hers." By this time, his voice trailed behind him as he headed to the living room.

"I have already arranged my ride to the airport, but thank you for offering." Her words came out drenched in bile.

The following morning could not come fast enough. She laid in bed thinking of the first time she and Mateo had been together. She'd taught him every little pleasure. You never forget your first fuck, and she was his. He'd learned a hell of a lot from her. Their time together had been bliss.

Then it hit her. She could easily transport herself back to her first time. She remembered the pain; there had been no pleasure. Her uncle had brutalized her in every way. He'd demanded she tell him how strapped he was and what a good fuck he was, and any girl would find it an honor to let them suck his dick. The first time, she had blood running down her legs. He didn't care. She remembered that teenage girl crying for him to stop. The more she cried, the more brutal he became, and he always ejaculated between her breasts, smearing his semen all over her. And because of him, it was almost impossible for her to have any normal sexual experience, except with Mateo.

৵৬

When she'd told Mateo her story, he'd cried with her, holding her like she wished her mother had done. Years later, Mateo had her uncle brutalized with a bat by one of his henchmen. After the brutality, he, himself, took delight in cutting off his manhood. The uncle cried like a little bitch. Then he sliced his throat and shoved his genitals in his mouth. Before the blood had started to coagulate, he was on his way back to Colombia. That was the first man he'd ever killed, and it had felt good to exact revenge.

৵৬

Morning came, and Marguerite dressed in her most slimming dress, with just a hint of make-up—he hated the painted look. She lightly touched her lips with passion-red lipstick. Maybe it was the knowledge she would see Mateo, or perhaps it was the missing face paint. Either way, her demeanor, and appearance were softer, more genteel.

She heard the horn of the cab, and off she went, without even saying goodbye.

৵৬

Marse got to the office earlier than usual. It was going to be a good day. Thibeaux was going to be the last nail in Smith's coffin. His original plan was to have conducted Thibeaux's interview the previous afternoon, but like so many things, plans got skewed. Marse expected him in before ten. He had made a list of the specific questions to ask and wanted to let him know about the proof of sexual impropriety. It would throw him off his game.

Robert Thibeaux had been made partner a year before Tom. He'd been with the firm eight years. He was an LSU boy from an average blue-collar family, hired straight out of law school, and had jumped ranks in the company at a good pace.

He'd also been on scholarship during his undergrad and was a four-point student. During the summer and on the weekends, he worked for an alumnus. The alum took a particular interest in him and offered to pay for law school. It just so happened when Robert met the daughter of his benefactor; he fell in love. When he graduated from law school and was hired by Tolbert, they married and had the token two children.

This little fact gave Marse a stacked deck. If anyone got wind of the sexual misconduct at the office, his father-in-law would have his balls, as would his dad for being so stupid. Yep, he was ready for him. He sipped his coffee and fielded some calls.

Robert was a nice-looking man. Clean cut, clean-shaven, he had an all-American look. A person couldn't help smiling back when Bob smiled their way. He was an easy-to-like kind of guy. He stood about five-foot-ten and maybe 180 pounds, blond hair, blue eyes, and sparkling white teeth. Bob was handsome and charming, a nice guy, caught in a nasty set of circumstances.

Marse got up and walked over to him, hand outstretched. "Thank you for coming in, Mr. Thibeaux. I thought it would be more comfortable to talk to you here. When I interviewed Mr. Smith and Mr. Tolbert, they seemed edgy, so I thought it better to get you out of the environment."

"Makes no difference to me, detective, and please, call me Bob. What can I do to help? I'm not really sure what this is all about if you could catch me up." He smiled earnestly.

Marse walked him into an interrogation room. "Let me be frank, Bob: your partner Tom Todd and his wife were both murdered, and things didn't add up. I was with Mr. Todd the night his wife was killed and was fairly certain he had nothing to do with it, but I knew something wasn't right. Do you buy the story Tom was dealing drugs?" Marse laid his hands flat on the table.

"No, sir. Tom had his faults as we all do, but drugs and Tom? No way." His sincerity was rare and refreshing.

"Are you aware Mr. Smith has a camera running at all times in the office?" Marse waited for the shock of realization that Thibeaux was in a most compromising situation.

The shock on his face was like something out of a cartoon. "No, sir, I'm not aware of anything like that." His voice quaked.

"And other things, too. Take a look at the monitor." He ran a segment showing Thibeaux getting a blowjob from Diane.

The man hung his head.

"Do you have anything to say? You are married, correct?"

He picked up his head and was wide-eyed. His eyes were misty. "I'm sure you have many more embarrassing situations on tape, am I right?" Marse nodded. "Clearly, I don't want my wife to find out. It's hard to explain." Bob's entire body was shaking.

"Um, I don't think there's anything to explain. It's pretty clear, Bob, Diane was giving you a blowjob on company time. I've seen more of you than I ever would want to see of you. At least you had manners and thanked each person for their services, unlike your partner Tolbert. We only got Smith when he was in your, Tolbert's, or Todd's office, and never a clear shot of his face, but we know it's him. Clear as the day, he walks in the office and out; we can't exactly see his face during the acts of degradation, but it's him." Marse nodded almost with arrogance.

"Everybody was doing it." Thibeaux dropped his head again. He was ashamed.

"If everybody was jumping off a bridge, would you? I bet you've said the same thing to one of your children. What's your wife's name?" Marse was still holding a confident, snarky upper hand, and he was going to push him until he broke.

"Cherie." His face was drawn with sorrow. "I love my wife. We have a great relationship. I didn't want to get involved in the shenanigans, but I caved. I don't want to hurt my wife; she would be devastated." The man was utterly deflated.

"I bet so. If you were to say there was a ringleader, who would that person be? Tolbert or Smith?" Marse looked him straight in his sad misty eyes.

"Smith by a landslide. It's based on the business brought in and the hours billed. Smith had only a few clients, but they brought in a lot of money. Always some petty something or other, but it was still billed hours. He runs the show. Tolbert is a wannabe Smith, but somewhere inside, there's still some humanity left in him."

"I see. Did Todd have humanity in him? He was pretty involved with some of the girls, but especially Diane, of course, he married her. Even if it was under duress."

"He loved her. There wasn't any coercion." Robert was sure, although the thought mystified him.

Marse told him the extortion bit between Tom and Diane.

"Holy shit. Oh my God." He ran his hand down his face in disbelief. "I don't think anyone knew about anything of the sort. Are you sure? Where would Tom get that much cash?"

"You didn't receive a lot of cash?" he asked. Marse thought they were all bought off by Smith.

"No, sir. I was an asshole to cheat on my wife, I admit, but I have never taken money from anyone. No, sir." Bob was straight-faced.

"Tom got the cash from Smith. I know Tolbert had some, too."

"I told you Tolbert was a wannabe Smith. He'd do anything Smith asked him to do or act any way Smith wanted him to act. Tom must have gotten wind or something. I don't think it would have been of his doing. Are you going to tell my wife, detective? I don't want to hurt her. I'll do anything to keep from letting her see those recordings."

Marse almost felt sorry for the guy as he pleaded.

"I heard you loud and clear when you said you didn't think Tom was involved in dealing drugs. Watch this."

He brought up the footage of the mystery man putting something in Tom's office.

"What the hell? You know who that is? That's Smith. I'll swear on a stack of Bibles."

"How can you be so sure?"

"Smith has this thing he does with his foot when he walks. Run it back. I'll show you." Marse reran the footage. "See, right there. He kinda kicks his foot out when he walks. I bet if you check all the footage you have, you'll see the flick of his foot. It's more attitude than impairment. From seeing this, I'd say Smith planted the dope and cash in Tom's office. I can't believe this." He drummed his fingers on the table. He was deliberating something in his head. Marse sat still and let him go through the hell in his mind. Eight minutes passed, and Thibeaux looked up with a determined look. "I have information, it might be of interest to you and help with the case, but I want total immunity and your word you won't tell my wife about the sexual indiscretions."

"Bob, if you tell me something like you pulled the trigger and killed the Todds, I don't have the authority to, nor would I, give you immunity. I guess it all depends on what you have to say, but I'm a pretty fair man and have a loving wife and three kids. It's a crapshoot. What can I tell you, but if it were me, I'd play my conscience. At the end of the day, we're all going to have to answer for our sins. You come across, despite the rampant sex, as a God-fearing man. Up to you, son."

Thibeaux put his hands together, took a deep breath, and let it out. "Smith ordered the murders of Tom and Diane. I swear I didn't know it was going to happen. I knew he was angry about something and wanted Tom out of the firm, but I had no idea. I swear." He started to tear up again. He wiped his eyes.

"Would you be willing to make your statement in a court of law? And I need to take a written statement. You didn't know what the plan was, which gives me some leeway, but the fact you didn't come forward is accessory after the fact. For your cooperation and the information you've given us, I'd say you're probably safe on the sex and the accessory, but you need to guarantee you'll testify to your statement. Otherwise, if you clam up, then the recording and accessory agreement will be null and void. We'll have to wait for an ADA, and then they'll bring the DA into this. Any plans you had for today are gone."

# NOTHING COMPARES TO YOU

Rainie took Michael's advice and had a mani-pedi the next morning, then went to his office. It was close to lunchtime. The girls at his office were thrilled to see her, raved about the wedding, and talked about her boys. She was one proud mom, and she missed them. Tears came to her eyes talking about them.

"I'm sorry. It's been a hell of a week, and I could use one of their hugs. I usually don't do this." One of the girls handed her a Kleenex.

The receptionist opened the door to the back from the waiting room and brought her to Michael's office. She sat in his chair and started reading a pamphlet about body sculpting. She looked over the top. Michael stood in the doorway with the biggest smile on his face.

"What a pleasant surprise. You need to do this more often, gorgeous." He bent down to kiss her. "Time for lunch?"

"Yes, and look." She wiggled her fingers. "It's called Tell Me About It Stud. Don't you love it?" She was excited as a schoolgirl.

"It looks beautiful, but what an odd name, it's really named Tell Me About It Stud?"

"Yep," she laughed. "Promise."

"Can you occupy yourself for another twenty minutes? And then we'll go." She heard him ask Beth to call his chef friend at the café.

Twenty minutes flew by. It was good to be out and doing things. She wasn't meant to be a homebody; perhaps it wasn't time to close the doors on the decorating firm. They exited the back door and were on their way to the café. He kept looking over at her, smiling.

"I'm stoked you came to see me. You look great, but then you always do." He patted her belly. "Hello, my sleeping one."

"I have a plan for tonight." She batted her eyes.

"Do tell." He raised his eyebrows in a flirty way.

"No way, it's a surprise," she giggled.

It was a wonderful lunch, in the kitchen again. The chef sat with them for a few minutes. The workings of the kitchen exhausted her just watching. It was go, go, go, but the aroma was irresistible.

Like any time with Michael, it went by way too fast. When they got back to the office, he walked her to her car and planted one on her.

"I love you, Michael. I can't wait until tonight." She squeezed him extra tight.

He asked her, "Should I be afraid? You seem almost too excited about tonight. I'm looking forward to my surprise."

"You're so silly, Michael. Afraid? Of me? No, just some fun, that's all."

He watched as she pulled away.

She called Mer to see if it was a good time to stop by. "Are you kidding me? An extra set of arms is always welcome. Besides, when have you ever asked to come over?"

They talked about the changes in their lives and how life was evolving. Rainie shared her thoughts about closing the firm but how she couldn't fathom not having the firm after only two days of nothing.

Mer agreed. "As soon as they're old enough for childcare, I'm all about getting back to it. We don't have to take on every project, like King's Court; even though we made out well, I don't think I want something on such a ginormous scale again. Time will tell, Rai, we aren't doing anything in a hurry."

It was good to hang with her friend. After Rand's death, she'd spent a lot of time at Meredith's. Her large family was a distraction from Rainie's emptiness. Her older brothers teased them all the time. One of their favorite gags was grabbing the girls, opening the huge chest freezer, and pretending to drop them in. Being girls, they'd squeal to the point her mother would come in, scolding the boys for being too rough. It was all part of the fun. The boys plotted numerous attacks against the girls but always evoking the same reaction—squealing laughter.

With a quick hug for Mer and whisper kisses to the girls, she headed home. She giggled to herself, thinking about Mer's brothers. When they all got together, they would revert to their teasing. Mer's sisters were considerably older. There were three girls, then three boys, and then Mer. She didn't remember much about the younger brother because the age gap had been substantial. He was the family surprise and babied beyond reason.

Michael called, "You have me very curious about tonight. It's all I can think about. Any hints?" He sounded like a kid begging to know what was wrapped inside the box.

"Are you kidding? No way, and Michael, it's nothing extraordinary." She pulled into the driveway.

"I have a stupid grin on my face and a boner extraordinaire!"

"Oh my, I can see where you may have a problem. Want me to come back, and you can examine me for a boob job or a butt lift?" She laughed. *This is hilarious. Tables turned, my friend.*

"That's not helping this situation. I still have two more hours of appointments. Maybe I need to excuse myself to the men's room and have you breathe heavy and talk dirty. That'll take care of this situation."

"Am I to take you seriously, or are you playing?" She was curious. *WTF? He's serious.*

"You choose." She knew that voice.

"I haven't done this before; I'm an amateur. Excuse yourself while I still dare to try, but I'm in the fucking car."

"I'm a few steps away from the men's room."

She heard the door open and close. She could hear him maneuvering to get ready. She closed her eyes. Rainie wasn't sure if she could do it without laughing. She set her mind, "Oh, Michael," she said in her raspy whisper. "Can you feel my mouth around your hard cock? I'm sucking it, stroking it, faster and harder. Oh, baby, I know how you like it rough. I will show no mercy. I'm going to take you down my throat. I'm sucking harder; I can't wait to taste you. Come on, Michael, I'm begging for it. I'm exploring myself, but it's no substitute for your hard-throbbing cock or your amazing, curious tongue." His breathing had picked up. She could picture him running his tongue across his teeth. "Are you ready to explode, Michael? Stroke it harder and faster. Here it is, it's right there, come on, baby. Give it to me, explode down my throat." She could hear him as the magic moment arrived.

Silence.

Back to her normal voice, she said, "Michael, are you okay? Did I do good enough? Did I get you there? It sounded like it, but I'm not sure."

"Wow, amazing, one for the book of first times for me. I almost feel like a pervert, but wow. My sexy, sexy, unbelievably sexy wife, all I can think is wow. Thank you."

Fighting back laughter, she said, "You're welcome. Glad I could help your sticky situation." She laughed. "Get it, sticky situation?"

She could feel his smile through the phone and hear it in his voice. "Yeah, Rainie, I get it. Very good." Then he put on a different voice, "Will you still respect me in the morning?"

"You're a jackass, Michael. Now go see your patients. I know they're waiting by now. Pick up something decadent on your way home, like Popeye's."

She could hear him walking back to the treatment rooms. "Popeye's, really? Spicy or mild? Sides?"

"You choose. I love you." She got out of the car.

"I love you."

As she got out of the car and went inside, she couldn't help but think her idea of reading parts of her book to him would seem lame. Had he not just gotten off with their phone sex, he would have found the reading exciting. She laughed to herself. The fact she could get him so turned on with a suggestion of a surprise said a lot about his lust for her. She'd go through with her plan. He'd appreciate the novelty. He might freak to think it was the kind of book his mother read, though. Hopefully, they too would be sex-hungry when they'd been married thirty-six years.

She went upstairs and ran the bath. Should she pretend she didn't know bubbles were off-limits for pregnancy or overlook it until her doctor told her? Maybe she'd just do candles and stay away from the bubbles. It would set the perfect ambiance to sip a great glass of wine, but sparkling water would have to suffice. Lounging in the tub, her hair pinned up on top of her head, she admired her newly painted nails. He was right; she needed to pamper herself more and accept the go, go, go when necessary, but when it wasn't, she should take advantage of the luxuries in life.

She closed her eyes in relaxation when she heard a whisper. "Rainie." Her eyes stayed closed, and she kept quiet. Again, "Rainie, do you hear me?"

Eyes closed, she answered in a whisper, "Yes." It was Rand's voice.

"What are you going to name your daughter? Please don't name her after me, I love you and am proud of you, but she needs a name of her own." The voice was soft and gentle.

"Please don't leave," Rainie said, eyes still closed and whisper ever-so-soft. "The reason I didn't have a sweet sixteen was—it didn't feel right without you. I haven't celebrated our birthday because it reminds me I don't have you to celebrate with, and it hurts too bad. I'm sorry if I hurt you. I'm getting better. On our next birthday, I'll be thirty-five, and I'm going to celebrate by letting the boys plan a party for me. I'll get them to help me blow out the candles like we used to. If I open my eyes, will I see you?"

Silence.

She hadn't heard the back door open or his footsteps on the stairs, or even his breath standing in the doorway of the bathroom.

"Who are you talking to?" he whispered.

Chills ran through her body. "Michael?"

"Expecting someone else?"

She slowly opened her eyes. He held a dozen beautiful red roses in his hand. The love emanated as he admired her, and he sat on the side of the bathtub.

He leaned in for a kiss. "My last two appointments canceled. Were you talking to Rand?" He cocked his head to the side.

"Yes. Could you hear her?" She had a look of wonder. Her tummy tingled, waiting for his response.

"No, but the bathroom is pretty chilly. My love, you need to make sure you lock the doors before coming up to shower or bathe. When the door was unlocked, I became alarmed."

"You want to get in the tub with me, or do you want me to get out?"

He put the roses down, reached for a towel, "Come here, gorgeous. I'll dry you off."

She got out, and he began to pat her dry.

Looking up at her, he said, "You know what I want to do?" With the tip of his tongue, he touched her belly gently.

"As much as that sounds irresistible, the roses need to get in some water. Did you get the Popeye's?" The way she asked sounded like she hadn't eaten in days.

With a laugh, he answered, "Yes."

"Great, I'm starved. Why are you looking at me like that? I know we ate only a few hours ago. I wanted Popeye's." She put on one of her robes. "Get comfortable unless we're going somewhere?" She reclined on the bed, ankles crossed and watched as he began to undress.

He began unbuttoning his shirt. "Nope. It'll be a night in. We need to pack for tomorrow. By the way, did you mean it when you said you were exploring?"

She gave him a look. "We can pack inside of ten minutes. It's okay if you just want to stay home. I do, too. And no, Michael, I was trying to have phone sex. I thought it might add an extra touch. You know I don't do that."

"You should." He gave her a devilish smile. "I'm waiting for the hand and the 'as if.' Chicken's gonna get cold. C'mon."

The Popeye's hit the spot. She couldn't remember the last time she'd had fried chicken. He'd managed to get one of each side. She sampled them all. As much as he questioned her about the choice of dinner, he was getting into it, as well.

"You had a surprise for me?" He began clearing the table.

"Yes." Together, they quickly cleaned the kitchen. "Sit with me on the sofa." They went into the den. "What I had planned may seem lame after today's little experiment. Get comfy," she said. They stretched out their legs on the sofa, facing each other. He was at one end and she at the other, by the lamp. She cleared her throat and started reading to him, changing voices with the different characters. He started to blush. She kept reading, panting, and groaning where applicable. She read for ten minutes before he interrupted her.

"Good gracious, is this what you've been reading? I knew it was sexy, but I had no idea, it really is smut, and my mom gave this to you? Christ! What is she doing reading this?" He looked like an animated character, his eyes wide with disbelief. It made her giggle inside.

She waited until he finished speaking and began reading again. This time she started acting out as she read. When the character spread her legs, so did she. Whatever the character in the book did, she did. It came to a part where her male counterpart was getting into the explicit action. After a few minutes, she tossed the book to the side, and they went upstairs.

They had taken love-making to a whole different level because of the love part of the equation. There was no doubt that she knew how to love; it was hard to accept having someone love her back as deeply—it had been foreign terrain, but, in the end, it was all about love, respect, and trust.

He kissed her over and over. "Have I ever told you just how beautiful you are? Rainie, you're something else; there are no words to describe. I want to be a better man for you, the best I can be." His eyes became glossed with a layer of tears. The sincerity flushed her with a warm wave.

"Michael, it can't get any better because you love me like you do. I love you, and there isn't a man out there that comes close to you." She gave him a devilish smile. "So, Dr. Stud, you liked my dirty talk?"

"And then some, my dear."

The ducks were all lining up. Marse was going to have Smith skewered—he wouldn't be able to wiggle anywhere, and there probably wasn't a decent attorney to take his case. After all, he'd had his partner and his partner's wife killed. Grayson Smith was nothing short of a cannibal. How would he explain it to the wife? No doubt he was destined for prison. The whole thing disgusted him.

Rick Marse had been faithfully married to his wife for years. Despite the fact he worked all the time, their relationship was rock solid. He had, like most cops, many opportunities to step out on her, but the thought had never crossed his mind. Nothing or no one was worth his marriage or his family. To see the debauchery on the video was unforgivable. He was disgusted, mainly by their treatment of the office personnel. How Smith hadn't been sued for sexual harassment was a mystery.

Marse wanted to get Tolbert for sexual misconduct, but he couldn't arrest someone just for having sexual relations with staff or being a pig. Maybe he could somehow advise one of the girls to register a complaint. He'd seen pictures and heard him tell a few of the girls to lean over the desk so he could fuck them up the ass. He was lewd, more so than Smith when it came to his comments.

The read Marse had on the whole sex thing was Smith seemed to like the group stuff, but he never showed his face. In prison, he would be guaranteed some group action, probably not the kind he wanted, but maybe so—he was pretty fucked up.

❧

The flight had been smooth; Marguerite had had a couple of beverages and was feeling relaxed and ready to see her friend—the only one who gave a damn about her feelings and all she had experienced. The silence in the aircraft and the drinks unleashed her mind to wander. She hadn't been a great mother herself, but she wasn't a bad one either. Her relationship with her kids was nothing spectacular but nothing unusual. They had grown, had their lives, and didn't seem to want to hang with their parents much. They got together on holidays and birthdays, but there had never been much huggy, fuzzy feel-good. They would die of embarrassment if they had any idea of what went on in the house now.

Grayson had always provided them with everything they wanted. He was a money dad. Even though Mateo was an important man in the cartel world, he would've been a better husband to her. His heritage was problematic to her parents. When they learned of the relationship, she obeyed and ended the friendship immediately, or so they thought.

As the captain announced the approach, she felt butterflies in her stomach. She wondered if he would be waiting, of course not in the airport—it would have been too dangerous—but in the car. They landed and disembarked, and waiting for her was a nice-looking man in a black suit with a sign displaying her name. He took her to claim her baggage. As they walked out of the terminal, the balmy atmosphere enveloped her. She felt as though she had come home. All the memories she had from Cartagena were happy.

The driver opened her door, and her heart skipped a beat. Mateo was in the car waiting for her. His smile was warm, and his eyes enchanting.

"Ah, my beautiful Marguerite, I trust you had a nice flight." The trace of his accent was still intoxicating; his English was almost too perfect, void of any contractions. It was eloquent. "Marguerite, my love, you, like fine wine, get better with the years. It is a perfect time for you to be here. We will bring the New Year in together, yes?" He was attentive and awaited her every word.

"I hadn't even given it thought, but yes, how wonderful to start a new year with someone you love. Words cannot express how grateful I am to be here with you, even if for a short time. You're my closest friend, Mateo. The only one I can count on." She smiled sweetly, like a young teenager in love.

"Let us think of only pleasant thoughts. You are away from all the negativity, bask in the sun, worry-free. I have a beautiful suite for you with everything you could want. I hope you will consider having dinner tonight with me at the hotel. Unfortunately, I no longer have the luxury of being in public places. My enemies have grown in number as my business has grown more prosperous." He closed his eyes and slowly shrugged his shoulders. It was the price he paid for success.

"Of course, I'd love to have dinner with you. I know how busy you are. I'm not expecting to monopolize your time during my stay. Don't feel any obligation." She put her hand on his.

He kissed her hand, "Being with you is no obligation, but my desire." He pointed to his heart. "Nothing has changed here for you. My heart still burns for you. It has been too long since our last meeting. Three years, maybe?" He kissed her hand again.

As they drove, she looked out of the windows. Cartagena had changed with the times and was far more commercial. It had always been urban, as much as she could remember, but as she looked down the streets they passed, it seemed in many ways poorer. The countryside in the distance was still lush, and brilliant flowers bloomed everywhere, but there was an ominous feel. One she had never felt or noticed before.

The resort, though, had been maintained beautifully and still had the feel of paradise on earth. They walked in the door surrounded by three other men; she assumed bodyguards and went straight for the elevator. Just as he'd said, the suite was lovely, almost palatial. Champagne was chilling amidst sumptuous platters of fruit, specialty cheeses, and delicious-looking pastries. The view from the terrace was spectacular.

"Mateo, this is lovely. You make a girl blush." Two of the men stayed outside the suite door and the other inside at the door. She looked at the man with a question in her expression.

"Ah, yes, they are with me all the time. There have been some unfortunate situations in the area lately. One can never be too cautious, but nothing for you to worry about, I promise. I am leaving Javier to watch over you in my absence." He smiled warmly. "I also have room 106 reserved." The way his eyes glimmered sent sizzles through her body. Life, this was life, and with him, she was alive.

She laughed girlishly. "Oh my, 106, that's where it all began, this wonderful friendship. I think you can release that unless you want it." She absorbed the beautiful view from the balcony.

"Maybe for a night. I love re-living the experience. Was it not a marvelous time?" He stood behind her, wrapping his arms around her waist.

"Yes. To think it all began when you brought me a few fruity drinks. There was something in your eyes. So sweet, Mateo, innocent and pure." She turned in his arms. They went back inside.

He poured her a beverage, tossed in some pineapple and mango with a cherry. "You desire any other food right now?" She shook her head no. He opened oversized French doors to a beautiful bedroom. The bed, elevated by steps, looked inviting and vastly larger. They walked in. "Do you like the bedroom?" He closed the doors behind them.

"My, yes. This suite is spectacular, but you didn't have to go to the trouble."

"No trouble, my beautiful lady, all my pleasure." He walked behind her and began to unzip her dress. "May I?" He slowly removed her clothes. She stood before him in heels and nothing else. He pulled the sheets down. "Still so beautiful." He began unbuttoning his shirt and then stepped out of his pants. He took her hand and led her to the bed.

"It seems the roles may be a bit reversed, as I remember," she said, glowing.

"Ah, but I remember always to relax my lips for a more succulent kiss." He pulled her to him and kissed her shoulders, gently caressing her body. He was loving and gentle, delicately touching her breasts. He laid down, making room for her next to him. "Come to me, my sweet Marguerite, do not be shy."

He made her giggle. "I seem to remember those exact instructions to you. Mateo, 'do not be afraid, do not be shy, I shall open a whole new world filled with ultimate pleasure.'"

"And you did." His smile broadened. "In one special day, I enjoyed my first kiss and learned from you about the pleasures of the body. I was a blank canvas for you. You could have told me anything, and I would have believed you. Yet, you were not selfish. I had never felt anything close to the feeling of you taking me in your mouth and then being inside you." He took a deep breath. "I was the shy boy, no girl had ever looked at me twice, and here you were, a beautiful American girl tantalizing me and teaching me the art of making love. Ours has been a love second to none. It has withstood a husband, a wife, your children, my children—but there was always my love for you."

"And mine for you." She kissed him gently.

He made love to her. There was no need for brutality or talking crudely. While very few people could arouse her and even fewer who could bring her to completion without punishment, Mateo brought out the woman in her with sweet sensuality. He delicately kissed her entire body. She could feel herself filling and releasing as though it were a natural thing for her. He didn't need to use gimmicks or toys.

"Are you okay, my sweet?" He was on his side, turned toward her.

"Yes." The tears started to roll down her cheeks. "You have no idea. This was perfect."

"Do not cry. Talk to me. I want to know what has made you unhappy."

Marguerite told him she had a developed an addiction to violent sex and about what she had been doing, the whores, the freaks, the brutalization she inflicted on others. She went into great detail. He listened attentively. She said Grayson liked to watch while the person was beating her or mistreating her, to the point of tearing sometimes. It was taking more and more to achieve pleasure. She took her frustrations out on whores. She felt bad because she knew she was scaring and inflicting pain on these young women, but that's what it took. It had become a vicious cycle.

"I'm embarrassed to tell you these things, but I guess I needed to tell someone, and you are safe for me." She closed her eyes with embarrassment, but her long dark lashes swept open as she felt his gaze upon her.

"You have no love in your life. You do not even love yourself; it is why you feel you need to do these things. It hurts me to hear this, but I will get you help." He laid silently for a few seconds. "Did I satisfy you? Tell me the truth." He took her hand and kissed the top ever-so-gently.

"Yes. I know it's strange. It's different with you. If someone else were to try to fuck me like—" Mateo interrupted her.

"Marguerite, I did not fuck you. I love you, and I made love to you. There is a big difference. Whores and kinky stuff is not what I desire. You taught me the art of making love, and I have never needed to venture down any other roads. My poor wife, I barely ever sleep with her anymore because I am always at work. I know she has a lover, and I understand; I do not give her the attention she needs. It has been the same man for years. I suspect he loves her, and I should probably let her go, but I cannot. One of my enemies could do something to her out of hatred of me. It is the only way I can keep her safe."

"You are a kind and considerate man. I only wish Grayson would be like—"

He stopped her. "You cannot ask a dog to be a cat, no? Grayson enjoys the affection of men, and yet, if that were all, so be it, but he seems heartless. Believe me, my sweet, I know heartless when I see it.

It takes one to know one, yes? Mine is business, his is personal, and I find him disgusting.

"I will get you help. You have always deserved much better. Are you physically okay now? I would never want to hurt you. Will you let me help you? Think of it as going to a health spa. I refuse to believe this woman you described to me is you. I think it is you running away."

She turned away from him, and he drew her close to him. Perhaps she had said too much, but it was all true. Peaceful silence enveloped the room. The fragrance of fresh flowers made it easy for the stress to drift away.

After twenty minutes, she spoke softly. "I'll go somewhere to get help, and as always, you're right. Grayson is in a mess he created by being careless. He'll have to get himself out of it. He's burned his bridges with me."

"What about this woman from his work? Are you willing to let that go?"

She began the story about Grayson's sloppiness, then how he'd felt compelled to make Tom a partner. She explained Diane's blackmail, the threats, and the eventual murders and how she felt confident the dead partner had told his ex-wife, the woman she spoke of, about Grayson, linking him to the murders. Having a spotlight on him would bring disgrace to their family. She couldn't bear the thought of being ostracized and humiliated; she felt she needed to make it all disappear and that included getting rid of the partner's ex-wife.

Mateo listened and laid silently next to her for a few minutes, thinking.

"It is inevitable. Grayson is going to prison, Marguerite. For once, I agree with your husband—this woman more than likely knows nothing, and if she does know, it will not affect your husband's fate. She must be left alone. The quicker the police get him away, the happier I will be. He has been bad for my business. And now, with all this, you need to be away until he is in prison. You do not need to be the doting wife. If you stay with him, as the rope gets tighter on his neck, he will treat you with even less respect."

The conversation went back and forth about Rainie, ending with Marguerite agreeing to leave her alone. She explained she didn't know what the fascination with her had been.

"Do you desire her sexually, my love? Is she interested in being your lover? Or is it darkness looming in you?"

She teared up again. "I don't know. She definitely isn't interested in me. She's in love with her husband; it is obvious." She let out a spelling sigh. "Part of me just wants to hear her say, 'yes, my ex-husband told me.' I want to be right to prove Grayson wrong, but I planned—" She became silent.

"To rape her, Marguerite. You know, it would be rape. Do you want to rape someone like your uncle raped you? It will not erase your pain. Knowing he paid for his transgressions should bring closure, not defiling someone else. I am sad to see you in this much pain, my friend. I am thankful you talked to me about these things. I will get you help." He stroked her hair. "Why do you wear it short? Your hair is beautiful."

"Because I'm no longer a teenager or in my twenties. It has gotten shorter and shorter over the years. Many women in America cut their hair as they age." He ran his fingers through her hair.

"I want you to grow it back, at least past your shoulders. Let the woman inside of you come back out. Let me take you to 106. You can teach me all over again, like it was the first time, yes?"

"Yes." She let him hold her in peaceful silence.

෨෪

The receptionist buzzed Grayson.

"Yes?" he asked in an annoyed tone.

"Detective Marse is here."

"What do they want this time? By all means, send them in." He was getting tired of the impromptu discussions.

"He's on his way to you already, sir," she informed him.

Detective Marse and two uniformed officers entered his office. "Good morning, gentlemen. What can I do for you?" There was irritation under the surface of his question.

Marse smiled as the uniforms began walking up to Grayson's desk.

"Grayson Smith, you are under arrest for two counts of conspiracy to commit murder and for two counts of first-degree murder. The murders of Diane Todd and Mr. Thomas Todd." He spoke with no emotion, merely stated the information respectfully.

"You wait one minute. You can't come in here accusing me of such things." Grayson was an arrogant bastard. He tried to back away, unsuccessfully.

Marse stepped forward with purpose and looked him dead in the eyes. He remained respectful, although he would've liked to haul off and slug him. "Yes, Mr. Smith, I can, and I am. You have the right to remain silent." He continued with Mirandizing him. Smith huffed and puffed to the point where if he continued, he would have passed out. One of the officers started to handcuff him.

"Is that really necessary?" he argued. Marse nodded. Smith watched as Tolbert, also in cuffs, was led out by two uniformed officers. "Why are they taking Randy?"

"Better to worry about yourself, Mr. Smith. I assure you, Tolbert is not worrying about you." Those were the last words Marse was going to say. The officers were going to deliver both Tolbert and Smith to Orleans Parish Prison, or as it was lovingly called O.P.P. Marse was going to pull every string he had to make sure there was no preferential treatment. They would go through the system like anyone else.

Grayson's mind was racing. Who was he going to call for representation? Who was his one phone call going to be? Marguerite? Mateo? No, he wanted someone with clout. It would be Sid. He hadn't seen him since he'd left Sherman and Andry several years back when he'd joined the firm with Tolbert. Sid was old school. At least he would give him good advice, even if he refused to represent him. He shouted back to the receptionist to call Sidney Sherman at Sherman and Andry.

Rainie made sure everything was packed. It was great going to Michael's parents. There was no need to dress up or make excuses as to why she wasn't drinking. She phoned her mom to let her know they were on the road.

Her parents went to the club for the New Year's Eve celebration every year—they put on a festive adults-only celebration. All their friends would be there, and at least it was only a couple of blocks away from home.

While the break, in some ways, had been good, Rainie missed the boys terribly. She wondered how they were doing and handling Tom's death. It was odd; she had complete trust in Missy and Jack to handle whatever came up. If it had been too bad, they would have called her for sure. The bond she felt with them had happened faster than she could have imagined, but then her relationship with Michael developed almost overnight too. It had started when she'd looked into his eyes and felt a twinge of wanting, and the rest was history. The first kiss blew her mind, and his magic moves, wow, still curled her toes. He was an amazing husband, friend, father, and lover. *Yeah, Mer,* she thought, *he's the whole package.*

"You seem lost in thought. Everything okay?" Michael called from inside his closet.

"More than okay, Michael. More like outstanding, amazing, it's like living in a storybook romance." She dashed into the bathroom for toiletries.

"Or smut," he laughed. "I don't know how I'm going to look at my mom the same ever again. Holy crap." He came out of the closet with a couple of casual shirts and jeans. "Rai?"

She poked her head around the bathroom door. "What, Michael, you don't think they play?"

His posture adjusted, and he was clearly on the defense. "Stop. I don't think about them like, give me a break. Shit, that's my mom." With angst, he removed the clothing from the hangers, continually looking back up at her, almost with contempt in his eyes.

She went back to gathering the items she needed from the bathroom cabinet, commenting. "You're almost forty years old and still get the willies thinking of your mom and dad?"

He interrupted her as he entered the bathroom. "What can I say? In that aspect, I'm still a child. What about you with your parents?" Leaning on the door case, she couldn't help but notice the definition of his bicep. *I could watch that body all day.*

"I probably would have said the same thing until I lived with them. My dad plays grab-ass constantly with my mom and does the whole 'babe' thing. It blew my mind at first, but I hope we're still bedroom-savvy at their age. They aren't old, Michael."

They loaded into the car and continued the conversation. He said, of course, he knew his parents still had sex, but he didn't want to think of things like his mom giving his dad a blowjob. The faces he made were like a little kid. She got a good laugh at his expense.

He changed the subject to seeing the boys. He could always divert her with talk of the boys. The ride there seemed to be getting shorter. The more she went, the quicker it felt. She'd begun to recognize the landmarks along the way, which perhaps helped mark off the time.

As they approached the gate, she saw the kids riding on the levee. Her heart dropped until she saw Jack come up from the riverside. The kids hadn't seen them. It would be a fun surprise.

Both Wendy and Michael's mom were waiting by the fountain as they pulled up. The greeting was par for the course.

"How was it, Rainie?" Missy inquired with sadness in her voice. "Both boys have had their moments of sadness; luckily, they didn't have them at the same time. We were able to give special time to each of them. Not saying they won't have more sad times ahead because they certainly will, but they're in touch with their feelings and express them well. Good job, Rainie. My boys still hold their feelings back, but as their mom, I can read them pretty well." She hugged Michael. "Right? I know you inside and out." She looked him in his eyes.

Michael seemed a little more distant than usual. His hug was quick with his mom, and he backed off fast. She watched him with curiosity. His demeanor seemed off and a bit cooler. It felt directed at her, not Rainie or Wendy. It was something only a mom could detect; she'd give it time before addressing the issue.

He carried the bags upstairs. He peeked in the boy's room, and as expected, it was as if a cyclone had gone through, scattering clothes. He went around and picked up Thomas' and Henry's things, stacking them in the dirty clothes hamper, and then emptied the hamper into the chute into the laundry room. He figured Wendy could worry about the others.

When he returned downstairs, his mom was going into deeper detail with Rainie about the episodes of sadness. "Yes, Thomas is far angrier, you're spot on, but this too shall pass."

Michael walked around the room, sat in his mom's chair, and picked up the book she was reading. He started to read it every few minutes, looking up at her, then put it down and went outside.

The boys had made it back to the stables and were cooling down the horses, brushing them down, so he pitched in. He took Henry's saddle and brought it into the tackle closet, which provoked thoughts of being there with Rainie.

He could visualize the experience, which brought a smile to his face, but then he was cast back to thoughts about his mom. He had to get a grip on himself. He was acting like a child. How would Thomas feel if he knew about the sexcapades his mother was partaking in? He needed to take his own advice: "Whatever was between a man and his wife was okay." He ran the thought through his mind a few times.

The hugs he had received from the boys had been sincere. They were anxious to get to their mom. "Y'all go. I'll finish up here. Mom has missed you two a lot!" His dad was helping little John; he took the saddle and put it away. As Jack came out of the tackle closet, he noticed a glare coming from Mike.

"What's up with you? You eat something bad? It looks like you tasted something off. You alright, son?"

"Yes, sir, I'm fine," Michael said, almost answering by rote.

"Like hell. Get your ass over here." He went over to his dad. Jack hugged him. "I haven't even had a chance to say hello, but something has crawled up your ass."

"I'm ridiculous, and I have to get over myself, that's all." He looked away. His face had a set jaw and distant eyes.

"Talk to me, Mike." His dad looked concerned.

Michael thought for a minute. "Mom gave Rainie a book." His dad smiled. "It bothers me that Mom reads that stuff."

His dad continued with little John's horse, then, after a few moments, asked him, "Does it bother you that Rainie girl reads them?"

"No, not really. No, it doesn't, but Mom?" He had a look of confusion.

"Mike, I don't want to be in your bedroom. Get out of mine. What's between you and your wife is your business and what's between Mom and me is ours. Besides, your mom likes the love story aspect.

She doesn't get caught up in all the sex. Maybe she used to, but not for years."

Michael's hand went up as if to say "enough." He didn't want to hear any more.

"No, sir, Mike. I don't want you to dwell on it, but I'm still extremely turned on by your mom. She's a vibrant, beautiful woman."

"Oh, dear God, Dad." He started to turn around in exasperation.

His dad grabbed him by the shoulder. "What the fuck is wrong with you? I know you're not a prude. Neither you nor John and certainly not Wendy—now that's something I don't want to think about—but the point is, I'm no one's fool. Wendy is as horny as your mom. I can see it all over her face when she talks to her husband. And whatever you and Rainie have going on is intense. Where do you think all of you got the loving spirit from? Mom and I have always been affectionate in front of y'all. Always. Sex was an open topic, or don't you remember?"

"I remember." Michael looked down sheepishly.

"I don't know if you were here or not, but when John was sixteen or so, your Mom caught him in bed, in his room with some girl. She told him, and I quote. 'No one is screwing under this roof except your dad and me.' John had a real come to Jesus. She kicked the girl out. Ask him next time you see him, he'll tell you. He couldn't imagine his sweet God-fearing mom coming out with such a thing. Personally, I thought it was fucking hilarious. Your mom is something. I can still see John's face." He broke out into a belly laugh. "Mike, as long as I can get it up, I'm going to use it. What do they say, use it or lose it? I choose, use it."

They finished cooling the horses down and put them in their stalls. The tension had lightened up. "You're right, Dad, absolutely. I hope at your age Rai and I are still madly in love. I guess you never want to think of your parents—"

His dad interrupted, "Then don't think about it. Worry about your erection, and let me worry about mine, deal?"

Mike had to laugh. "Deal, Dad."

"Let's get back to the house. Mom's going to send out the militia."

They walked back toward the house, and out came the four younger boys. They were squealing and racing to the go-carts and mini-bikes.

Michael grabbed Henry for a quick hug. Looking up at Jack, he commented, "I haven't seen Sam. How are things going there?"

"He's a good boy, a bit immature and strange, but okay. I figure you're an adult for a long time, might as well stay a kid as long as you can, right?" He put an arm around Michael's shoulder, and the two walked into the house.

"Right. What grade has Sam completed?" Michael had lost the strange, weird feeling after talking with his dad.

"He's fourteen. I would think maybe eighth, seventh. Mom's been working with him. When school starts back, we'll have to get his records to get him into school. She thinks he will test into ninth, but I don't know he'd be mature enough.

"He hasn't been the slightest bit interested in any of the girls comin' around. You know news travels fast around here. A new boy at the Landry's usually results in teenage girls hanging around." They entered the mudroom, both washing up after tending to the horses.

"I never realized, I guess, Dad." It had been a most thought-provoking day.

"Damn straight. Why do you think we told y'all over and over, 'If you take it out, wrap it up?' Many country families in these parts hope their girls land one of y'all, one way or another."

They walked into the kitchen. The older boys were involved in some board game on the floor in front of the hearth. Michael walked up to his mom and gave her a big hug. "I love you, Mom."

"I love you too, Michael. I was getting worried I did something to upset you." His mind flashed to Rainie reading the book to him. His mom smiled and whispered to him, "Like you didn't approve of the book I gave her."

He shook his head and scoffed, "As if. You know me better."

She smiled knowingly. "Good. I love my stories, and as I told Rainie, I'm not much bothered by the sex; it's all about the relationships. I was concerned you might get upset at the thought of me reading such things." She laughed, but she knew. Dammit, she always knew.

Jack asked Michael and Dave, Wendy's husband, to help set up the fireworks on one of the trailers. The evening looked like it would be frigid but calm, which made for a much better fireworks display.

The gate buzzed. Missy answered the buzz. "Yes?" It was the catering company dropping off the food. They brought tray after tray into the dining room. The only time Rainie had been in the dining room was on Christmas Eve and during Michael's grand tour. Some of the decorations had been taken down, and it had a homier feel. They delivered the food for the night and New Year's Day. All of it, casual and easy.

They heard a couple of whistles and pops. Wendy commented, "Testing the fireworks. I don't know if Dad does it more for the kids or himself, but the kids get the benefit."

Once all the food was set up or stored away for the next day, Rainie went upstairs to lie down. It was the first time she had thought about her conversation with Rand. She wondered if Stella had talked to Rand or if it was a coincidence. Rand had asked her what she would name the baby and asked that they not use her name. She, she, she—Michael was going to be over the moon. Both their families would be thrilled with a granddaughter. It was going to be perfect; she would be able to go to school and play with Mer's girls. Perhaps the twins would be a grade above, though. Rainie thought back on when she might have gotten pregnant—Labor Day weekend, when the boys were with Tom, popped into her head, but they'd find out in a few days.

❧

Labor Day weekend had been a great time. She felt a warm flush down below. She thought about how funny Michael had been about his mom and dad when he was all about oral sex himself. Although he said he didn't have a favorite type of sex, it felt to her that he was obsessed with his head between her legs. Not that she minded, she laughed. For her, when it came to him, she was sure it was all about controlling him. The actual act could be exhausting, depending on when his last ejaculation had been. The second one always took longer than the first.

The door creaked open. "You okay?" Michael sat on the bed and looked at her with caring eyes.

"I'm fine, I wanted to rest, but I've been thinking about you, which negates any chance of rest." Her eyes twinkled with invitation.

"Ah, that kind of thinking." He slid his hand down her leggings. "Yes, you have been thinking about me." He got up and locked the door. "Tell me, what have you been thinking about exactly."

She laughed. "Your talents."

He raised his eyebrow and watched as her body showed signs of arousal. How far could he take it without actually touching her?

She wiggled out of her leggings and panties, shifting slightly on the bed with a most provocative attitude. Michael touched the top of her thighs, for a second, with his fingertips. No doubt it was working. Things were pinking as the blood rushed in.

He spoke softly, "You're so in tune with your sensuality; you can completely control your completion. I know you want to feel me but imagine it for now." He took a purposeful slow breath in through his mouth, gently biting the tip of his tongue.

Her breath became more rapid, and her eyes widened as she touched herself. Michael watching her turned her on even more. She totally got into the new adventure and finally held her breath as her body released.

He witnessed it. There was no doubt. Rainie's body physically responded to her thought with only minimal touch to bring it on. Could she be any sexier? It made him want her that much more.

"Michael, what you do to me. That was weird." He smiled contentedly.

"Me? Baby, that was all you this time and so damn arousing to watch. You're the sexiest woman ever." She could tell he had wanted to touch her all along but was doing his voyeuristic thing, which she found interesting. They were perfect for each other. They explored every avenue and pushed the envelope, but it was together.

"My beautiful lady, it gets better and better." He sprawled next to her in the bed.

She stared into his eyes with a devilish smirk. "You bet it was all me. Talk about burning brain cells. Do you have any idea how many brain cells I burned conjuring up that orgasm? I have to admit. It certainly helped to watch you watch me. You wanted me, oh yeah, you were like putty in my hand. Oh, and the touching myself, don't expect that to happen often." She gave a sassy giggle.

He was holding his breath so as not to laugh. "I love it," and the boisterous laugh boomed out.

"You sound like your dad when he laughs. That really got you." At this point, she was laughing, which encouraged him.

❧

There was knocking on the door. It was Henry. "Let me in. I want to come in and play, too." They both lost it, gasping for air and wiping tears from hearty laughter.

"Okay, boo. One second while I go potty." She quickly pulled up her leggings and straightened the bed.

"D.M. Dad, you can open it." Henry was persistent.

Michael did a quick check around and unlocked the door. "D.M. Dad?"

"Yeah, we're trying on different names. That was Thomas's idea. It means Doctor Mike Dad, but I don't think it's gonna work." Michael picked him up and tossed him on the bed, tickling under his arms and the backs of his knees.

"You said you wanted to play, yes?" Henry's laughter was from the belly. Pure and perfect. Rainie came out of the bathroom. He held him down. "Here, Mom, have yourself a tickle. Did you hear they're trying on names for me? This new one is D.M. Dad, but Henry doesn't think it's gonna work." She tickled him. He was squirming under Michael's big hands.

"I didn't feel like being outside anymore. I was wondering where you were. Then I heard y'all laughing."

"I bet everyone else is wondering where we are as well. Come on, Rai."

"Yeah, come on, Mommy." Henry took both of their hands, pulling them to the door.

# Wants and Needs

They pushed his head down as they loaded him in the police car. A crowd had gathered around. It was most embarrassing. He hoped the dumb fuck of a receptionist called the right person. That would be his luck if she didn't.

The back of the police car smelled foul; it was a combination of urine, body odor, and general human funk. As they pulled up, other cars arrived with horrible, disgusting-looking people. Certainly, they were going to find a different place for him and Tolbert to wait. Speaking of, he hadn't seen Tolbert get out of any of the cars, only a bunch of low-lives.

They let Smith out of the car. "Would you please release my arms? It's not like I'm going to try and run away." The officers didn't respond, acting as though they hadn't heard a word. They chatted among themselves about a ballgame. "Officers, would you give me the respect of answering me? I said, would you please release my arms? This is most uncomfortable."

"No, sir, you better try to get comfortable." They went back to talking ball.

Grayson was one of many in line being processed, and he was bringing up the rear until the police brought in another wave of bad actors. Some were stumbling drunk or high. It was a mixture of people crying and begging, to people cursing and thrashing around. He had been at the back of the line at first but could see Tolbert at the front.

He wanted to ask what was happening next but kept quiet and to himself, observing everything around him. They had already emptied his pockets and patted him down. The officer brought him to the holding cell.

As he'd feared, he joined a group of animals. The caged area smelled even worse than the back of the police car. There were puddles and splashes here and there, and he could only assume it was piss. One of the drunks started throwing up. No one thought anything about it. The vomit ended up on some of the people, inciting yelling in the cell. No one responded because none of the guards gave a hearty shit.

He heard Tolbert's name called, and off he went with an officer. It was hours before Smith's name was called. He moved through the array of degenerates, trying to avoid any of the wet spots on the floor. The officer led him out and into a courtroom for his bail hearing. He saw Sid in the room. Because of the charges, the judge set bail at two million. Sid agreed to the bail, and Grayson was going to be released.

He turned to Sid. He put his hand out, but the attorney pulled his hand away from Grayson. "Don't blame you," Grayson said. "Who knows what disease you could get."

"I had to give it a great deal of thought before coming down here, Grayson. Your receptionist did a good job of pleading your case to me. You owe her—oh, and your firm paid the bail. Seems you are in deep shit, and the best I can suggest is a plea. Truthfully, I'm surprised they let you out. The charges are pretty substantial, and from what I understand, the police have you lock, stock and barrel." Although he was trying to conceal it, Sid was smiling on the inside. "Grayson— you're fucked. As I said, the best you can hope for is a plea."

"You know me, you know I could never do what they said I did," Grayson whined. He looked like a panicked animal.

Sid stared him in the eyes. "Problem, Grayson, is I do know you and know what you are capable of. I don't doubt for one minute your hand is somewhere in this tragedy."

Once released, Grayson took his belongings and rushed out in a hurry. "Sid, why'd you take the case?" He truly wanted to know.

Walking side by side with him, Sid answered, "Because everyone deserves representation. I almost turned it down, but your girl at the office was relentless. She was afraid; she didn't say as much, but I could hear it in her voice. I don't know what you've got going on over there, but I'm pretty sure it's reprehensible." Sid drove Grayson to his car and handed him a piece of paper. "This is how it's going to go. When it says be here or there, you damn well need to be here or there."

Grayson got out of the car and into his own. He thanked him profusely, but Sid was having none of it and took off. He got on the phone and tried to call Marguerite. No answer. No surprise there. He tried Mateo. No answer again. They were probably together. He called the receptionist on her cell.

"Tiffany? This is Grayson Smith. I can't thank you enough for calling Sid Sherman. He said it was because of you he took my case. Thank you."

"You're more than welcome, sir. I hope things work out for you." She was a sweet girl.

"Thank you," he said, and they hung up.

Grayson drove home to an empty house. He thought about Marguerite and started to think about how the madness began. It seemed like one day they were raising kids and doing PTA the next, she was abusing whores, and he was engaging in all sorts of perversions. He enjoyed the doing but never allowed anyone to violate him. In that case, he was still a virgin. He wouldn't suck a man's dick either, but he'd let anyone suck on his and did quite often. He preferred men because they knew intimately how the dance went—when to stroke, speed up, grasp firmer and suck forcefully.

Marguerite had been a good lover until she'd discovered toys and developed a taste for women. Perhaps it was the same thing—a woman could do a woman better, except for their favorite whore, James. He could hurt her to ecstasy. It was titillating to watch. It was when Grayson had his best erections. Just thinking about it provoked a phone call. It had been a horrible day, and he needed someone to make him feel better.

"James?" He was boldly matter-of-fact.

"This is Jamie. Is this Mr. Smith?"

"Yes, it is. Are you busy tonight?" Surely he was available for the right money.

"I'm afraid I am. You have to give a girl more notice." James was sarcastic, with a vile guttural return.

"Marguerite went to Colombia, no one is here, and it's been a stressful day, to say the least." He was whining like a child wanting their way.

"Sorry to hear, honey. I can send someone to you, but my friend has strict limits and distinct tastes. If he needs to bring a friend, you willing to pay?" It sounded like there was no bargaining.

"Yes. How much?" Smith rolled his eyes.

"I'd say fifteen hundred for the two, and they'll stay no longer than one hour. Do you hear me, one hour tops?"

"That's robbery, but I'm in need."

"Make sure to put on your costume, dearie; they dress up. I'm telling you, the man has distinct tastes," he warned him.

Grayson squinted with a menacing look. "Make sure they know my rules."

"Tootles, Gray, and they'll be there at ten." The phone went dead.

He wondered what James had meant about distinct tastes. He poured a drink, downed it, then poured another. He looked through the mail, wandered into his bedroom, and pulled out his favorite leather chaps. After taking off his clothes, he looked in the mirror at his naked body. He looked pathetic. He fiddled with himself to see if there would be any response. None. He turned on some of his favorite porn and gave it a go, but nothing. He didn't want to take one of the pills, but he doubted the newcomers could complete the job without the drugs.

He swallowed one and chased it with another cocktail. He watched more of the video, but it was only at half attention at best, and that was after an hour plus. It might take some more time for the pills to do the job considering the stressful day.

Hours went by then the doorbell rang. Grayson put on his trench coat over the costume before he answered the door.

The guy had a coarse biker look with a build that could be on the front of a gym magazine. His companion was a very short girl with a good bit of meat on her bones. Grayson offered them a cocktail, but they declined.

He led the way to the bedroom.

The man told him to lie down, and he had a specific order to his service. He told Grayson to do what he said or else. It started well; he took Grayson in his mouth, but his grip was a little too firm and his movements harsh. The man climbed on top of him and attempted to stick himself in Grayson's mouth.

Grayson yelled, "I don't do that. You're here to pleasure me."

No was not an answer. The girl grabbed Smith's jaw and squeezed at the joint, which opened his mouth, and the guy shoved it in, almost choking him to death. Any moves he made were aggressive. The big man rolled them over, maintaining the position, and the woman began spanking Grayson, threatening all kinds of things. She began massaging his balls, then slid her finger in his ass, then two, then three. The act was gagging him, and even though her fingers were tiny, it wasn't his thing. There was no getting away from them, and his fear caused a shrivel effect. The man got up and looked at him.

"I can't do anything with a worm."

"I'm sorry, but I don't do those things. I'll get it back." He was in a state of fear and shock.

The man grabbed him and proceeded to move things along. "Marcia, get his soldier up. I got the salad." Very roughly, he spread Grayson's cheeks and ran his tongue across his asshole until there was saliva dripping down Grayson's legs, then forced his full package into Smith.

He screamed, "Stop, you're hurting me."

"Relax, you'll enjoy it," the brute commanded.

"No, no, stop." The more he fought, the more it aroused the man and the harder it went. He started slapping Grayson's ass. The girl was working her part, making slow progress.

"I know Marcia can suck a dick. What's wrong with you? I don't think I've ever fucked an ass this tight. It must be your first, but whatever." He was getting ready for the finale, and the girl had managed to get him almost there. Then the man went faster and faster with hellish jolts, "And this is for all the pain you've caused

Marguerite." The girl had some implement that sent burning shocks through his balls right at the point of ejaculation.

Grayson screamed. He had blood dripping from his ass with the seminal fluid. He was horrified the guy had ridden him bareback.

The big guy zipped his pants, grabbed his bag and the money from the dresser. "Your hour is up. Better get used to it. I popped your cherry, but the boys in the can, some of them are hung like horses, you better start stretching it, or you'll be getting stitches." They walked out of the door.

Grayson sobbed. For the first time, he saw the monster he had become. He yanked off the chaps, gathered all the sexual paraphernalia he had, and put it in a trash bag. The videos, the books, anything and everything of that ilk. Then he gingerly soaked in a tub.

He cried some more. Faces flashed through his mind of all the people he had defiled, all the women and men who had cried for mercy at his punishing hands. What had happened to him was minuscule compared to some of the things he had done to people. The guilt crashed down on him. He was alone, bleeding, and heartbroken about the man he had become.

After soaking for a while, he slid into bed. He called Marguerite. It went to voicemail. "I'm sorry for all the years I hurt you. I don't blame you for leaving. I've become a monster, and I'm sorry. If it's worth anything, I miss you."

৯৩

"Henry Williams, please. It's Sid Sherman." He waited while the music played. It didn't take too long for Henry to pick up.

"Hey Sid, how are you?" Henry asked in his usual jovial way.

"Thought you might find this interesting, and I shouldn't be telling you, but it'll be all over the news anyway. The police picked up Grayson Smith this morning, conspiracy to commit murder, two counts, Tom and his wife. He called me for representation. Get a load of them apples." There was a tone of amusement.

"I've always thought he was a bit sleazy, but I would've never imagined him part of a murder plot. I'm glad Rainie divorced Tom, thank God. I'm sure they'll have the details on the news." Henry got up and closed his office door.

"He's out on two million," Sid told Henry. "I was surprised the judge optioned bail. The charges are substantial. Everybody deserves their day in court, I suppose. From all I've heard, the police have him dead to rights. They picked up Tolbert, too. I don't know who's representing him or if the charges were conspiracy or prior knowledge. Whatever, it's a cluster." He sighed.

"What about Thibeaux?"

"He seems absent. Maybe he's a key witness. I wanted to give you a jingle. The whole thing is a damn shame."

"It is. Thanks for calling. Take care." Henry hung up the phone.

He couldn't help but be thankful his girl wasn't anywhere near the situation.

Marguerite's time spent with Mateo had been outstanding. He offered to get her a house if she would move to Cartagena. She'd want for nothing; he would provide it all. She had one more night. He asked her to stay.

He knew it would be best if she didn't go back yet. One way or another, he would make sure she didn't leave.

She had a relaxing day by the pool and had retired to her room. The time away had done her good. Her head was much clearer. There were going to be some changes when she got back, whether Grayson liked it or not.

There was a knock on the door. "Yes?"

"Room service, ma'am." It was Mateo.

She opened the door. He held a tray with one of the fruity drinks from the pool bar, reminiscent of their first encounter.

Mateo whispered, "I would like to see you after I get off work, only if you can." It was the exact conversation from decades before.

She laughed. "Do you know of any place we could sneak off to be alone?" she asked, playing the role.

"I get off in an hour." He raised his eyebrows and puckered his lips.

Still whispering, she said, "Tell them you need to get off now." She giggled because, at the time, he'd had no idea exactly what she meant. It was a double-entendre.

He shifted his eyes back and forth. "Okay. I know a place." Back in the day, he had told her to stand by the outside stairs.

Marguerite was still in her pool loungewear. He led her down the stairwell to the ground floor. They slipped out, and the first door to the left was 106. He quickly unlocked the door. Things in the room were much different than they'd been back then. It had become an actual guest room and not a junk storage area for the odd table, lamp, and old mattresses.

Walking toward the bed, she motioned for him to come closer. He acted shy. She took off her loungewear down to her panties. He remembered she had taken off her bathing suit top. Her breasts were full like something out of a girly magazine. He remembered the burn in his loins. He slowly walked toward her; even as a grown man, his loins burned for her. Her breasts, while older, were still beautiful and full. He started peeling his clothes off as he approached her until he was down to his white underwear. Now they were silk; back then, he wore threadbare cotton. She laid down in the bed.

She cooed, "Don't be shy. No need to be afraid." Mateo climbed in next to her. "Do you want to kiss me?"

"Si, yes." He puckered his lips and closed his eyes tight.

"Mateo, relax your mouth." She ran her tongue along his bottom lip and went in for the kiss. They kissed, filling each other's mouths. She pulled back. "Would you like to kiss my breasts?"

He didn't answer but leaned over and kissed each breast briefly.

"Is that all you want to do to my breasts? You won't break them." Mateo grinned, remembering how scared he had been but how she'd offered herself to him.

He caressed her. Never, as a boy, had he felt skin as soft. She put her hand over his and squeezed her nipple, making it ready for him to kiss. She put her hand on the outside of his underwear. She could feel him draw in a deep breath, as he had the first time. They made out like when they were teenagers, petting each other's bodies. He was in disbelief that she remembered each detail.

"These have to go." She giggled as she pulled his underwear down.

While he was now a man, she remembered the embarrassed young boy. "It's perfect, Mateo, don't be embarrassed. Now close your eyes." He did, and she took him in her mouth.

"Dios Mio," he exhaled. He could bring that first moment to the forefront of his mind. She had perfected the art already, thanks to her uncle. His hips began to flex. He put his hands on her shoulders, but she didn't stop. She encouraged his release. "I am sorry." As a man, it took a bit longer, but he remembered to apologize.

"You shouldn't be, my friend; that is the desired outcome. You grow up under a rock?" She laughed. "Did you enjoy it?" His eyes widened as he grinned from ear to ear. He was playing the part of himself as a young man to perfection.

She inched up his body, and he held her close, whispering into her neck about how beautiful she was, and he loved her.

"No, you don't, Mateo. You're confused. You may have loved what I did, but not me; thanks for saying so, though, it felt nice to hear." She kissed him. He was a quick learner; his kisses were passionate and perfect.

"I think I might have this now. Can I be on top?" He smiled, looking into her eyes.

"Okay, but if it seems like you need more demonstration, I'll climb back on top again." She rolled onto her back. He had picked up the game as a young man and was born to be a lover. Back then, he didn't have any control; whatever his body did, that was it. As a man, he made sure to make it last as long as she desired.

"Oh, but you were mistaken back then, my sweet, I did love you. I knew it deep in my heart and my Marguerite; I still love you. While I cannot marry you, I wish I could; that is how much I love you." His voice was sincere and coated in love.

Hearing him declare his love for her had an aphrodisiac effect, breathing life into her pleasure. He remembered the experience had ended with them laying side by side, holding hands. "I am going to improvise. I hope you do not mind, and then we can hold hands and lie side by side." He smiled down at her then moved down her body. She received his affection willingly. As promised, when Mateo had fulfilled her desire, he laid next to her and held her hand. "Want to sleep the night in here or go back to your suite?"

She snuggled into his arms. "Here is fine, Mateo. I have a late flight; I'll have plenty of time to get ready," she whispered, her breath stimulating him.

"You are not leaving tomorrow. I canceled your ticket."

⁊◌

Rainie's OB appointment was first thing in the morning so that it wouldn't screw up Michael's day. The New Year's celebration at the Landry's had been fun for everyone, but truth be told, she was happy the holidays were over, and routine could once again return.

They drove to Michael's office in separate cars so that they could ride together for their first appointment. She had butterflies of excitement. From experience, Rainie felt sure they would hear the heartbeat. Michael's face would be priceless.

She pulled up alongside him and put the window down, "Where ya going, good lookin'? Want to take a ride?" She whistled at him.

"Rainie Landry, you're a hot mess," he teased as he got in the car.

"Michael, are you excited?" Her voice bubbled with happiness, and a warmth surged through her body, filled with love.

"You know I've been looking forward to this since I found out. I have all kinds of questions. We need to have the right vitamins, what meds you can take, like for a headache or heartburn, a list of off-limits food, um—" He hesitated as he thought. "I remember some obstetrics, but not a lot, and I'm sure things have changed."

"Do me a favor, wait on your questions until after the doctor has said his part." She turned her head to look at him.

Eagerness was the only word to describe the look he had on his face, like a kid awaiting cotton candy watching as the vendor rolled a paper cone around the big drum of spinning sugar. "Of course, I don't think I've ever met him. What's his name again?" She could picture his internal contact list as he sorted through it.

"Dr. Adelson, Abraham Adelson, on Prytania Street by Touro." She was trying to prompt a memory, but nada.

"No, I'm sure I don't know him." He seemed sure.

They pulled in, and Rainie led the way. The nurse called them back after a couple of minutes. She knew the ropes: pee in a cup, the dreaded scale, then the questions. She couldn't recall her last period. The fact she couldn't remember boggled her mind; how strange to not notice. She guessed September, maybe August. In conversation, Michael said they thought perhaps they conceived around Labor Day.

Smiling, the nurse hooked her up to a monitor. Rainie watched Michael's face as he heard the heartbeat. He couldn't contain himself; he was smiling ear to ear, fighting back tears.

"Sounds strong, Mom and Dad. Dr. Adelson will be in momentarily." The nurse exited.

There was a brief knock, then Dr. Adelson, the nurse, and another doctor came in. Michael stood and turned. "Daniel, I didn't know you ended up in OB. It's a small world." There was an element of surprise in his voice.

Dr. Adelson cleared his throat. "Rainie, good to see you. It's been a while." He shook Michael's hand and introduced himself. "Rainie, I'm not delivering anymore; Dr. Dupuy has taken over the obstetrics. I hope that's okay."

"If he's good enough for you, then he's good enough for me." She put her hand out to the new doctor. "Sorry, Dr. Adelson, this is my husband, Michael Landry."

"Dr. Landry as in the doctor of the fountain of youth?" Michael smiled at the compliment. "My wife is a big fan of yours." He chuckled.

"Always nice to hear."

The tech took a few moments to evaluate the image.

Dr. Dupuy watched intently. "Mrs. Landry, based on your best guess and the development so far, I suspect fourteen, maybe fifteen weeks. The baby looks perfect, about the size of a sweet potato. At your next appointment, which will be in a month, we'll do a more detailed ultrasound, and you can choose to find out the sex if the baby cooperates. Your due date will be the last week in May, but we'll know better at your next appointment.

"Congratulations, Mike, you ready for this?" Daniel patted his shoulder.

"Been ready. End of May. Can't wait."

Rainie wanted to know how late she could fly. Dr. Dupuy told them the new rule was anytime up to thirty-six weeks if all was good with the pregnancy.

"Michael, we're good for New York."

After the appointment, riding to his office, they agreed she would order the "big brother" shirts, and as soon as they came in, they'd tell the boys.

Rainie phoned Missy. "We just came from the OB, and it looks like we'll be good for the New York trip. We're due at the end of May."

"Spectacular." Missy's voice bounced around the car. "John is coming home in two weeks; he has someone he wants to introduce us to." Rainie dropped her jaw.

"Wow, Mom, John bringing home a friend?" Michael said. "Uh-oh. We'll make sure to be there, this I must see. So not this weekend, but next?" he confirmed.

"Yes, Michael." His mom was in a hurry to get off the phone.

"Hey, if you don't want us to be there, it's okay. We don't have to be there."

She answered abruptly, "Don't be silly. I'll talk to you tomorrow." She hung up.

Michael and Rainie looked at each other; something was most definitely up with Missy. Michael worried something was wrong and couldn't leave it. He called her right back.

"Mom, are you okay?" She said yes. "Dad okay?" Once again, she said yes, only this time exasperated.

"I'll talk to you tomorrow, Michael." Click.

He looked at Rainie. "Tomorrow, it is."

Still feeling sorry for himself after the ordeal from the night before, Grayson called Tolbert. On the third ring, he answered. "Hey Gray, how's it going?"

"How's it going? It's a fucking nightmare. Marguerite left me a few days ago." He was still whiny, in shock over the brutality forced upon him, and scared about the situation of pending prison time. Whoever had said he would be an easy target was right—he'd be lucky if he lived a week.

"Bad timing, buddy, for a fight. You need to get her back; promise anything to get her here. It'll speak to your character. Shit, promise her whatever she wants." Tolbert was right.

"How're things with your wife? Did you tell her anything about the recording? God, I wish I hadn't had security all over the office. I'm sorry, I thought I was protecting my investment," Grayson rambled.

"I can't believe you had it either. For fuck's sake, I brought you into the firm; I have no idea what you were thinking. The recordings are going to be a nail in our coffin. The crazy sex was great while it lasted, and hell no, I didn't tell her. Since she bailed me out and felt sorry for me, I brought her to the jeweler's for a thank you to the tune of two carats. The thank-you sex was outstanding. Who knows what it'll be like once the cat's out of the bag and she watches the video. Did Marguerite know about the recordings, and that's why she left? Leaving you now is going to look bad."

Grayson poured another drink. "No, it was before. She has no idea about all this mess. She doesn't know I was arrested or any of it. Our argument was over a more personal thing, and I said some harsh things to her. She had every right to leave me. I've been a bastard to her for a long time. Marguerite is convinced Tom told Rainie everything. She thought going to lunch with her was a good idea. She thinks she could get the truth out of her. My wife has some problems, Randy. I told her 'absolutely not,' and the next morning, she was gone. She hasn't answered her phone or called. I should've said 'fine' in hindsight." He gulped down the whiskey even though it was still mid-morning.

"Just hypothesizing; if your wife is right, maybe we could find out what she knows if Tom did tell her something. Hey, we're planning a renovation. My wife, Connie, could meet with Rainie for a design concept," Tolbert said. "Also, as a gesture, the firm could always fund the two boys' college or something. My wife can warm up an ice cube. We have a small window of time left, and if she does know something, we need to find out soon. Think about it." He could tell Tolbert's wheels were spinning.

"It's worth thinking about." It was a better option than Marguerite luring her into the room of horrors. She was hot for Rainie, he had seen the same look on her face many times before, but it was always whores or people with the same persuasion. This was different— Rainie would go to the police for sure if Marguerite tried to assault her.

If Marguerite didn't call him back within the next day or two, then they could put Tolbert's plan into action. Truly, he felt all this was much ado about nothing and convinced Tom had not spoken to her. Tom looked at Grayson almost as a mentor, a pseudo father figure. What difference would it make anyway? They had the video. Besides, anything she said he said would be hearsay.

❦

"Mateo, why would you cancel my flight? I can't stay here too long," Marguerite griped.

"Have I not offered you a beautiful life here with me? You would want for nothing, my love."

"I have a life, a house—besides, we couldn't be together always. You're married and have a family, and what of my family? I don't live here. I have no friends, no life." She was getting worked up.

"There is much I cannot tell you. Please trust me. Besides, you said you wanted help. Consider this a good time to get help. Relax." Mateo was smooth and patient with her.

He did not want to tell Marguerite about Grayson's arrest or late-night visitor. Mateo made sure his message to Grayson was loud and clear.

She was not happy. Even though she said she wanted help, a big part of her didn't want to let go of the fantasies. How long would she be satisfied with Mateo? How much time could he possibly give her with his business and family?

"I want to go back to the suite." She was perturbed.

"Do not be angry with me. You will see it in time; it is the best for you. I can protect you like no one else. We will arrange everything to your liking. You will be mine and want for nothing." Mateo tried to kiss her, but she turned away.

He told her to get dressed. Javier would escort her to her suite. He would see her the following day.

She put her clothes back on and walked out of the door. Javier stayed with her but spoke not a word to her. Still in silence, he opened the door to the suite, went in, did a search of the place, then asked her if she wanted anything. She didn't, so he said he would be outside of her door should she want something. She shut the door behind him then looked for her phone. It was nowhere to be found. Mateo had had all the phones removed from the room.

She was pissed and opened the door. "Javier, where is my phone, and why are the phones taken from the room?"

In a very broken accent, he offered to call Mateo for her or order whatever she needed.

"I want to make a phone call," she said spitefully.

He started to call Mateo, but she stopped him, saying she wanted to call her husband in the States. The man shrugged his shoulders and continued his call to his boss. They spoke briefly. Javier stepped inside the suite, shut the door, and stood in front of it, staring ahead.

She would have to use her feminine wiles to soften him. She started to take off her top. He continued to look ahead. She went to grab at his crotch, but he moved, saying no. She began to rant and rave, throwing a temper tantrum.

Mateo entered the room, watching her demonstration. He signaled Javier, who picked her up and held her on the bed. "This is for your own good, my love." He injected her with a sedative and tucked her into bed. He leaned over and kissed her forehead. "Sleep well."

Thibeaux and his attorney sat with the D.A., going over his testimony. They spent a few hours working on it, and this was only the beginning. He would tell the story exactly as it had happened. He knew Smith's attorney would try to make him look as guilty as the rest and would out him on the sex. He might be able to keep his wife away from the courthouse during his testimony, but surely it would be plastered all over the news. Maybe he should tell her, but it would hurt her to the core. He sorely regretted his participation in the sick games, but he hadn't wanted the guys to think he was a wimp.

The case was coming together well for the D.A. He had testimony from Thibeaux, Diego's confession about a hit call, and the recordings lining up the whole story. It was teed up and ready to be spanked down the fairway. While Diane's murderer was already dead, it was a moot point as far as Marse was concerned. A hit on a hitman usually ended in a cold case file. Another team would be assigned to it and re-hash all the evidence or lack thereof.

However, nothing made sense about the Grayson Smith-Mateo Moreno connection. One plus one did not add up to two—it was a mystery. Maybe once Smith's head was on the chopping block, he might be able to make a deal for more info. Any way it sliced, Smith was going to do time, and Marse didn't have one sympathetic bone for him. Grayson Smith was a snotty, arrogant prick. The images of the hidden man from the office tapes played through his mind. He couldn't help but think, *What a twisted bastard*. It seemed like he derived pleasure from inflicting pain. Smith would get his comeuppance, no doubt about it.

With all the evidence Marse had, he couldn't see where testimony from Rainie would be necessary. It would be thrown out as hearsay anyway. She'd get her wish and remain out of the equation.

☙❧

When Marguerite awoke in the morning, Mateo was going over papers at the table. He had breakfast set up for her. She sat in the bed, looking at him.

"Good morning, my lovely. Do you want some breakfast?" he offered politely.

"Go to hell. How dare you keep me against my will? I want my phone. I want to go home." She glared at him.

"You are still angry with me? In the long run, I promise you will thank me. Now get dressed. We have an appointment this morning."

"No, I don't think so." She turned her back on him.

"Marguerite, I do not want to have harsh words with you. Do as you are told. One way or the other, you will be dressed, and you will be present at your appointment." While attempting to mask his emotion with love, she could see the coldness in his eyes and knew she had no choice. He was not a man to be denied. The love he showered her with was real, but his word was the last one. Period. There was no telling how many people worked for him; she speculated thousands. He was a powerful and dangerous man.

"Okay, Mateo. Can you please give me the courtesy of letting me know the plans you have for me?" There was a coldness in her voice.

"Of course. Today we are going to tour a wellness center. I promised you help, and I have all intention of delivering on my promise." He spoke with patience and love, but there was an underlying message that they would be doing things his way.

Her mind rolled over and over. It had been a mistake to tell him all she had. It was a gross mistake on her part. She bought into the happily-ever-after with him. But there was too much damage for her to realize the dream.

The countryside was beautiful as they flew down the road. The car drove away from civilization. After an hour ride, they pulled up to a luxurious resort.

"Welcome to Vida Curativa, ma'am," the young woman said in near-perfect English.

She began with her pitch. The facility dealt with all types of addictions. She said almost all addictions resulted from an imbalance in the body's chemical makeup; however, the psychotherapy they offered was second to none.

The facility was beautiful and had all the imaginable amenities, but Marguerite didn't want to be locked up. She was being held against her will, but fighting or trying to tell anyone she was a hostage was pointless. The entire situation was all because of her spitefulness toward Grayson; she'd brought it on herself.

The young lady led Marguerite to a luxurious bedroom equipped with everything she might need. It was lovely and overlooked a most picturesque view. For being held prisoner, the facility was the best of the best.

"How often will I see you?" she asked Mateo sadly.

He smiled warmly and took her hand. "I will have dinner with you at least three times a week." Mateo kissed the top of her hand.

"When can I leave here?" she said spitefully.

"We shall take one week at a time." His voice, while silky smooth, had an air of authority. There would be no negotiation.

She wanted to throw herself on the ground and scream, but it would be to no avail. There was no running away. Her frustration mounted.

"Will we have any private time?" While the corners of her mouth turned up as though smiling, her voice was laced with malcontent.

He laughed. "Be patient."

"What about my needs?" she pushed.

"My love, that is exactly why you are here. Your perception of want and need are—" he searched for a word, "confuso, hacia atras." He thought it through. "Mixed up, my love."

"I need you. Can we have time before you leave me here?" Marguerite's eyes begged him.

He put his finger up to ask a question of the facility person. She quickly answered a definitive "No."

Marguerite gave the prissy bitch a look of contempt. "I understood her. She wants you to fuck her. She can't bear the idea of you wanting me."

He hugged her. "Do not talk foul, my love. I want you protected and to get well."

# WITHOUT YOU

The package was due at any time. Rainie couldn't wait to see the boys' expressions. Every time they had been around the twins, the baby requests would start up again.

Allie was working in the office when she came in from dropping off the boys at school. She was on the phone and scribbling away. "I can either come meet you, or you can come by the office. Whatever works best for you." She gave directions and said she'd see whoever soon.

"What was that about?" Rainie wanted to know.

Allie was pumped. She told Rainie the client, a woman, was doing a house reno and wanted them to do it. Rainie was not quite as enthused as Allie; she suggested they talk to the lady but maybe pass depending on the extent of the renovation.

About an hour later, there was a knock on the door. Allie answered the door. "Connie? I'm Allie. Did you bring your ideas?" The lady had stacks of pictures cut out of magazines.

Rainie looked up; she couldn't believe her eyes. The new client was Randy Tolbert's wife. There was no way in hell they were doing her project. She had never been a big fan of Connie, and now with Tom dead, it was out of the question. Who knew what involvement Randy Tolbert had in the shady situation?

"Hi, Connie," Rainie said.

"Oh, my God, is this your firm? Isn't the world small? Your firm did a job for one of my friends, and she gave me the number. I had no idea it was you." She had the same fake smile she always had and made sure she flashed her hand adorned with a good-size sparkling rock.

"Connie, let me be frank. Given the recent death of Tom, I've been focusing completely on the boys. It was devastating for them. Allie is more than capable of handling anything you might need, but I'll be unavailable to assist." Connie looked uncomfortable.

"It's a big project. Maybe we can put it on hold until your life settles down," Connie said and smiled.

"If that's what you want to do, or if Allie wants to go with it, she's great." Rainie had thrown the ball back at Connie, and she was somewhat unnerved.

"I guess she can start on it; at least get the ball rolling." She didn't stammer, but Connie was clearly disappointed by Rainie's comment.

"Allie, find out if it's something you feel comfortable with considering you have upcoming school. I left my phone inside. I'll be a sec." Rainie got up and went back into the house.

Something about the whole thing with Connie Tolbert didn't feel right. She didn't believe it was a coincidence, but why go through the charade? Maybe she should call her bluff.

She dialed Michael. "Hi, it's Rainie. Have him call me when he has a moment." He must have been standing there because he took the phone.

"I'm available. Everything okay?"

"Weird is all I can say. Connie Tolbert, as in the wife of Randy Tolbert, one of Tom's partners, called us for a renovation she's doing. She acted like she didn't know it was my business. She said a friend recommended us. It's squirrely. Do you think we should take the job? I wonder how much Randy knew about Grayson's shenanigans. He could've even been involved in it. It feels hinky, Michael. Maybe you should call Marse and get a read from him."

"You go ahead and call. Thanks for the head's up, my love." She could hear his smile. "Bottom line, Rainie, if it doesn't feel right, don't do it. I love you."

She sent a kiss through the phone. "Later."

Following her call with Michael, she called Allie. "I have a funny feeling about this. Figure a way to get out of it, or I can come in and nix it."

"I already have," Allie said, and they hung up.

Rainie looked out the window but didn't see an unusual car, so she walked out to the office. Allie told her about her discussion with Connie and that it seemed more like a quiz. How long had she been working with Rainie? She was intrigued by her being the nanny. Had she known Tom? How close had she and Tom been? What about Rainie and Tom? They spoke for maybe a minute about the project, leaving it with Connie calling her back. Allie thought the whole thing was strange.

"I'm going to call Detective Marse." Allie raised an eyebrow at her. "I spoke with Michael, and he told me to. I've been a good girl and left the mess behind."

She left a lengthy message for him. It had barely been a minute when he called her back.

"As usual, Mrs. Landry, your senses are spot on. Haven't spoken to the wife, but she bailed him out. I'm betting she doesn't know the half of it. I don't know anything about her, but Tolbert is a scumball in an expensive suit, and it's going to come to light in time. Stay away from anybody having to do with the law firm."

"Thank you, detective."

The brief bit of information was enough to keep Allie and Rainie speculating for hours. The shirts for the boys came in, prompting a change in the topic of conversation—they discussed how the feel of the business was different now. Life had changed to the point that Rainie couldn't even classify her old life as a faded memory. It was as though it had never existed. It seemed like everything had changed. She was married, had a baby on the way, even the business was different, and she missed the day-to-day time with her friend. There was a looming sense of melancholy; perhaps it was the after-holiday blues or the massive hormonal change taking place in her body.

While she and Allie were close, it was different not having Mer. Their constant banter had smoothed out life's wrinkles and energized the business. A ding from the clock interrupted her thoughts and signaled carpool time. They rode together to pick up the boys from school, which generally indicated the workday was over.

A newly domestic Rainie prepared dinner and planned the shirt reveal. Michael would go along with whatever she had planned, which made it easy. She went through the checklist: homework completed, dinner finished, boys playing in the yard, so now it was time to wrap the shirts. Finally, the only thing left was waiting for Michael to come home.

Time seemed to stand still until he arrived home, but once he did, life was complete. Rand's voice rattled in her head: "This is what it's supposed to be like, Rainie." Michael was a mass of questions about Connie Tolbert's visit and Detective Marse's comments—he found the whole thing bizarre and troublesome. She went over the plan to give the boys their presents, and dinner went like any other night until Rainie brought out the wrapped boxes. Both boys were excited but then looked curiously at the shirts.

"Henry, can you read your shirt?" Rainie asked.

"Yes, ma'am, but I don't get it. I'm not a big brother. I'm a little brother."

Thomas figured it out quickly and asked Henry, "Why am I a big brother?"

"Because I'm a little brother." He was still perplexed.

"But, if there was someone younger than you, like a baby—" Thomas coaxed.

Henry got it. "Mommy's having a baby!" A flurry of excitement was sparked.

They could hardly contain themselves. Questions came like gangbusters. Was it a boy? Was it a girl? When would they have the new baby? Was it going to be twins like Auntie M had? They let them go on and on until Rainie said, "We don't know if it is a boy or a girl, and there is only one baby in my tummy. We will meet this new little person after school is out for the summer. That's the scoop, guys."

"Mommy," Henry questioned, "how did the baby get in your tummy?"

Michael gave Rainie the look of "hope you got this one."

"Excellent question, Henry. You know how plants and trees come from seeds?" He nodded yes. "It's the same way with people, only the seed isn't put in the ground but inside the mommy."

To Henry, it made sense, thank God, at least until next time.

"Mom, can we wear our shirts to Mimi's and surprise them?" Thomas asked.

Michael said he thought it would be a fun idea, and of course, they would. Allie came into the dining area after being on the phone in her room. Both boys screamed out the news as fast as they could. Allie dropped her jaw, feigning surprise, but, regardless, there was no denying the excitement in the room was contagious.

"Mom," Thomas noted, "you're gonna have to get a bigger car like Auntie M's, so we can all fit." He continued to look down at the shirt with pride.

"I suppose you're right. We have lots of time, but we can start looking. How about that?"

Michael winked at Rainie. "Right now, we need to head over to Mimi and Poppy's."

᳀

"Get a load of this," Marse said as he walked back in the interrogation room, "Tolbert's wife tried to hire Rainie Landry, Tom Todd's ex, for some work at their house. She said she got strange vibes." He pulled out the chair and sat across from Thibeaux, trying not to give him a judgmental eye.

Thibeaux was quick to respond. He warned, "Rainie better keep distance from Connie. She can be conniving and manipulative. She's going to lose it when she sees those videos. Some of the cracks I can remember him making embarrassed me at the time. It's not going to be a pretty picture at all." He hung his head, looking at his left hand and his wedding band.

The D.A. questioned him, "Do you think Tolbert had any idea about the plans to murder—" Bob shot a glance at Marse, who slightly nodded his confirmation.

"I don't think so, but I can't swear to anything. Randy didn't seem surprised and acted like I was a fool for not knowing." Thibeaux was remorseful. "I'm still having a hard time wrapping my head around it all." Any moment now, his balancing tears were going over the brink.

"You need to be concise with your testimony, and don't muddy it up." The D.A. looked toward Marse. "Any idea where Mrs. Smith is?" He unconsciously twiddled his pen.

"No sir, nobody has any idea where she is or when she went missing. We're still trying to run it down." Marse was exhausted. The case had not only consumed his time but drained him spiritually, leaving him without an ounce of energy. This one was going to make him dig deep for patience.

The D.A. continued questioning Thibeaux.

"I've got cases on my desk at work. When can I return to work?" Thibeaux asked the D.A.

He responded quickly and vehemently. "Sever your ties. The preliminary hearing is the day after tomorrow. So far, the defense hasn't produced anything. They have a couple of employees, but it's weak. From what I can tell, Smith's trump card is his defense attorney, Sid Sherman, from Sherman, Andry. He's a formidable opponent but a stand-up guy for a defense attorney. Grayson Smith used to work with Sid years ago. My take is Smith left them on questionable terms. I don't think there was any love lost between the two. Candidly, I'm surprised he took the case."

Rick Marse was the cop to have on the stand. He couldn't be rattled; he was pleasant and professional, matter-of-fact. Marse didn't have an ax to grind. The facts were the facts, and he stood by his testimony— he refused any speculation. He had handed this case to the D.A. on a silver platter. There was enough evidence it should be a no-brainer, but nothing in the law was ever opened and closed.

❦

Tolbert was reading the paper, and the biggest story on the front page of the *Times-Picayune* was the scandal at Tolbert, Thibeaux, Smith, and Todd. He put the newspaper down and turned on the television. Over and over, they showed footage of the police loading Grayson into the back of a unit. "How'd it go with Rainie?" he inquired as his wife walked in the room.

"I spoke mostly to her assistant. She was busy with something else when I got there. I got the feeling she didn't want to do our job. What that means is, who knows? What's your interest in her, anyway?" She sat on the edge of a chair, studying him.

Tolbert quizzed Connie off and on for most of the day. She wasn't sure what he was looking for, but, whatever, something was amiss. After several failed attempts at asking why he had been arrested, a sickening feeling conjured the thought that he'd had some kind of involvement or had at least known something about the murders. Did he genuinely learn about it after the fact, and why hadn't he called the police when he found out? She anguished over having to borrow against their house for his bail. What would happen if they found him guilty?

"I think you need to worry about us, Randy, and what's going to happen. What do you think Rainie can add or subtract from this problem? It's more than obvious she has moved on in her life. She showed no interest in Tom or anything about him other than he was dead, and her boys were the ones feeling the fall-out. The impression I got, she and Tom were barely on speaking terms. I don't get what's going on? This whole thing is scaring me. You're scaring me."

Just as a precaution, Marse called his counterpart, Jake Little, at the Jefferson Parish sheriff's office. They chatted for a few minutes, briefly going over the latest Orleans Parish scandal. Then Marse told him about his history with Rainie Landry and to put her on his radar. He said what he could of the current investigation, how he was concerned for her. There wasn't a specific reason, just a gut feeling. "I'm giving Mike Landry your number should a need arise."

Next in line was a quick call to Dr. Landry to give him Jake's number. When the receptionist gave him the message, Michael called Marse immediately.

"Dr. Landry, everything is fine, no worries. Sorry if I raised concern. Since you and your wife are in Jefferson Parish now, I wanted to give you a good contact there should you need one. It's out of my jurisdiction." He gave him Jake's number and said he had filled him in on the situation, concentrating on the recent murders and Rainie's distant relationship in the case.

Michael thanked Marse for his attention, commenting he certainly hoped there was no need to call Jake, then thanked him again.

The day couldn't end fast enough; Michael wanted to be with Rainie and the kids. Marse's call had stirred an uneasy feeling inside, and the sooner he could leave work, the better he would feel.

Whenever he turned on the news or picked up a paper, the firm's scandal was front and center. Michael had to take care of his patients and couldn't give up his practice, but he felt like his family was exposed, making him anxious, like waiting for the other shoe to drop.

❦

The weekend came quickly, and it felt great to get out of the house, away from it all. Going to Michael's parents' house was a complete escape. They rarely had the television on, and the atmosphere was far more relaxed. The boys were excited to wear their new shirts. They had told anyone and everyone about the baby on the way.

Rainie and Michael reconnected on the ride to Baton Rouge, both decompressing. In general, the rat race of life felt burdensome and demanded Michael spend time away from her, but the latest drama had increased the intensity of those feelings. Missy was waiting for them as they pulled up to the fountain. She made a big deal over the shirts and the exciting news, winking at Michael.

It didn't take long for the boys to be back on the track with the mini-bikes and go-carts. Sam joined them when Poppa Jack brought him home from school.

Jack, Missy, Rainie, and Michael sat for a spell, catching up on life.

"Mom, is everything okay here?" Michael asked. "You seemed funny on the phone and just as elusive in our next calls."

He watched as she carefully chose her words. It was more than obvious she was perplexed.

"For crying out loud, Dad, what is going on?" Michael was getting nervous.

His Mom began, "It's about Sam." There was a sigh of relief. Anytime people acted cagey, it brought out the worst-case scenarios to mind.

"What's up with Sam, Mom?"

"Mike, it's actually Samantha." She had a strange look on her face.

"Samantha?" Rainie asked with her face all askew.

"Sam was born Samantha. We have him in counseling, and we're going to counseling. This unique situation is a first for us, and neither your Dad nor I feel comfortable. We've said Sam was small and slight for a boy his age but figured it was from malnutrition in childhood or whatever. He seemed different than any of the other Lost Boys. Sam's what the counselor calls transgender. While he has all the parts of a girl, and they're starting to show, he's all boy. He has become fond of one of the young girls on River Road,"

Rainie interrupted, "She's a lesbian? I don't get it."

Michael jumped into the conversation. "What confirmed her or his identity?"

All four were shifting positions; no one truly comfortable with the conversation or maybe the idea. "He got a cycle. While cleaning Neverland, we came across a stash of underpants with bloodstains. At first, we thought something had happened. It was strange, but he plainly said he was a boy trapped in a girl's body when we asked him. I have to say, I've never thought he seemed girly. He's always been a boy in our minds. Then the dilemma came up. We don't take in girls; you know that. We've been struggling with this to the point we started getting help to try and understand. Long of the short, when he turns eighteen or when we think he seems fully grown, he can undergo some surgical procedures."

Both Michael and Rainie sat with their mouths agape.

Jack scratched his head. "This is a new one for me. I've worked with homos, but never with fellas who thought they were girls."

"Gay, Dad, not homos," Michael nudged.

"Right, gay. Sam wants the surgery as soon as possible, but the doc says to wait. He put Sam on mild male hormones, which will slow the female things down. It's befuddling, to say the least."

Their glances to one another seemed to dance around, no one quite knowing what to say.

Michael walked into the kitchen, grabbed two bottles of water, and returned to the Hearth. "A couple of facilities are specializing in gender reassignment, but I think y'all are wise doing counseling and holding off surgically. I can get any information y'all may want. Wow, that's not something I saw coming."

Missy sternly instructed, "Y'all are not to say one word to him. Wait for him to say something to you."

The momma bear came out in Rainie. "I don't want him saying anything to the boys. They're too young to understand—hell, I don't get it," Rainie tried to be supportive but wanted to get her point across.

They were all in agreement. Missy said she had already told Sam not to say anything to the younger kids and explained that they wouldn't understand. Missy also said even if she hadn't said anything to him, Sam wouldn't have said anything. "The kid's dealing with a lot. His hormones kicking in is upsetting his apple cart."

The boys came in from playing. They heard the buzz from the gate—John had arrived, and everyone was anxious to meet his new friend. He parked and bounded out his fatigue-green Jeep. From the other side emerged a tiny woman. She was maybe five feet tall, had straight blond hair and wide doe-like eyes. Unlike most blondes, her complexion was darker, almost olive, but not quite. Everything about her was tiny but perfect. Her small stature made John look like a giant.

He did a group introduction, "Everyone, this is Aimee; she's Dominique's cousin." They welcomed her with open arms. The conversation centered on her extended family and how they were happy to meet her. They spoke highly of Dominique.

Aimee was equally as spunky as the rest of her family. Her accent wasn't as thick as Dominique's, but there was a trace of Cajun. She had a bubbly personality and seemed maybe a fit for John. The jury was out, though. Missy instructed John to take their bags upstairs. Rainie remembered how nervous she had been the first time she'd met Michael's family. Aimee didn't appear shaken in the slightest. If Rainie were to lay odds, she'd say the two of them were two ships passing in the night. She'd never seen John in love, but the way he looked at her, he was hardly in love with the girl. The question, why bring her to meet Missy and Jack?

While Aimee was cute and fun, there was a rough side to her. John later revealed Aimee was a federal agent and worked in conjunction with the Port Authority. Perhaps she was more aware and direct than unpolished. She and John had been friends with a twist for well over a year. Neither of them interested in anything too serious. It was about having a good time while it lasted.

She had Missy and Rainie spellbound with some of her work stories, but when asked if she was working on anything at present, she side-stepped the question, and it was apparent she wasn't going to say much. Rainie wondered if Missy could read her mind, too.

Aimee knew the whole Rainie-Mikey story, commenting it sounded like something out of a fairy tale. She was candid about the nature of her relationship with John and made some comments about it being more rated "R" than a fairy tale.

It had been a lovely weekend with family, and meeting Aimee made things feel more balanced; nonetheless, it was good to get home. Life, in general, was progressing. Allie had her appointment with Tulane to get the low-down on law school and her next steps. It was going to be an exciting year—lots of changes ahead.

# When A Man Loves A Woman

Rainie stood in front of her bedroom mirror, looking at her naked body. There was no doubt she was pregnant. Her breasts had already begun to fill out, her waistline wasn't as well-defined, and the baby bump was far more pronounced. If it hadn't been for fashionable belly bands, low-rise pants, and her wardrobe of knit dresses, she would have had to shop for maternity clothing already. Even so, that time was around the corner.

The slower pace was beginning to feel more comfortable. Rainie sipped her herbal tea, lit a few candles, and drew her bathwater. It was the perfect temperature, and she submerged into it. Thoughts danced through her head regarding baby names, godparents, nursery décor. She almost missed the soft voice calling to her.

The voice whispered, but with urgency, "Rainie, get up, go, now." She thought it was peculiar.

"Rand? Stella?" she whispered back, but nothing. She got out of the tub and could hear someone coming up the stairs, but it didn't feel right. She picked up her phone and dialed Michael. She hid in the back of his closet, crouched in a ball, behind the long clothing bag housing his tux and tails.

It was Michael's third patient of the day. She was a breast reconstruction

case due to a radical mastectomy. They were in the midst of a light
conversation when his phone rang. He saw it was Rainie; he put a
finger up and said quickly, "Hold on a sec."

☙☻

Rainie could hear the person walking into her bathroom. Chills went
up her spine when a man's voice commented, "This is convenient. Your
wet footprints are leading me straight to you. Come on out, Rainie.
Don't make me come after you."

She stuck her phone in the corner, hoping he would hear what
was going on. The voice was familiar, but she couldn't place it. She
closed her eyes tightly, trying not to breathe. The closet door opened,
he started moving the clothes until he found her. She opened her eyes
with a start. Standing above her was Randy Tolbert.

"What the hell?" She stood up, holding onto her towel. "What
the hell are you doing?" He seemed menacing. "You scared me half to
death. What do you want? Not cool. I think you better leave."

He pulled her towel down. She stood there, naked. "What do I
want?" he asked with a scary-sounding voice. He looked her body
up and down. "Rainie, I want information from you, but right now,
I want something else. " He unzipped his pants but then noticed her
baby bump. "Pregnant? What a turn-off. Put these on." He threw her
the dirty clothes from the bathroom counter.

"You don't intimidate me, Randy. Get the fuck out of here."

He slapped her across the face. She tried to hit him back. "Put the
fucking clothes on."

She started to walk past him. He blocked her, shoving her to the
floor. "You are fucking crazy. Get out of my house." She scrambled to
get to the phone. He kicked her in the ribs.

☙☻

His patient said, "Your bride? Take the call, Dr. Landry." He put the
phone to his ear and could hear what was going on. He called into the
phone, "Rai!" He listened to the slap to the face and struggle. "I'm

outta here," he told the nurse. "Call 911 send them to my house." He dropped everything, heading home at break-neck speed, keeping the phone on speaker.

❧

"Rainie, I don't want to hurt you, but I will. Get dressed now." In her head, she heard Rand. "Cooperate, Rainie. Be calm. You'll be okay. I'm right here with you."

She put the clothes on quickly. Tolbert grabbed her arm, dragging her down the steps. She managed to keep on her feet, but barely. He pulled her close to him and put his hand over her nose and mouth. That was the last thing she remembered.

❧

Michael's tires screeched as he made the turn onto Stella. He pulled in the drive, slamming the car into park, noticing that the kitchen door was wide open. He ran into the house shouting, "Rainie!" and raced up the stairs. It was clear there had been a struggle. He saw the full tub, the water still quite warm, footsteps heading toward his closet where the door was open. From the sight of the closet, there was no doubt it was the scene of the abduction. There were a few drops of blood.

He dialed 911. "Someone has broken into my house and taken my wife! This is Mike Landry. My office just called and asked you to send the police to my address." The voice on the other side of the phone told him to calm down and explain again. "Someone has taken my wife from our house." He remembered the name Marse had given him. "Patch me through to Jake Little." The voice on the other side of the phone said she had already dispatched the officers to his address and called it out to confirm. He hung up the phone and called the Jake person.

"Detective Little," a calm, professional voice answered.

"This is Mike Landry. Rick Marse gave me your—" The guy cut him off.

"What is the problem, Dr. Landry?"

"A man broke into my house and abducted my wife. It couldn't have been more than twenty minutes ago if that." He could hear the detective shuffling papers.

"You at home? Stay there; I'm on my way." The 911 operator called back again; Michael had ignored the first two calls, but this time, he answered.

"Sir, the officers should be arriving within minutes. Please do not hang up again and do not touch anything." He heard the police pull up. He met them, still on with the operator, but told her they were there and hung up. He was in a panic. He tried to explain to the officers that he knew his wife had been in the bath as the tub was still filled with water. Obviously, there had been some sort of altercation in their bedroom, actually his closet, and she was missing.

Detective Little pulled up with a screech of the tires. He found Michael. "Mike, Rick Marse told me a bit about the current situation. Any idea who could have taken her?"

"She tried to call me. I heard it as it happened. My first inclination is Grayson Smith, her ex-husband's partner, but I don't know. What I do know is we need to find her before he hurts her." His calm demeanor had vanished when he heard the struggle. This was Rainie, and some son-of-a-bitch was going to pay.

Jake called Marse. "They have Rainie Landry. From the house. No, no witnesses, but it's obvious it was against her will. Dr. Landry heard the struggle on the phone." The two men talked briefly.

"Last week, Connie Tolbert, one of her ex's partners' wives, showed up at her house; maybe her husband has something to do with it," Marse interjected.

Jake tried to settle Mike down to no avail.

Mike knew he needed some big shoulders to lean on. He called his dad. "They have Rainie, Dad." He heard his dad call John, who picked up the phone.

"Mikey, she's gonna be okay. Aimee might have more resources at her fingertips than the locals. Give her all the info you have." Mike went through the Smith possibility, Connie and Randy Tolbert, the strange visit. Aimee told him to give her fifteen minutes, and she promised to call him back whether she had any info or not. He didn't want to hang up with his dad.

His mom picked up another phone. "Michael," she was stern, "you listen to me. Rainie's going to be fine. Trust in God, Michael. We'll be praying here. John's girl already has a lead on something. You've got to have faith and trust, Michael." They hung up.

His dad, in a hushed voice, told him, "We'll find the motherfucker, Mike, and no one will ever see him again, do you understand me? We got this, son. Be strong and Mom's right; trust in God."

☙

When she started to wake, they were flying down the highway. Randy had her hands tied and a gun on the seat. She tried to reason with him. Her head was still foggy, and her lip felt sore. "Randy, what has gotten into you?" *Stay calm, hold it together.*

"Rainie, you know too much. You're a liability."

"Too much about what, Randy?" She wanted to try to keep it familiar and not be too hysterical; maybe he'd come to his senses. Her head was pounding, but she kept telling herself to stay calm. Rand said, "Perfect, Rai. Stay focused. He's a bad man."

"Don't try to play that game with me. I know Tom told you about Grayson and me and Diane and Tom?"

"Told me what? Tom and I haven't spoken amicably since I caught him cheating. Of all people, y'all knew how bad things were between us. Y'all probably knew he was cheating, t'boot, and thanks for nothing." She took a deep breath, trying to fight the tears. "You're not making any sense. I'm sorry he's dead, but I don't know anything about how or why. I certainly had nothing to do with it if that's what you're implying. Talk to me. What's going on?"

"Shut the fuck up." He was crazed.

"I don't understand. Connie was at my office the other day. You're acting crazy, Randy. Think about this. We were friends, what's happened there? I get y'all were on Tom's side if there even was a side, but we were friends. What's going on?" She tried rekindling a connection with him. She tried everything she could. *Please stop. Take me home.*

He was taking the old highway, running toward the lake and fishing camps. He pulled up to one, got Rainie out of the car, pushing her along to a fishing camp next door, still condemned from Hurricane Katrina.

There were a few wobbly makeshift steps. The place had gaping holes in the walls and floor, and then Randy threw her into a corner. "What did Tom tell you, Rainie?" He towered over her.

"The last time I spoke with him was when he picked up the boys for his weekend. That's it. I haven't seen him since I got married in mid-December. That's it." She tried to remain calm.

"Bullshit. You're lying. Tom told you, didn't he? He told you Smith killed Diane." He was pacing like a caged animal.

"What? Grayson, Diane, what? Grayson is a sweet, gentle man. I think someone is lying to you, Randy." She was frustrating the hell out of him, and he smacked her across the face again. She let her body go limp. *I have to play along, or I'll never see my boys again.* Rand's voice bellowed inside her head, "No more thoughts like that. You will be with your boys. Stay strong."

She listened to him as he ranted. "This is fucking great, Raaainnie." He nudged her body with his foot. He called her name again. She heard him as he walked out of the building. All she could do was pray, hoping Michael had heard her on the phone, but the odds were not favorable. Rainie heard the car door slam and felt the camp sway as he climbed back up the stairs. As Randy walked toward her, the floorboard creaked under the weight of his body. The dilapidated wreck of a building shuddered every time he moved.

He doused her with water, startling her and drawing her attention to his face. Her cheek throbbed in conjunction with her lip. What would be the alternative now? He started pacing again.

Talking to her as well as himself, Tolbert said, "If you didn't know before, then you know now. I can't ignore this. I don't have a choice, do I?"

"A choice about what, Randy? You're not going to hurt me. We're friends. Take me home, now. It would help if you talked to someone, Randy. I know a good therapist; I've been seeing him for years off and on." She tried to sound sympathetic and concerned, but there was a definite quiver of fear in her voice. He sat there looking at her.

"Un-fucking-believable." He shook his head.

∾

Marse had Connie Tolbert picked up. The officers walked her into his office. He stood until she sat.

"Mrs. Tolbert, we're looking for your husband. Do you know where he is?"

"I don't. Why? You could have asked me this at home and not made me come here, especially in a police car. My neighbors will be talking, for sure." She was exasperated and had an attitude from hell.

"He's missing, ma'am, and with all the strange occurrences from his place of work, we're trying to keep account of everyone. I know you posted bail, so I'm to understand you're aware of his situation."

"Alleged," she said snootily.

"No, ma'am." He turned his computer screen to face her. A video played footage of her husband engaged in a sexual act with one of the office girls. He ordered the girl what to do using foul language and a pornographic commentary. He was crude and demeaning. Marse fast-forwarded through one episode to another, showing a different girl walking into his office being ordered to give him a blowjob. He complained about the way she performed, telling her how to improve. Connie could hardly recognize the animal on the screen. He was sick, perverted, and she loathed him. It was apparent she had no idea about the office games.

"Any idea where he might be? By the way, I have hours of video of your husband and his office activities should you wish to see more."

She was embarrassed, hurt, angry, plus a plethora of other emotions. Her face had paled, and her jaw set. Her tone was deliberate and unforgiving, dripping in sarcasm and hate. "I don't know where the bastard is. If he's not at the office, he's off screwing around with someone." She pointed at the monitor. "You might want to ask Grayson Smith or check the fishing camp along Irish Bayou. Try contacting Tom Todd's ex. He's been fixated on her, probably screwing her, too." It was obvious she was done.

"I'm sorry you had to learn of your husband's infidelity this way.

From our conversation, I thought you knew. I would have been more sensitive to the situation. You've been helpful. Hopefully, we find him. It seems people from his office are dropping like flies. The officer will give you a ride back home." Marse looked at his notes as she walked out.

"He's going to wish he was dead," Connie added. "And, by the way, he wouldn't be living at the house if I had any knowledge of his disgusting activities. He won't be coming back there, that's for sure." As she walked out of his office, he could hear her calling Bob Thibeaux's wife. *Oh well,* he thought, *shit happens.*

Fifteen minutes later, his phone rang. It was Bob's wife. No surprise there.

❧

Aimee told John, "We've located Tolbert's car."

"Where?"

She told him, and as she was telling John, he was telling Michael. Jack came into the room and told him to tell Michael not to leave his house. They were on their way.

Michael told him he wasn't waiting, period.

❧

Mateo was due any minute for dinner. Marguerite had gotten caught trying to seduce some of the staff. Nobody was willing to come anywhere near her sexually. She wondered if it was fear of Mateo or dedication to their job. If she were to bet, her money would be on fear of Mateo.

A staff member called her to the dining area. Mateo looked scrumptious; she could've devoured him. He kissed each of her cheeks. "You look lovely, Marguerite. I hope you are doing well."

"If well means playing by the rules, then yes, I have no choice. I tried to get the attention of one of the staff members, but he turned me down," she pouted. "I long for you, Mateo. When can we be together?" she whined. He pulled out her chair, whispering as he took his seat.

"Soon, my love, soon. I have something I want to tell you, but you need to start eating before your food gets cold." He watched as she took a few bites. "I have news from America. The police arrested Grayson for conspiracy in the murders of Diane and Tom Todd. His trial will be quick, and he will be going to prison. I am sorry to say I do fear for his well-being in prison." While what he said was horrible, and his manner was almost sympathetic, but not.

Her eyes filled with tears. "Isn't there something you can do? Find someone to watch over him. I feel horrible I'm not by his side while he goes through all of this. I know he and I have had our problems, but we've both been wrong." Her countenance reeked of desperation.

It hurt him to see her sad; for once, it was for someone besides herself. "There is nothing you or anyone can do, but I will arrange for you to be with him in America for his trial, but then you will come back to me. I need to know you will keep your word. I don't want to have to bring you back. You know I will." His voice left no wiggle room.

"Please, Mateo. I need, no want, to be with him in this difficult time."

"Tomorrow morning, then, my love. Do not disappoint me." She wasn't sure if it was a warning or a plea from a friend.

☙❧

Michael's speedometer hit 120. He prayed the whole time he would find Rainie safe. It had only been a couple of hours since the phone call. He slowed down as he came upon the fishing camps. He spotted the only new-looking car in the area. He pulled in a few camps down. His phone rang, it was John. He didn't have time to talk, nor did he want to. "I'll call you back."

"Don't be stupid, Mikey. I know Dad wants us to take care of our own business, but Aimee makes a good point. You don't want to end up on the wrong side of the law. You have too much to lose."

"I hear ya, John." He dropped the phone on the seat.

He got out of the car and approached the camp. Climbing the stairs, he tried to be quiet. There was complete silence, and from all appearances, there wasn't anyone inside, but his peripheral vision picked up movement in what remained of the camp next door.

It was going to be challenging to get inside the dilapidated building unnoticed. The stairs were all but gone. The wind alone made the boards screech. The area was desolate—the bastard could have held a gun on her, or she could have been screaming at the top of her lungs, and there wasn't a soul around to hear. An old rope hung down from one of the beams underneath the building, and the far back corner walls were completely missing.

Michael took off his shoes, shirt, and tie and emptied his pockets. Sliding down into the water, he glided over to the rope. He tested his weight on it and found it solid. Hand over hand, Michael climbed the rope, eventually getting to the beam. He assessed the layout and could hear heavy footsteps pacing the floor with a few outbursts from her captor. He prayed she was okay and worried even more because he hadn't heard her voice. The guy must have stepped on a rotting board because there was a loud crack followed by cursing.

He used the noise of the cursing to scale to the corner piling, pulling his body onto the small patch of solid flooring. He crouched down.

Rainie was still trying to keep the situation calm. "Good God, Randy, you're going to fall through the floor. I want to help, really, I do. I've no idea what you're ranting about, but none of it makes sense to me. Just untie my hands, and we can leave here. I'll help any way I can."

"I'm not gonna tell you again; shut the fuck up." He loomed over her like a lion stalking its prey.

She was scared but wasn't going to show it. "What do—" Smack. He slapped her. She screamed. "Don't touch me again, Randy." Smack, he popped her again, at which time Michael dove through the air, bringing Randy to the floor. The boards cracked loudly under the weight of the two men. Michael had taken Randy by surprise, giving him the advantage. The raging fury racing through his body gave him even more of an edge. He had Randy pinned to the floor. He slammed his head into Randy's, almost knocking his wife's captor out, which gave him time to shove his elbow against his throat. An audible sound of crunching could be heard as Randy's trachea crushed beneath the force of Michael's elbow. The grip Randy had on the gun released. Michael picked it up and shot him between his eyes. Cold, callous, and unforgiving.

He rushed to Rainie, removing the rope binding her hands. Her face had a blank stare. No tears. No screams. Just blank. He kissed the top of her head. He swept her up, made his way to the back corner, knowing the make-shift stairs could not bear the weight of the two of them. Holding her, he went into the water. He got her onto the grass over the bulkhead, leaned over to gather his keys and wallet. Just as he had her in the car, his phone on the seat buzzed. He didn't recognize the number.

"Mike Landry," he responded when he answered the call.

In a slightly broken but smooth Spanish accent, the caller spoke, "Dr. Landry, take your wife and leave immediately. My cleaner will be there momentarily. No more concerns for you and your wife; it is done. My regards." The call disconnected.

She had spoken not a word. "Rai, you're going to be okay." He pulled onto the highway.

His phone rang again. It was his dad. "Tell Mom and John I found her. She'd been left in an old fishing camp on Highway 11. She's safe now, and other than a bruised cheek and split lip, she appears to be okay, but we're getting her checked out."

They spoke for a few minutes. Michael's parents wanted to talk with her, but he said they'd call them back later. He realized her parents hadn't a clue about any of it. Perhaps it was a Godsend.

She held his hand. He could feel a slight shake; he squeezed her hand. "You're going to be okay, Rai. I love you."

Softly, she told him she loved him, then remained quiet. Understandably she was freaked out and probably in shock. Her mind was blank; she was having trouble connecting the dots to what she had witnessed—the recent terror. Would she ever be back to normal? What had started as a relaxing bath turned into a nightmare in mere minutes. The whole thing had been bizarre, and then to see her sweet loving husband kill another person without even a blink was too much to wrap her mind around.

Michael was fully prepared to take responsibility for his actions.

Something didn't sit right about throwing the body in the river by his dad's house. There had been rumors about intruders being killed and thrown in the river, but he didn't want to carry on the tradition.

Who was the mystery caller, and how had they known what was happening? Nothing had been part of a plan. Who would have known Randy Tolbert had kidnapped Rainie to an abandoned fishing camp? Was someone watching them, and if so, for how long and who could it be? Had it been the police, they wouldn't be sending a "cleaner." He assumed a cleaner was someone who cleaned up untoward incidents. Certainly, no one he knew would have the kind of lifestyle that required a cleaner. His mind drifted as he drove.

He brought Rainie home at her insistence. The story would have to be she was mugged or maybe tripped in the house.

The phone rang—it was her mom. Rainie didn't want to talk. "She's indisposed, Leslie. Can I have her call you back?" He worked hard at regaining his usual demeanor.

"Certainly, Michael. I was just checking on her. I had a weird feeling she wasn't okay. Just being a mom, I suppose." He looked over at Rainie.

"No, ma'am, your senses were dead on. She had a tumble, enough to call me home. She cut her lip and bruised her cheek. She looks like she went a couple of rounds in the boxing ring, but she's okay."

"Do you need me to come over?" He could hear the panic in her voice.

"She's good now, but maybe check in with her in a bit." They hung up.

Pausing after the call, he walked over to Rainie and took her face in his hands. Rainie's world regained some calm because he was back to the person she knew as Michael. She held onto him, whispering, "That's what I'm supposed to say? If I say Randy took me, then the police will want to do an investigation. Then, there'll be more and more questions. I just want a simple everyday life."

"What do you want to say, my love?" She shrugged in response. "When we were leaving, I got a phone call from some person I don't know saying for us to leave and get on with our lives. They had the situation under control. I have no idea how they knew anything or who they were, but if it means life can go back to normal, I'll take it." He wanted to make it right again.

She held tightly onto him. "It'll never be normal again, Michael. I can't believe it all happened." She looked him in the eyes with an expression seeking an answer. "I can't believe you found me. I didn't think I'd ever see you or my boys again." Her tears began to fall, "I tried to talk him down, but he was crazy. He was going to kill me, Michael." The sobs began.

"From what I heard, Randy sounded disturbed, and you handled it perfectly, not showing fear and keeping control of what you could." He told her wanted to take her to the O.B.

She shook her head no. "Physically, I'm fine, Michael. Mentally I'm anything but." She dropped her head. "You killed him—you didn't even blink. I heard his throat crack as it crushed, then you shot him without thinking." She spoke between sobs.

He turned her face toward him, "I don't remember any of it clearly. All I knew was I wanted you home safe and sound. I heard him hit you and lost it. Instinct took over." A tear rolled down his cheek. "I'm sorry he's dead, but I would do it again without hesitation. There's nothing in this world that means more to me than you. I will have to make my peace with God. It's not going to be easy."

Marguerite's flight arrived on time, and she cabbed it home. She entered the house, calling out, "Grayson."

She heard him coming out of his bedroom. His eyes teared when he saw her. "Marguerite, I'm sorry for all the years of torment I put you through. I'm sorry I made a mockery of our marriage. This all falls on me."

"No, Grayson, it falls on both of us. I've been at a facility for people with addictions. I know I'm screwed up. No matter the reason, I should have gotten help a long time ago. The unfortunate thing is I developed a taste and desire for perversion. I guess some people can partake in alternate lifestyles and still have a normal relationship. I've learned a lot, and I have a long way to go." She held her arms out to him.

"So much has happened, Marguerite. The police arrested me for ordering Diane and Tom's elimination, but much more has come out. They have the recordings from the office of all the extracurricular activities. It's an embarrassment for the firm and will be the demise of Tolbert and Thibeaux's marriages, I suspect." She nodded as he spoke. For the first time in a long time, she had kindness in her eyes.

"Grayson, you never lied to me. Randy and Bob played the game but kept their wives in the dark. We have our problems, but at least we've been out in the open. I'm sorry we let it get out of hand. We've lost too much time together, wasted with hate."

He told her about his late-night visitor and what had taken place. He also told her he'd be going to jail, and perhaps it was best if they divorced because then she could move on. She consoled him during his telling of the brutalities. The story sparked more apologies from him about what he'd encouraged other people to do to her, and he didn't understand why he found it arousing. He said his perspective of excitement and intrigue had done a complete turnaround in a matter of one hour. She told him she was going back into treatment after the trial was over but wanted to be by his side until the verdict and sentencing.

He was happy to hear she had been in therapy and not in the arms of Mateo. He told her how Mateo had gone silent from him, and it sealed his knowledge that he was on the outs, and he was going to prison. She didn't have the heart to tell him his feelings held water. Inside, Marguerite was disappointed Mateo had been responsible for the brutalities performed on Grayson, especially after the accusations he'd made about her wanting to rape Tom's ex. She no longer felt the tickle between her legs thinking about sexually abusing Rainie. However, her appetite for sex had not diminished.

She and Grayson made amends deciding they would at least share a bed until prison. They made a pact; it would be the two of them in her bed. No whores, no threesome, or group play. Whatever was between the two of them together was all fair game.

A few hours went by with benign chatter, watching television and avoiding any sort of news. Marguerite fixed them some hot toddies and snacks, and sitting on one of the crackers was his little blue pill. She gave him a flirty smile.

❧

"How did you find out about everything so fast?" John asked Aimee. "You're amazing. I hope Mikey took your advice and let the police handle everything. We generally take care of our own stuff, but we need to get up with the times and do things right."

"I'm happy to help any way I can," Aimee said. "It was fortunate the guy had already been on the radar, or it may not have been such a piece of cake." She radiated confidence and calmness.

He had already shown her the stables and the fields, and then they'd gone for a walk on the levee. She had made it a long weekend to meet the family, putting faces to names. She had gotten along well with Missy, Jack, Rainie, and Mike. Their family was all he had said they were and more. While the family was into happily ever after, it wasn't her M.O. She was more into the three "F" rule. It had worked well thus far in her life. She didn't have time for relationships.

"Gotta call Mikey, check on him," John said. "What an ordeal. I can't imagine how crazy he must've been." There was a quiver in his voice.

Aimee excused herself to the bathroom. She had her contact on speed dial. "Mat, you da bomb, ma frien'. No, no one has any idea an' won't." John knocked and walked in. "Donde pusiste el cuerpo? Que usaste como plomada? Bueno. Te amo." She hung up. "You make a habit of walking in on girls in the bathroom, Big John?"

"Sorry, thought I heard the flush; besides, you don't have anything I haven't seen up close and personal." He smiled. He put his arms around her. Aimee had a deep in the soul kind of kiss, leaving the recipient wanting more. "Ma girl, you make me a crazy man."

"Big John, that an invitation?" She jumped down and unzipped her jeans.

"Hold the thought." He grabbed a condom out of the medicine cabinet. The girl's drive matched his toe to toe. She knew him well enough to screw but had no idea of his linguistic skills. Although she'd switched to Spanish, he understood—and it gave him great cause for speculation.

There was no doubt in his mind. Aimee was a dirty fed and

somehow was mixed up in the law firm debacle, something he would keep to himself until he and Mikey could talk in private away from everyone. While he enjoyed the banging, he would be happy to drop her off at Port Authority in the morning.

☙☞

"Jake, this is Rick Marse. I know it's not my case, but out of curiosity, Rainie Landry back home?"

"Yes, sir, she is. It's a tad odd. It was her husband who found her. Don't know how and don't care how. I know he's some who's who doctor, but he's a straight-down-to-earth guy, and if he got a tip from somewhere, I don't need to know." Jake Little had put the case to bed.

"I've gotten to know the two of them over the past two years when there was that big cartel bust, and they're good people with no ax to grind. Unfortunately, the missus was at the wrong place at the wrong time and witnessed some cartel business; she has a knack for that." Marse said. "I'm glad she's home."

"We're about to have the double murder case a done deal. It's been the fastest I've seen the judicial system work in some time, and while the murderer is pushing up daisies, we got the guy who put out the hit. There are some sick S.O. B.'s out there. My bet, the tabloids will wind up with the story, and it'll be one people will read and say 'yeah, right,' but it's one hundred percent true. It'd make one helluva porn miniseries. Bunch of sick bastards. Who woulda thunk a law firm could be such a den of deviance?" A reel of the depravity rolled in his mind. Deviance hardly described, more like one of Dante's rings of hell.

"Rick, keep on keepin' it real, brotha."

"You, too. Thanks for staying on top of the Landrys." He tapped end.

After hanging up, Rick felt good. While he probably shouldn't have called Tolbert's wife in and definitely not shown her the video, he felt good nonetheless. He felt for Thibeaux since he'd helped put the nail in the coffin, but NOPD hadn't spilled his secret to his wife. The bottom line, they'd all gotten their just desserts. He wondered how long it would take, if ever, for Randy Tolbert's body to be found.

John happily dropped off Aimee, and when he got back home, his mom was waiting at the fountain.

"I'm glad you brought her back to where she came from. She may be cute as a button, but something isn't right there, John. I hope I haven't hurt your feelings, but I had to let you know. Personally, I think you and Dominique would make a cute couple." She was never one to hold her tongue or thoughts.

"Thanks for the thought, Mom, but I've known her way too long; besides, it would be awkward since I've been seeing her cousin off and on for about a year, but I think that fascination is over. It'd be like dating your girlfriend's sister, not good." He shook his head and put his arm around her. "Mom, I love you, ya know that?"

They walked back into the house. It was good to be back piloting the river. He started to feel like he had a life.

"I hope I didn't disappoint you, John, about Aimee," Missy said.

"No, ma'am. We have fun, but she and I both know it's not going anywhere. She likes the single life. I'd like to settle down one day in the not-so-distant future, but nobody has turned my head enough. I might see Mikey if he has time. He had to be freaked, the way he loves his lady. I'm glad Dad turned around and came back home. Y'all don't need to get all involved in New Orleans drama. Rainie's fine, and that's what matters, right?" He gave her a tight hug.

Loading the dishwasher, she grinned up at him. "Right. I think he'd love a visit from you. Your soulmate is around the corner; I can feel it in my bones. Before long, it'll happen, and we'll have more grandbabies on the way." Missy loved her kids, no doubt.

"Like the Rainie girl says, 'let's not get hysterical.'" He winked at his mom. "If I haven't told you lately, you, Mom, are the best. The problem is nobody compares to you. If I could find someone as loving as you, it'd be a done deal." He gave her another big hug. "Gonna get going soon, the old man out back?"

He went to the stable and called up to his dad. He went upstairs, and they jawed before he made his way to the city. While it had appeared everyone liked Aimee, he learned nobody thought she was the one.

Plain and simple, he'd brought her home because he liked fucking in his own surroundings, and she was as sexually driven as he was, which made for some fun frolicking.

৩৩

Traffic was a beast going into New Orleans; John had spoken to Rainie so that the visit wouldn't be an unwelcome surprise.

Michael looked forward to seeing him—he needed to talk about what he had done and the weird phone call. He and Rainie were good about bouncing things off each other, but she was on the fringe of shock from the horrendous scare.

The first thing John did when he got there was hug Michael and check on Rainie.

The state of her face brought blood coursing to his face in anger. Tears welled in his eyes. "My Rainie girl. You're the only one I know who makes a split lip and bruised cheeks look good." He kissed the top of her head. "Fucking bastard."

The boys were running around downstairs, and Allie was trying to keep them at bay. They had freaked out when they'd seen her, at first. Henry still couldn't look at her without crying.

"Not trying to make you relive it, but what happened? I want the real story, not the one you've concocted for the rest of the world." He looked back and forth between Rainie and Michael.

"Real simple, John," she said. "I drew a bath, got in the tub, heard unfamiliar steps coming up the stairs, jumped out the tub, grabbed a towel, and hid in Michael's closet. Randy Tolbert, one of Tom's old partners, was the one out to get me. He pulled me from the corner of the closet. I had tried to call Michael and left the phone on, hoping he would hear what was going on. Randy ripped the towel off, and the only reason he didn't rape me was that he found my baby bump a turn-off. Thank God.

"He somehow drugged me, brought me to a condemned fishing camp on the Irish Bayou. The place was half torn down. Holes in the walls and floor, and one of the exterior walls was practically gone. He was going to kill me. He was crazy ranting and raving."

A tear started down her cheek. "I'm sorry." She re-grouped. "Michael came flying from the back of the place, knocked him down." She looked at Michael, and he nodded. "Then, he put his elbow into Randy's throat. I heard it crunch. Michael picked up the gun and shot him in the head. He helped me up, we went down in the water, he got me to the car, and that's about it. Randy popped the piss out of me a few times. He was going to kill me."

"Mikey, I kinda knew what happened. Here's the weird—"

Michael interrupted, "After it all, my phone rings, I think it's you or Dad, but I didn't recognize the number. I answered anyway. I don't care what might happen to me; I'd do it again every time. Fucking bastard threatened, kidnapped, tied up, and smacked around my wife and would have killed her for sure. He was a lunatic, but I answer the phone, and it's this smooth Latino voice telling me to get my wife out of there, and he was sending his cleaners. Oh, and then he says the shit is done and have a good life kinda thing. But, ya know, I have my wife, she's basically okay, probably traumatized for years, but she's alive. I'll have to make my peace with God. I didn't take your advice and did go old school Dad, don't tell your girl." He put his hands in the air like he was giving in.

"Mikey, she's my fuck, not my girl, and she's a dirty fed. The reason she found the guy as fast as she did was she's connected somehow to the bad guys behind the bad guys. I overheard part of a conversation, and as soon as she knew I could hear, she switched to Spanish, asking where they put the body and what'd they use for sinkers. She knew your cleaner person. If they sunk the body in Irish Bayou, there'll be nothing left to find. It's thick with gators." John was matter-of-fact and didn't seem the least bit surprised at the outcome or his brother's actions.

Rainie loved hearing the two talk, but she needed to make sure John got the story right. "John, we've told my parents I tripped, and Michael had to come home and help me. My parents couldn't handle any other kind of information. They couldn't, no way. I don't know what your parents know, but whatever, if they know, tell them never tell my momma and daddy. You hear, never? Momma came over for a bit to check me out." She gave a half-hearted smile.

"Looking at you, she probably thought Mikey roughed you up," John said.

"You're a bag of chuckles, John. God, I hope her parents wouldn't think I'd hit her. I'll meet you downstairs. This one looks like she's nodding off." Michael gazed at Rainie with misty eyes. "She's my everything."

John kissed the top of her head again. "Get some rest, pretty lady."

Michael snuggled next to her for a minute, putting his arm around her. She winced. "That hurt, Rai?" He looked at her side. "Jesus, Rainie, we need to go see the doc. You're black and blue." He felt her ribs, but everything seemed intact. "Let's go to the E.R. to make sure."

"No, Michael. Tomorrow will be fine. I'm okay, I promise. Kiss me and let me go to sleep."

# THE PROMISE OF A NEW DAY

A few weeks flew by, and the cards all fell into place. Grayson was sentenced to twenty-five years. His attorney speculated it would more than likely be fifteen at most. Through their many years of marriage, Marguerite had never expected Gray to end up in jail. He had changed throughout the years, but she still cared for him. Tolbert's body still had not shown up. Thibeaux's wife and Tolbert's wife had both filed for divorce. Sherman and Andry bought out the law firm, and two of the junior partners were made senior partners, making it Sherman, Andry, Stockton, and Spruce.

Marguerite had been reading and re-reading the paper from the morning after the trial. It was bent and stained, but she read it every day like it was something new. The doorbell rang; she slowly got up and went to the door. She could see through the glass a young dark-haired girl.

"Can I help you?" she asked the girl.

"Marguerite?"

"Yes, what can I do for you?"

"You need to pack a suitcase. I have your ticket right here, and it's time for you to go home." She was a soft-spoken attractive young woman, but Marguerite knew who she was in an instant.

"Let me call, Mateo. I'm home already, and I don't want to go back yet." She took her phone out of her robe pocket and called. "It's me. I don't want to come back now. I like being in my own home, Mateo. Can you understand?"

He reminded her of their agreement and how he had kept up his end, and now it was her turn to keep up her end of the bargain. "If you do not agree to come now, I cannot promise your safety. We can bring your family here or go there for the holidays, but you must keep your word to me if I am to trust you. It will all be good, my love. I have a place for you with a magnificent view, and you will be in the lap of luxury, Marguerite. Pack your bags, bring whatever you wish. I have been more than fair with your time away from me."

There was no point in arguing. Either she went, or she'd have a bullet to the brain. "I will be able to come back occasionally?" she asked.

"Yes, Marguerite. You need to get your bags packed. I will see you for dinner tonight."

She invited the woman in and went to her room. The woman stood at the door, almost like Javier had at the resort. Marguerite threw most of her closet into four big suitcases, making sure to wrap some of her more personal items inside nightgowns. Within an hour, she was dressed and packed. She went around the house to check windows and doors were secure and walked out to the awaiting car. The driver loaded all the bags in the car.

On the way to the airport, the woman provided Marguerite with a new driver's license, a Colombian passport, and a new U.S. passport. She was now Rita Smith Moreno, with credit cards and money in a new wallet. The girl asked for her old wallet. To die or live a kept woman? It could've been worse. He didn't have to give her the new life, he could've erased her, and that would've been that. She wondered if she'd be able to see Grayson ever again.

She checked in along with her new best friend, or was it, bodyguard? They took their seats in first class, soon to be in the air, and arriving at her new home. Things could've been worse. She had a brand-new life. How pleasurable she made it was all up to her.

Rainie and Michael had two days to wait until the big ultrasound. Following the nightmare almost four weeks earlier, they had gone to the doctor only to find all was well, and she had to take it easy. All bruises were healed, the split lip had mended, the story of the injuries had all been accepted and was no longer the topic of interest. Everyone was on the edge of their seats to find out the sex of the baby—only two more days.

Life had gotten back into a routine. Running the kids to school, the beginning of Mardi Gras, and crazy Botox Thursday, the Botox deal day, was even crazier than ever with the upcoming Mardi Gras balls. Her baby bump was getting more pronounced but was still only a bump. She'd never heard from Connie Tolbert again, which was hardly surprising, and Mer could only shake her head when Rainie finally divulged the whole story of Randy Tolbert. Rainie didn't tell her Michael had killed Tolbert. It was his story to tell. The version Mer heard skipped the crushed throat and shot to the head, but still, in all, Michael was the hero and Rainie, his damsel in distress.

She let the boys go to the gender reveal appointment. Both sets of grandparents, Allie, Michael, and the boys, watched as the tech squirted the lubricant on her stomach and rolled the transducer ball over her belly. All eyes on the monitor, finally, the baby cooperated. Michael got a massive smile on his face.

The tech asked him, "Dr. Landry, do you want to tell everyone the gender of your baby, or do you want me to?" She smiled.

He wiped his eyes. "Looks like we're having a girl, y'all!"

To see what happens next, check out a few words about *A Strike Past Time*...and if you enjoyed Half Past Hate, please be kind and leave a review on Amazon, Goodreads, BookBub, or most book sites.

# A few Words About A Strike Past Time...

The Cartagena Cartel has a mole inside the New Orleans Police Department. Detective Rick Marse, from A Quarter Past Love and Half Past Hate, is investigating the disappearance of Randy Tolbert, the law partner that abducted Rainie in Half Past Hate. On a gut feeling, he suspects Rainie knows something. In an informal meeting, Marse discusses the oddity of the disappearance of Randy Tolbert and the debauchery at the law firm. He asks Rainie pointedly if she knows anything at all. Was it Tolbert who abducted her? And Why?

Mateo Moreno, head of the Cartagena cartel, contacts Michael, and a wicked twist in the plot reveals Mateo's desire to get out of the dark world and his dependence upon Michael to assist him in the endeavor. A friendship forms between the two men. A few of the secondary characters in Book 1 and 2 develop in A Strike Past Time, giving another dimension to the story. Throughout the journey, the closeness between Rainie and Michael continues with even steamier sexual encounters. And, of course, the case gets solved, the mole caught, and they live happily ever after. But...there is one most crucial development in the storyline that you'll never see coming. In the end, the story gets tied in a perfect bow, and the Censored Time Trilogy closes at A STRIKE PAST TIME.

# Acknowledgements

Many, Many Thanks...

...To those of you that have loved my Rainie, through all her craziness, that have laughed, cried, and swooned at their breathtaking love, and to those that venture forth with them on their journey as it continues.

...To my extraordinary husband, who loves me amazingly and shares me with the cast of characters that consume much of my thought. Doug, you are the most wonderful man alive...thank you for loving me so.

...To our children, their spouses, and our grandchildren that have supported me along the journey with their wonderfully biased opinions and the splendorous attention as though I were a rockstar.

...To Mark Malatesta, who still believes in my writing, my editors: Julie Mianecki, editor extraordinaire, and Paige Brannon Gunter, my go-to for "is this good or am I an impostor?" and her on-point suggestions.

...To Gene Mollica, who once again designed an impactful, beautiful, sexy, and just-what-I wanted cover design. You rock.

...To Cyrus Wraith Walker for his beautiful interior formatting and patience.

# About the Author

Born and raised in the enchanting city of New Orleans, the author lends a flavor of authenticity to her story and the characters that come to life in the drama of love, lust, and murder. Her vivid style of storytelling transports the reader to the very streets of New Orleans with its unique sights, smells, and intoxicating culture. Once masterful event planner, now retired, she has unleashed her creative wiles in the steamy story... *Half Past Hate*.

CPSIA information can be obtained
at www.ICGtesting.com
Printed in the USA
BVHW032333170821
614224BV00003B/3/J